STEALING

ALSO BY MARGARET VERBLE

Maud's Line
Cherokee America
When Two Feathers Fell from the Sky

STEALING

A Novel

MARGARET VERBLE

MARINER BOOKS

New York   Boston

HarperCollins books may be purchased for educational, business, or sales promotional use. For information, please email the Special Markets Department at SPsales@harpercollins.com.

FIRST EDITION

Designed by Jamie Lynn Kerner

Library of Congress Cataloging-in-Publication Data

Names: Verble, Margaret, author.
Title: Stealing : a novel / Margaret Verble.
Description: First edition. | New York, NY : Mariner Books, [2023] |
Identifiers: LCCN 2022026039 (print) | LCCN 2022026040 (ebook) | ISBN 9780063267053 (hardcover) | ISBN 9780063267091 (paperback) | ISBN 9780063267084 (ebook)
Subjects: LCGFT: Novels.
Classification: LCC PS3622.E733 S74 2023 (print) | LCC PS3622.E733 (ebook) | DDC 813/.6—dc23/eng/20220603
LC record available at https://lccn.loc.gov/2022026039
LC ebook record available at https://lccn.loc.gov/2022026040

ISBN 978-0-06-326705-3

22 23 24 25 26 LBC 5 4 3 2 1

For my cousin, Leisha, with love

STEALING

1

I thought the cabin was still empty until I saw the red rooster out in the road. He was really flame orange, but people call those roosters red, and he had a big, bright green feather curling over the top of his tail. I had on my sneakers and was walking in a smooth gully the rain had created. So I wasn't kicking gravel or making any kind of noise, and he didn't look up from his pecking until I was close on him. Then, he cocked his head to the side and looked me over, slit-eyed. It was March. I hadn't been down that road since fall. And by the tilt of the rooster's head, it was clear to me he'd been around some time, maybe all winter. He owned that territory, or at least he owned the chicken part of it, and he wasn't going to give ground scared, or even in a huff. He lifted a foot, held it up in a claw for only a second, and then he walked off like he had business in the weeds he'd been meaning to get to all morning. I admired him for that.

Mama always called the cabin "the cabin." It was really more like a shack, but "shack" isn't a good word to describe where people live, particularly if they happen to be your kin. So when my great uncle

Joe lived there, Mama said it was Uncle Joe's cabin. And when he was killed, I still said it was Uncle Joe's cabin for a while, because I didn't forget him just because he was dead. Every time Mama and I visited Uncle Joe he gave me a new and interesting rock to play with. He called them river stones and said that the Arkansas River had made them smooth and shined them up. But I never actually saw Uncle Joe go down to the river. He spent most of his time sitting in a rocker on his front porch. Next to his rocker on one side was a spit can and on the other side was a brown paper bag with his bottle in it.

Uncle Joe was sort of watery in the eyes, and he was black-headed and dark, like most of Mama's people. But he was the only one of them who lived close to us. I don't know why we lived off away from the rest of our family, but we did. And Mama told me, "Kit, this is my uncle, your grandmother's brother" more than once. I guess she did that because I was so young she was afraid I'd forget it. She knew she was dying and probably wanted me to know who I belonged to before she left. Or, maybe, she had a feeling for the future and hoped Uncle Joe would rescue me and take me to her parents and sisters. He probably would have, too, if he could've stayed sober and alive.

The rooster wasn't the only new sign of life at the cabin, just the first, him being out in the road. When I got closer, I could tell somebody was living in there. The door was open, its hole covered only by a screen with a tear in it. And I heard a noise from inside. It was somebody humming. I craned my neck as I walked past, thinking maybe I could see who'd moved in there. But I couldn't see anything except the outline of a refrigerator inside the door in exactly the spot Uncle Joe had kept his refrigerator in.

So there was only the humming and the refrigerator, and then, past the cabin in the ruts of the lane forking off to the east, some chickens and a couple of black and white spotted guineas. One of the guineas was large and one bitty and both of them screamed. They were for the snakes, and they told me that whoever had moved into the cabin knew what they were doing, because it was definitely not safe to be out and around in the summer without some warning system for snakes. I always carried a stick to swing at the weeds whenever I got off the road into the pasture. But guineas work in the opposite direction. They warn people about snakes, whereas sticks warn snakes about people.

I kept thinking maybe I'd run into a dog, too. It's unusual for anybody to live out in the country and not have one. But a dog didn't turn up, and I walked on down the ruts wondering who was in the cabin behind me and not really wanting to go fishing at all. But fishing was what I'd set out to do, and fishing is what I did. Not that it did me any good on that particular day. I only got nibbles and one tiny perch that I threw back because he was too small to make a meal by himself. But I may have cut the fishing a little short out of curiosity. Not much happens out in the country, and you don't want to miss anything when it does.

When I walked back, there was a car pulled up into Uncle Joe's yard. It was two-toned green, with a curvy line of chrome down the side that separated the two colors. It was sort of shiny, but not very. The car wasn't new or flashy, but it wasn't old either, and it looked like it belonged to somebody who took care of it. The obvious question was, did it belong to people who had moved in or to somebody else? I slowed down, thinking maybe if I could take long enough I'd get a glimpse of the hummer or the car's driver before I got directly in front of the cabin. But I didn't. Even the guineas and chickens weren't in sight, and the door was shut.

I went fishing again the next day. After Mama died, that was my habit during the spring and fall on the weekends and even on some weekdays during the summer. We could use the food and there wasn't anything else to do. There weren't many other children out in the country and Daddy didn't want me working in the fields with men and boys. My work was in the garden and the house.

The house wasn't big—a living room, a bedroom, a kitchen and bathroom—but it was painted. And there wasn't much housework to do, except cook breakfast, wash the dishes, cook supper, and get the quilts out of the closet, spread them on the couch at night, and put them away in the morning. There was a little stool in our closet to stand on to shove the quilts up on a shelf rather than leave them on the floor with the shoes. And I knew even then that we were lucky to have a closet, because some people didn't. But I never could've guessed how much of my time I would spend in one (here at Ashley Lordard, not back at home). And that being in the closet here would make me feel safer than I feel anywhere else.

At home after Mama died, the place I felt best was on the bank of the bayou. It fed into the Arkansas, but it wasn't deadly and wild like the river. It was more smooth and still and quiet, except for the sounds of the insects and the fish and the frogs hopping and flopping. If the fish were biting, they kept me busy, and I'd bring home supper. But even if the bobber wasn't bobbing, sitting on the bank was always entertaining. There were those sounds and plenty to watch. And when you stay quiet yourself, everything else starts moving.

I once even saw a wolf up close there. Wolves were always around, but generally they kept their distance. I'd only heard them at night in bed or sometimes seen a lone one way off in a field. But this one came down on the other side of the water directly across from me. He drank quick, looked up, sniffed, didn't catch my wind, and drank some more. He made me think of one of the stories Mama told me before she left. She said one day when her grandma was down at the water washing clothes, the wolves came in a pack. It was after the War Between the States. All the poultry and game had been killed for human food and starving wolves were roaming everywhere. Mama said her grandma had a baby and a sack of biscuits with her, and she heard the wolves and knew she was in trouble. She threw the biscuits out of the sack just as they appeared, then she grabbed her baby and ran. I believe that story is true. Or I hope it is, because nobody wants to think their mother lied to them. I'm also glad her grandma threw biscuits to the wolves, not the baby.

Anyway, when I went fishing the day after I first saw the rooster, the car was gone and the door was open again. But I didn't hear any humming. However, there was a long splash of wet cutting across the ruts in front of the cabin. I could tell by that wet spot somebody had been cleaning something up. There was a pump in the front yard east of the porch, and it was clear that a bucket or a little tub of water had been slung out into the road from close to the pump. I stepped right over the spot, but I looked toward the cabin when I did, thinking maybe somebody would notice. But nobody did, and I went on toward the bayou.

The fish were biting that day. I caught three catfish, each about a foot long. They were so same in size that I decided they were brothers and had come from the same litter. They were mud cats, dirty brown in color. I've heard here at Ashley Lordard that some people won't eat catfish at all, and I know some people won't eat mud cats in particular. But their meat is white and tender, and everybody I knew then—which wasn't a lot of people, true—all thought mud cats were delicious. So I was pretty happy with my catch, and on my way back down the lane I thought about going up to the door and offering the third catfish to the hummer who had moved into Uncle Joe's cabin. Daddy and I would only eat one fish each. And usually I would've stopped fishing at two that size, because there's no use wasting food you can leave for another day. But probably somewhere back in my mind I had already formed a thought about catching another fish to give away.

When the time came, I chickened out. Because just as I was coming upon the cabin, the front door shut. I saw it, but I heard it more. And after that, it seemed like I couldn't walk up onto the front porch and knock and hold out a fish. People close doors for reasons. Not that I thought the door closing had anything to do with me. I think it was just a coincidence. But it was a bad one for my purposes, so I kept the fish.

That night at supper, Daddy pointed at the spare fish with his fork and said, "Save that for breakfast." He never talked much during meals, so I took that as a chance, and said, "There's somebody in Uncle Joe's cabin."

Daddy belched.

I figured that was because he was eating fried food. He'd had trouble with his stomach for as long as I could remember. So I waited for the gas to pass, hoping he knew, and would tell me, who was in the cabin. But he just got up, went into the living room and turned on the radio. I washed the dishes no wiser and hearing a baseball announcer talk about statistics and players and all the things they yap about before the game actually starts. Then, when I was through, I went into the living room and sat on the floor at the table in front of the couch. Daddy is a Cardinals fan, so that's what we always listened to. The Cardinals and the Pirates. I never could get too worked up about baseball. But I liked Daddy's company and I mostly played solitaire.

2

It was spring, so school was still going. I didn't go fishing all that next week because the bus didn't get me home until about 4:30. We lived so far out in the country that I was the first kid to get picked up in the morning and the last one to get dropped off in the afternoon. That made for a long day and some boring time on the bus. I tried making friends with the driver, but he didn't like children, and nobody really wants to be known as the school bus driver's pet, so I didn't try very hard. Mostly, I just sat at a window and watched the fields go by. There were always the cows to count. One day, my top one, I counted thirty-six.

When I lived at home, school was okay. Everybody was mostly nice to me. The upper-grade town kids ran the place, and even down in the third grade I could tell that was the way it had always been and would be forever. The country kids stayed in one group. We were outnumbered, and we didn't have the clothes and lunch boxes the town kids had. I know that mattered to some, but it was okay with me. I wasn't very outgoing or friendly. Mama died when I was still in the first grade. And she'd spit up blood long before that. The first thing I ever remember knowing her by was her cough.

But I did hope that someday, when I could get to feeling better, I could make everybody like me. I studied the popular girls while I waited for that day to come. But I wasn't an outcast or anything like that. I just had troubles. All the other kids knew what they were, and that there was no fixing them. So everybody just tried to be nice and sort of let me be.

But here at Ashley Lordard, some of the kids are mean. And we're told stories about how even little children are naturally evil and about how we're all born with some sort of sin that has to get washed off of us. But I think the kids here are mean because they're unhappy. They probably came here unhappy, and being in a children's home doesn't improve on that. But, in my experience, grown-ups are a lot meaner than kids. And I never heard the born sinful idea when I lived at home and I haven't taken to it since. Although people are working on me about that. I just act like I'm going along with them. That seems to make them happier, and it's easier for me.

When I went fishing again the next weekend, there was a different car pulled up into the yard. That car was green, too, but it wasn't as nice as the first one. It was a Ford and its back right fender was busted. It looked to me like it'd been busted a long time and nobody had done anything about it because the dent was just a little bit rusty.

The cabin door was closed, and on the top step of the front porch was an empty whiskey bottle that reminded me of Uncle Joe and made a lump come up in my throat. But I swallowed it hard and went on past the cabin and down the lane looking for signs of poultry. I didn't see any. Whoever lived in the cabin hadn't let the chickens out yet. It was about 9:30, so that told me a lot. Drinking people can be sloppy about taking care of animals. When Mama was having good spells and the weather was nice, she'd sometimes take me down the road in my wagon far enough to see if Uncle Joe's chickens were loose or still cooped up. We had to go on to his chicken house and lift their latch more than once.

On down the lane, when I cut off through the field on my way to the bayou, I got to adding up everything I knew about who was in Uncle Joe's cabin. I decided, first off, that whoever lived there didn't have a car of their own. But they had friends who had cars. And those friends drank liquor. But even more interesting was that, in five whole trips past the cabin, I hadn't seen any sign of a dog. That seemed to settle the dog question. But it was puzzling. Almost any man would have a dog.

I tried to think if I'd ever met a man without a dog. And I couldn't think of a single one. Everybody in the country had one, and even Mr. Elliot at the feed store had Babe, a hound who was always either fat with puppies or nursing them in a big box in a pen in the back. I visited with Babe whenever Daddy took me to the store because he and Mr. Elliot would get to talking and there wasn't anything else for me to do. I asked Daddy once if he thought he wanted to buy one of Babe's pups, but he shook his head and said they were too expensive. He said Mr. Elliot sold them all over Oklahoma and Arkansas and even up in Missouri and Kansas, and he raked money in on them. After that, I inspected Babe pretty closely, but I never could tell that she was much different from any other kind of hound. Most people I knew had setters or retrievers.

But we didn't have either one. Daddy didn't hunt birds. He stuck to hunting deer because deer give more meat for less work and expense. So we had a terrier. His name was Randy. Daddy said that when Randy was young he had gotten himself a whole bunch of puppies. But when I knew Randy, he was only getting snakes and sometimes a squirrel. And he didn't really get them, he just barked them up. That was useful for the snakes, but aggravating to the squirrels, who were just trying to mind their own business and never bothered him at all. Randy was a rat terrier, but I never knew him to go after a rat. I don't think we had any out in the country.

I caught all the fish I needed early that day, but hung around the bayou just for the pleasure and didn't walk back by the cabin until I started getting hungry. Again, I had three fish, pounders each one, even though they were perch. They were yellow-headed and just as pretty as they could be. I carried them on the stringer, but tied the stringer to the end of my snake stick and balanced the stick on top of my shoulder so that the fish dangled off behind me. A little kid with clothes smelling like fish isn't very attractive and I wanted who-ever was living in the cabin to like me because we didn't have many neighbors. And I got lucky on that trip. The car was gone. And the red rooster, chickens, and guineas were all out in the lane before I got to the cabin. Guineas, of course, can't keep a secret. They started screeching.

When I got closer to the cabin, Bella came out the front screen door and stood with one hand on her hip. I didn't know her name was Bella then, but I did know she wasn't like anything I'd ever seen before. She wore a dress with sleeves that just covered the tops of her arms and it was open at the collar. It was a normal dress, Mama had had some like it, but it looked different on Bella. She was tall for a woman, and slim, but with curves, too. And she didn't have on any shoes or any hose, although it was still early in the year for a grown-up to be dressed so cool. But mostly, what struck me about her at first sighting, beyond just the way she was standing there with her hand on her hip and her head cocked like she was waiting for me, was that she had the prettiest hair I'd ever seen.

It was brown with a sheen. And it sat on her shoulders like puffy clouds do on the ridge on the far side of the river on some fall and winter mornings. The top of her hair was pulled back so that her fore-head showed. It wasn't high or low either one, it was more just right. And her eyebrows arched so high that I could see their curves from a distance. That let me know more than anything else that the woman standing on the porch of Uncle Joe's cabin, which was really a shack as I have said, wasn't a countrywoman at all. She was a woman who plucked her eyebrows.

Not only that, she was dark, and it was only the first week of April.

She was watching me like I was watching her. Not hiding anything, more directly than most people watch. And I walked right up to the porch, took my stick off my shoulder, and held my catch out in front of me. I said, "Want a fish? I got an extra."

Bella threw her head back, laughed and shook her hair.

I pulled the fish in closer. I didn't mean to get laughed at.

And Bella must have realized she surprised me because she got quiet quick and said, "I'd love one. That's the best offer I've had in a long time. What's your name?"

I said, "Kit. My real name is Karen, but everybody calls me Kit."

"I'm Bella. Have you got a last name?" When she said that, she gathered her skirt and sat down on the porch so that her legs hung off and we were closer in height.

"Crockett. Have you got one?"

She smiled and said, "No. Just Bella."

Well, I knew that wasn't true. Everybody has a last name. And I must have frowned, because Bella said, "I'm teasing you. I have a last name, but you can call me Bella because you've offered me a fish and I'm pleased to have it."

At that, I set the fish right down on the porch and started getting one off the stringer. And Bella got up, went in and came back out with a bowl. She sat down again with the bowl in her lap. It had a wet rag and a couple of eggs in it. She picked one egg up with her thumb and forefinger and said, "Want a boiled egg? It's all that seems handy for lunch."

I nodded and she held out the rag to me to wipe the fish off my fingers. I set her fish in the bowl and took it. Then she and I both peeled our eggs together, which, because they were so fresh, was a little slow. While I was chipping away, I hoped she'd say, "Let me get us some salt." But she didn't, and I didn't ask for it because I thought maybe she didn't have any because almost everybody salts their eggs. I ate the egg unsalted and didn't even lick the salt off my arm to help with the taste. But the egg was good enough. I was hungry.

That was the beginning of this whole awful mess. It was only four years ago. But now, it seems like it was a long, long time in the past.

3

Bella wasn't like any of the town women either. They ran to types that were as easy to drop into holes as eggs are to put into cartons. The older ones wore their hair pulled up in buns or mashed down by hairnets. Most of them were stout and had big bosoms and smelled of heavy perfume. But there was a skinny group, too, and they were flat-chested and smelled as stale as clothes left too long in the closet. All the older ones, both stout and skinny, wore the same shoes, thick-heeled, laced-up, and black. There didn't seem to be any other kind of shoes to wear once you reached a certain age, although I can't tell you what that age is, except that it's between being young enough to have children and so old that you only wear broken-down house shoes and people have to be careful around you.

The younger women, the ones who had children in school and were about the same age as Bella and Mama, were different mainly in how much they talked. Some of them talked too much and in high voices and they waved their arms around when they were in groups. They used perfume, too, and makeup on their eyes and powder on their noses. There was another younger type that was quieter and wore glasses, but not much makeup and perfume. Most of the teachers at my school at home fit into that hole, although one of the fourth-grade teachers was one of the high talkers. You could hear her cackle all the way in the next room. When I first got to the third grade, I thought they were having more fun in that room and I looked forward to getting over there the next year. But after about three days of listening to that cackle I realized that Mrs. Farris didn't have any more sense than most of the mothers of the kids in my grade. She, somehow, just got to be a teacher.

One thing all those women had in common was church. And that was something that Daddy didn't approve of. Mama didn't much either, in my opinion. But she nodded like she was going along with the church women who stopped by with pies, green beans, and potato salad because she was sick. I was glad she was nice to them. Sometimes she didn't feel like cooking and the food they brought us was good.

But Daddy said they every one had an agenda. He thought they didn't much care if we went hungry or not, they just wanted to save our souls because they were sure we were all going to hell. My parents discussed that a lot when Mama was still well enough to eat in the kitchen, or at least well enough to sit at the table and move her food around with a fork. She contended that those women were trying to help us out, doing their Christian duty. Daddy thought that was hogwash. His father was a Baptist preacher in Georgia, and Daddy said, "Peggy, you weren't raised around Christians, so you don't understand. Everything they do is for a reason. That pie isn't just pie and it wasn't brought to banish our bodily hunger. It's to make us feel obligated. And to make us think they have things better than we do so we'll convert easier." He said that again and again, but he always ate the pie.

Mama nodded to Daddy like she nodded to the women. She never got worked up, and I think now she may have been saving her energy. She always told Daddy, "Jack, people do the best they can do. They're bringing us food. Let's be grateful." And every time a church woman came with food, Mama would give her a dozen eggs. That was a trading thing. She didn't want to be beholden, and eggs were the easiest food for her to collect. She kept them in cartons and handed them through the screen door because the women never came inside or even stayed long on the porch. They were all afraid they'd catch the consumption. But if Daddy wasn't around, one of them would offer to take me into town or, more often, to church. Mama talked to them through the screen, but she never even once said I could go, which was a good thing, because I didn't like being away from her.

So anyway, pretty much that first day when Bella and I ate eggs, I had some things figured out. It was obvious that she was trading eggs for other food, just like Mama had. That told me a lot. She had some pride. She wasn't just going to take a fish and not give something back in return. She wasn't trash. But she was poor, because she didn't have much to eat for lunch except eggs and, maybe, not even salt. And, of course, anybody with any money at all wouldn't have ended up in Uncle Joe's cabin. So I figured out from the start that Bella was like Mama in more ways than just in color, and that made me like her right off.

I didn't stick around too long that first day after eating my egg. Daddy had taught me that people don't want other people's children hanging all over them. So, after I licked my fingers, I picked up my other two fish, my pole, my snake stick, and bait sack, and backed away from the porch saying, "Thank you."

Bella said, "No, Kit, thank you. I'll fry this fish up for supper tonight."

I opened my mouth to ask if she was going to have company for supper, and I thought just for a minute that maybe I should go back down to the bayou and catch another fish if she was. But I closed my mouth before I said anything about that. People don't like to know you've been watching their comings and goings.

When I got home, Daddy wasn't around. I cleaned our fish by the pump, threw the guts and heads to the chickens, and put the bodies in a bowl of salt water in the refrigerator. I thought again about whether Bella had any salt in the cabin and decided that she probably did. Everybody has salt, even if they can't afford anything else. But some people have to go without salt for medical reasons. I didn't know what those are and still haven't found out. But I began to feel some fear that Bella was sick, and I knew whenever I start getting afraid about illness, I better distract myself.

So I went back outside and watched ants. There were two great big mounds in the orchard under one of our pecan trees and the ants marched in lines carrying things back and forth between those mounds. I had read a Life magazine article on pyramids in Egypt, and the pictures of the pyramid builders made them look a lot like ants. So seeing ant mounds as pyramids was easy, and I could entertain myself for hours by watching ants and thinking about ancient Egypt. That day, I must have been especially deep in thought on the subject, because I don't recall hearing Daddy's car drive up or Randy barking, which he must have done because he always did.

However, the orchard is behind the house a ways, so it's not like I was being invaded by people from Mars and missed seeing their spaceship land. I did hear when Daddy rang the cowbell for me. It startled me out of ancient Egypt, and I jumped up off the ground and headed to the house.

We had our orchard, but not enough planting land to make a living on. Fifteen acres, maybe a little more. We also had chickens and used to have a cow named Sweetie Pie, but Daddy sold her when Mama died. My hands were too puny to get the good strong hold on an udder you need to make milk squirt, and Daddy didn't like milking and thought cows could be dangerous to children. One of the boys in my grade at school was kicked in the head by a Hereford when he was about four, and he wasn't right after that, and everybody, except his mama, knew it. So Sweetie Pie was first thing to go when Mama died, and afterwards we drank bottled milk that Daddy picked up at the store.

But we did pasture a few calves before they were butchered and we had apple trees as well as pecans. We also had a garden, a hen house, a garage, a couple of out buildings for tools and junk, and a large smokehouse where hams we cured for a hog farmer hung from the rafters. That smokehouse smelled like salty grease, and sometimes now I pretend this closet I'm in is really the smokehouse and I try to get that delicious smell back in my nose.

Daddy had come in that day with fertilizer and declared that it was time to put tomato plants out. We grew our own from seeds under lights in the garage, and they were about eight inches high. Daddy said the chance of frost wasn't really over, but the weather prediction at the feed store was good and the almanac said it was going to be an early and hot summer. He said we were going to take our chances, and that would be better than waiting another week because he had a full five days of hard work ahead. So we worked in the garden before we ate, and I didn't mind it at all. There's something real tender about young tomato plants that makes you want to be around them and hope they do well.

That night after supper, Daddy listened to another ball game and drank beer. Daddy has his faults, that's for sure, but he's not a big drinker, and into the fifth inning and third beer, he fell sound asleep on the couch. That was bad for me, because that's where I slept. But he had done it before, and if he didn't wake up by the time I was ready to sleep, I just got in his bed. Now I don't sleep well except in this closet, but it seemed like back then I could sleep almost anywhere, even after Mama died.

I liked to sleep because sometimes I dreamed about her telling me stories, rubbing my back, or throwing balls of socks at me. The sock game was my favorite. I don't know who invented it, but while Mama could still do the wash, I'd help her take it off the line. She'd fold the clothes up real nice and set them in the basket and I'd ball the socks. Then when we got back in the house, I'd hide behind furniture and she'd sit in a chair and we'd throw the sock balls at each other.

It was pretty exciting to see socks whiz through the air, and we'd laugh hard when we got hit or hit each other. Some of the kids I know whose parents have died have bad dreams about them. But I never had those, and Mama never appeared in my dreams sick. She was always laughing instead of coughing, and I wish I could dream about her again.

But back to that night, Daddy was asleep on the couch and I didn't figure on him waking up, so I slipped out of the house and headed toward the road. Randy started following me. Usually, he stayed at home guarding the house, and at first I thought I'd tell him to go back because I didn't want him yapping, it being too early in the year to really need him for snakes at night. But he kept his nose to the ground and went off into the weeds just to lift his leg, so I decided to keep him with me. There's nothing unusual about a child taking a walk with her dog.

I just happened to walk in the direction of the lane, and while I was going that way, I decided to look in on Uncle Joe's cabin and see what was going on there. I didn't plan to get right up to it, but it sat on a turn and there were some trees in the way and there was a new moon. I had to get fairly close before I could see anything at all. One of the cars was there. A light was on in the kitchen that I could see only through the window because the door was closed. Bella was standing with her back against the sink. She was holding a glass in one hand and her other hand was on the sink's pump. She was talking to somebody in the room, but I couldn't see who it was. She stayed like that for a while, and whenever she moved her head her hair shook, too.

I wanted to see more than I was seeing, but I was afraid to get any closer. I wished I could tell which car was there, but it was parked away from the light and it was too dark to make out the model, and I don't know much about cars anyway. After a while, Randy started whining. I sure didn't want that going on, so I gave up and walked home. Daddy was still asleep when I got in, so I took my bath and crawled into his bed and read a Nancy Drew mystery. I was going through the whole series.

4

The next morning was Sunday. We didn't ever go to church, but we didn't work, either. Daddy liked to carve, and Sunday morning was his carving time. His specialty was frontiersmen with rifles. He had made a bunch of them before I could ever remember. Most were the size of his hand, except some were crouching and they were shorter and wider. The newer ones lined the mantel, but the older ones were in boxes. While he carved, I'd get the boxes out from under the bed and play with the older frontiersmen on the floor or the porch. Some of them had on coonskin hats, and as our name is Crockett and Davy Crockett had just been a big deal a couple of years earlier, it all made perfect sense to me. I think it made perfect sense to Daddy, too. He said we were descended from the same line of Crocketts that produced Davy, and he was proud of it. I think that was the whole reason for his hobby.

While Daddy was carving and I was lining the frontiersmen up on the porch and making them shoot at each other from behind the legs of the chairs, Uncle Russ drove up in his truck. Uncle Russ is not kin to us in any way, but he was, and still is, Daddy's best friend. He hopped out of his truck like it was on fire and yelled, "Jack, you're goin' to hell for not being in church." When he got to the porch, he grabbed me and lifted me up eye to eye with him. I pinched his nose and said, "Uncle Russ, put me down, I'm playing." He did, and I went back to the frontiersmen.

Uncle Russ is married to a woman named Jean, one of those talkative, perfumed, hand-flinging types. Aunt Jean is a church-goer, and I guess that's where she was that morning. That's where she was every Sunday morning. Mama and Aunt Jean were nice to each other, but they were kind of opposites, and as soon as Mama died Aunt Jean started bringing her friends around to see Daddy. I didn't like that, and to his credit, neither did my father. So Aunt Jean stopped coming around much, and I didn't miss her. But Uncle Russ got to come on Sunday mornings when he could duck out of church.

I guess, as I think back, Daddy was lonely and sad. He didn't seem to have any interest in women, or really any interest in anything except carving frontiersmen, baseball, and working. But I don't really know. Daddy would let me work with him, and he showed me things, but he didn't talk to me much except to correct me. He did talk to Uncle Russ about the weather and the crops and I could tell they were buddies and Uncle Russ has been a good friend to him through everything. But I think it was hard for anybody to know what really went on in Daddy's mind. That morning, they talked about a setter of Uncle Russ's that he was trying to breed. He kept saying he hoped she could produce a litter. She had set him back a lot of money and Aunt Jean didn't like being around a dog in heat.

Daddy and Uncle Russ went out to the garden, and I played with the frontiersmen for I don't know how long, but after a while they came back and Uncle Russ left. I waited until Daddy started in carving again and then I said, "I think I'll go on fishing."

He said, "We can have bacon for supper tonight."

I said, "We better save that for the middle of the week."

He nodded and I went inside and made myself a peanut butter and jelly sandwich to take with me.

When I got to Uncle Joe's cabin, the car was gone and Bella was out in the front yard hanging clothes on a line strung between a porch post and a tree at the side of the house. That might sound odd because most people hang their clothes on a line in the back, but Uncle Joe's cabin sat on a ridge that dropped suddenly to lower bottomland and the Arkansas River, and the backyard was really more of a slope. So the clothes were hung out front whenever Uncle Joe got around to washing. That wasn't that often, but now, I sometimes wonder about what happened to them when it was hot and dusty and somebody drove down the lane. It looks to me like cars would kick up dirt and wind would blow it all over the clothes. But I didn't think about that then and I don't know that it ever happened. Nobody much ever drove down that lane except Mrs. Burnett, who lived at the end of it. She didn't have many friends to come visiting and she didn't go much of anywhere except to church.

So I just said hello to Bella and put down my snake stick and fishing gear. We fell into talking, and when she got through hanging the wash, we sat down on the porch and dangled our legs off. Bella asked me questions, like what did I like to do most? Did I like school? What grade was I in? And what was my teacher's name? I told her all of that, and then I asked her about where she came from. She said she was born in Nacogdoches. (Hard to spell. I had to look it up.) But she had been all over since then, and had spent a lot of time in New Orleans. I wanted to know what New Orleans was like, and Bella said it was nice if you had money and rough if you didn't.

I wondered which category she fell into while she was in New Orleans, but didn't know how to ask that, and while I was trying to figure it out my stomach growled. I didn't want Bella thinking I had come to be fed, so I quickly said, "Want part of my peanut butter sandwich?"

Bella said, "No, thank you. I didn't eat breakfast until late. But I have some potato chips that might taste good with your sandwich. Stay here and I'll grab them."

Bella was talking to me like I was a grown-up. I felt good about that, and it made me think maybe she'd never had any children and hadn't learned the voice most people use when talking to us. While she was inside, I inspected her clothes on the line. There wasn't a wind, so they weren't flapping and blown out and I could easily tell they weren't much like Mama's. Mama's underwear was sort of square, and had been hand-made. But Bella's drawers were skimpy, and the leg holes were like half moons in their cut. Her slips had lace on the tops, but Mama's had been scoop-necked and plain. However, I had seen underwear like Bella's in the Sears and Roebuck catalogue, so it didn't come as a total surprise to me.

Bella brought two Coca Colas with her, as well as the chips, and she drank hers while I ate. We talked about the red rooster who was in the lane and watching us like we were going to give him something to eat. Bella said he'd been a present from a friend and was going to be a daddy real soon because she had a setting hen. I asked her how many eggs and she said nine.

We went on and talked about other things, mostly just what we could see in front of us, the trees popping out leaves, the Johnson grass and how sharp it was. I showed her my finger where I had gotten a deep cut the summer before and told her I didn't even know I was cut until I saw the blood dripping down on my leg. Bella said I must be a tough little girl and I agreed with that. Mama told me again and again before she died that I needed to be strong and that I come from a line of strong people.

When I finished my sandwich, I threw my last bite of crust to the red rooster. He went for it, of course, and Bella laughed and said, "Chief'll grab at your fingers if you aren't careful."

I said, "Chief's his name?"

"Sure. Don't you think it fits him?"

To tell the truth, I thought it was risky to name a farm animal except a milk cow or a dog. Things happen to animals and you just don't want to get too attached to them. But Bella had already named that rooster, so I didn't say that. Instead I said, "Are you an Indian?"

Bella laughed. Then she put a hand on my shoulder. "I'm all mixed up, Kit," is how she answered my question.

I said, "Me, too. Daddy's white, but Mama was an Indian."

Bella peered at my face then. It is, I should say here, flat, and my cheekbones are high. I'm dark in the summertime, but lighter in the winter. My eyes are what you call hazel and my hair is near black. It's also thick. Back then, I wore it in a long ponytail because I never ever like pigtails and Mama wasn't around to braid it right. Bella said, "Cherokee?"

I nodded. "How about you?"

Bella shook her head. "Don't know. Around Nacogdoches everybody has been married into each other for generations. I'm like a stew. My ingredients are thrown in and cooked all together."

I thought about asking Bella if she was part colored, but then I thought better of it. She didn't much look like a colored, and if she was she'd probably lie about it, because colored is a dangerous thing to be, even more so than being an Indian. Nobody had ever done anything to Mama except keep a distance from her and try to convert her to Christianity. But people can be so mean to coloreds that they have to be careful and watchful like animals. So if Bella was part colored, I didn't want to know about it, because then I'd have to take that into account and worry over it. I didn't want to have to do that.

In that same conversation, Bella asked me my parents' names. I think that was her polite way of asking why I'd said "was" when talking about Mama. So I told her their names, and went on and said that Mama was dead, even though I didn't like hearing those words coming out of my mouth. It was still awful to say and I didn't have much practice at it because everybody else already knew. Bella's forehead crinkled up and she said she was sorry to hear that. I could tell she really meant it, and I changed to another subject fast because I didn't want her feeling sorry for me.

5

That conversation with Bella got me to thinking about Mama dying all over again. Toward the end, Daddy took her to the hospital. That was a mistake because she never got out of there, and it was expensive and Dr. Fletcher had come to the house whenever she needed him. He was real nice to me afterwards, but there wasn't anything he or anybody else could do about the dying. Mama had had TB since she was a girl. It went away and came back. When that happens, according to Dr. Fletcher, it's going to get you eventually. That's its nature.

When Mama was about to die, we camped out at the hospital, and Mama's sisters, Aunt Lou and Aunt Rosa, came and stayed in town with us. Aunt Lou is just as pretty as Mama was, darker though, and bigger, but not fat, just heavy compared to Mama, who was wasting away. Aunt Lou is quiet and sizes people up before she talks. Aunt Rosa is dark, too, but little bitty, and acts more like a white person or a bantam rooster than an Indian. She could be one of those talkative women I've described earlier, but she has lots of sense and, of the females in the family, she's always leading the charge. Aunt Rosa tells people what she thinks right out and she does the writing for the whole family. She and Uncle Mark are doing the fighting to get me out.

But there wasn't a fight going on when Mama died. Everybody was real peaceful and just trying to make the best of a bad situation. Daddy didn't like the hospital, and he sat in the corner all day long with his mask on. Everybody had masks on except me, and that's because TB shots work on children. Everybody else around Mama had shots, too, but since they don't work well on adults nobody wanted to take any chances. And the hospital people wouldn't let them, either.

Anyway, we went to the hospital during the day and then at night we slept in a little motel named the Starlite. It was shaped like a horseshoe and had eighteen rooms and an office attached on the east end of it. In front of the office was a sign saying "Starlite" that was lit up at night. On top of the sign was a crescent moon, which was sort of odd because the motel wasn't named Moonlight. At the bottom of the sign was the word "No," and one I didn't recognize, as I wasn't yet good at my spelling. Daddy said it was "Vacancy." But the V was burned out and the "No" was never lit up the whole time we were there. So the sign really said "acancy" at night. I remember that because achy is the way I felt and the word seemed to fit me pretty well.

I had never been in a motel before, so it was a little bit exciting even though the reason we were there was so sad. Our room was orange and brown. The carpet was both colors in stripes, but the bedspread was orange alone, and the walls were brown, except for the ones in the bathroom, which were orange. I don't know if it had anything to do with the colors or not, but the room smelled like the inside of a shoe and made me sneeze. So Daddy and I slept with the window open and I curled up next to him to keep warm. That was the only time I remember sleeping with Daddy, and he wasn't too cuddly. But I laid right up against his back, and he gave off so much heat that I didn't have any problem, even though it was January and cold outside.

My aunts slept in the room next door, and every morning, the four

of us ate breakfast across the street at the Dusty Roads. It was the first
restaurant I ever ate in. The linoleum on the booth tops was new, but
the booth benches needed to be replaced. There were holes in the
seats and sometimes the broken parts poked my legs. Usually Daddy
just put his jacket under me. But one day, the woman who waited on
us pulled her golly rag off her shoulder and gave it to me to sit on while
I ate. Every morning we sat in the same booth and ate the same thing,
eggs, bacon, and toast. The grown-ups had coffee. I drank orange
juice. We sat in that booth at night, too, but we ate different things,
mostly the specials.

Those days in the Starlite and Dusty Roads seem like a big part
of my life and it seemed at the time they were going on and on forever.
But now, five years later, I think it probably wasn't more than part of
two weeks that we were there. I only remember Uncle Mark and Uncle
Dennis coming to be with us twice, and I bet that was on weekends,
because both of them work. Uncle Mark runs a hardware store and Uncle Dennis works at a gasoline station. Uncle Mark is married to Aunt
Rosa and he's white. Uncle Dennis is Aunt Lou's husband. He's also a
Cherokee and he acts like Uncle Joe.

The night Mama died, there came a hard rain. I think the doctors
must have known she was dying because we got to stay in the room
long past the time when they usually made us leave. And I remember
looking out the window at the rain and seeing the reflections of the
grown-ups behind me huddled inside the curtain and over Mama's
bed. There was another person in the room, on the other side and outside our curtain. She was an old woman, but she never had any visitors
and she didn't have any teeth, either. She never said anything, but if
her curtain was open, her eyes would follow me and she'd show me
her gums. I didn't know what to do, so I pretended like I didn't notice.

The night she died, Mama was peaceful. For several days before
then her breath had been raspy. So we could hear something was different, but the silence told me something bad was about to happen,
so most of the night I tried to keep it away by watching everybody in

the reflection and thinking about the raindrops rolling down the pane. The only excitement was when the preacher came through. He prayed loud over the old woman in the bed closer to the door and then he poked his head through the curtain and asked if he could step in. Aunt Rosa said he could.

But Daddy said, "No, thank you."

I turned from the window to see what was going to happen.

The preacher said, "Now, Mr. Crockett, I understand your wife isn't doing too well." He was a tall old white-haired man. (I got to know him better later and will tell the total truth about him when I can get around to it.)

Daddy said, "That's correct."

"Well, don't you want a little insurance?" The preacher said that with a smile on his face like we were at a happy occasion.

Daddy shook his head.

Aunt Rosa said, "Jack, he's trying to be helpful."

Daddy said, "That so, Rosa? When's the last time you went to church?"

"Why, just three Sundays ago. I didn't go last Sunday or the one before because I was here." She shot a look to Aunt Lou.

Aunt Lou said, "Pastor, why don't we go out into the hall just a little ways. I want to ask you something about my sister." And she moved out away from the bed, over to the curtain and parted it.

They left the room. And the first thing Daddy said was, "You lied to a preacher, Rosa."

"What if I did? It's the best way to deal with them. Just go along. Keeps them from turning mean."

"You weren't raised with one. They don't need excuses to be mean."

"Well, I've found if you deal with them in a civilized manner, most of them don't spend too much time on you. They go on to aggravate other people."

Daddy raised his eyebrows and they both sort of smiled. They weren't really having a fight.

They turned back to Mama, and after a while Aunt Lou came back in alone. Aunt Rosa said, "What did you do with him?"

"I told him that our brother-in-law was upset and that my sister had been prayed over earlier by the Methodist preacher."

"How did you know he wasn't the Methodist preacher?"

"I asked him his leanings first thing. He's the Baptist one."

Mama died later that night, not prayed over by any preachers. By that time, Aunt Lou had opened the window so her soul could get out, and the rain had gotten better, so we didn't have to use any towels to mop up the floor. It was chilly, but I didn't care. I'd been feeling like I was in a cage, and I was hot all over from the inside out.

My two aunts whispered a lot of things in Mama's ears, and Daddy held onto her leg and cried. It was a real pitiful situation, and not one I like to relive. At the end I got to where I didn't want to touch Mama or have any of the grown-ups touch me, either. If they tried, I just stiffened up. And that night instead of huddling against Daddy, I slept in the room with my aunts. Neither one of them wanted to sleep. They walked the floor. But I just wore out and fell asleep in the middle of the bed by myself. It wasn't cold in their room because the window wasn't open, and the smell didn't bother me because the pillow I was using smelled like my aunts. They didn't have to use perfume. They smelled sweet naturally, like Mama.

6

Grandma, Granddaddy, my aunts and uncles, and some of Mama's other people came to the funeral. But my grandparents didn't look like themselves. They were wearing new clothes. Granddaddy had on a suit and tie. Usually, he wore overalls and a long-sleeved shirt. Grandma had on a black dress. She always wore a dress, but you could tell that one was new. I'd never seen it and the cloth was stiff. She also had on a hat with a little net on it. Usually she wore a scarf or one of Granddaddy's straw hats. My uncles looked more like themselves. Uncle Mark had on a suit and tie. Uncle Dennis had on clean overalls and a jacket.

The casket was in a big room, and there were both people there I knew and ones I didn't know. Mostly, I stayed in a little back room with Grandma and Granddaddy. Grandma doesn't say much to strangers. If she has public talking to do, somebody does it for her. Mostly, Granddaddy. But while we were in that little room he went out to the bathroom and left us alone. A woman came in, one of those stout types. She had a handkerchief in her sleeve, and when she saw me she just swept me up into her bosoms and cried all over me. I pulled away and the woman said something to Grandma. Grandma didn't say anything back. So the woman said something again. I can't remember what it was because I was trying to shut her out. But then she got right down on my level, said, "Does she speak English?" and looked up at Grandma. The woman's eyes were real big, like she was in the room with a dangerous person. I said, "No, but she understands it a little."

The woman straightened up and said real loud, "I'm right sorry about your daughter." My grandmother nodded. Then the woman left.

Afterwards Grandma said, "Who's she?" She said it in English because that's the only language she speaks. None of my family speaks Cherokee. There are reasons for that that I didn't understand then but know more about now. And to set another record straight, we don't live in tepees either. Plains Indians live in those and can still talk their own languages. Cherokees live in houses and mostly talk English. Mama got me a picture book that shows the differences between the Civilized Tribes and the Wild Indians. But most people, for some reason, don't realize that all Indians aren't the same. And to tell you the truth, I'm not as certain we are now as I was then. I'm nearly 12 now and I've been around some other kinds of Indians. So if there's a real difference it's something I'm beginning to doubt.

Not long after the woman left, Aunt Rosa came in and got us. We went out with all the other people and listened to the service. A preacher, not the white-haired one, gave it and he read out of the Bible. I know that sounds strange after what I've said about my family, but I think he was there just because there probably isn't any other way to get buried. I've still never heard of anybody being dead and buried without a preacher talking over them. They always want to have the last word.

After the service, we brought Mama back close to the house to bury her. There was a little graveyard in a clump of trees down the road from us in the opposite direction from Uncle Joe's cabin. Daddy said it'd been there since Indian Territory days and he liked it a lot better than the cemetery in town. The grown-ups had talked about taking Mama over to the rest of her family and burying her there. But Daddy decided he wanted her close by, so that's where they put her.

Afterwards, we all went back to the house, and my aunts and Mama's cousins served dinner to anybody who wanted to eat. People brought food, but nobody other than family and Uncle Russ and Aunt Jean hung around for long. I don't know if that was because they were afraid of the TB germs or afraid of Mama's family. I think people who can take one Indian alone are uneasy around clumps of us.

After Uncle Russ, Aunt Jean, and some of our people left, the grown-ups still there got into a discussion. They couldn't send me outside because it was too cold. I was only six, so I think they pretended like I couldn't understand what some of the talking was about. But I picked it up and have remembered it ever since. I want to set it down here so if anybody ever reads this they'll know what was said.

It got started by a phone call from Daddy's parents in Georgia. I'd never met them and I still haven't. But they called, and Daddy talked to them. He kept saying things like, "It's not the time to discuss that," and, "No, I'm not doing that." All the rest of the room got quiet, and Uncle Joe picked his bottle up and went to the kitchen. Granddaddy and Uncle Dennis went with him.

But Aunt Rosa had her radar up. And when Daddy got off the phone, she said, "Jack, I know what your parents thought of my sister, and I've never held it against them."

Daddy looked at me. He said, "Kit, go to the kitchen."

I said, "I'm not hungry."

Rosa said, "We can talk as adults."

Daddy said, "No."

"We can't even talk about it?" Aunt Rosa had a whine in her voice.

Daddy shook his head. "I can't let her go. We can make it. She'll help with the work."

Aunt Lou spoke then. "I suspect there'll be plenty of women around trying to do housework soon enough." She said that with a sigh.

"Don't be so sure, Lou. Women are looking for men who have something. I've got fifteen acres, a cow, a smokehouse full of somebody else's meat, and a big hospital bill. Besides that, everybody's holding bets on whether I'm infected or not."

Grandma shook her head. She reached out and pulled me close to her.

Uncle Mark bent over with his forearms on his thighs. He was trying to quit smoking, and I could tell he wanted a cigarette because his fingers were squirmy. He said, "Now, Jack, I don't want to get in your business. But you know that Rosa and I would give Kit a good home. And we'd give her an education. She's whip smart." He looked at me and smiled. "She'll need an education and will make good use of it. Could be really something. You could visit her any time and she'd still be yours. There wouldn't be any papers or anything. And if we ever have children of our own, we'll still love her all the same. Rosa wants a child powerful bad, and Kit's her flesh and blood. You've had a hard time with this sickness. We've got the means to keep her up."

Daddy didn't say anything. He just shook his head.

Aunt Rosa started crying. And so did Aunt Lou. And to my surprise, Grandma said something. She said, "A little girl needs women around her." She didn't say that directly to Daddy. She said it to her shoes and fingered her braid.

But Daddy said, "I appreciate that, Mrs. Glory. All y'all are welcome to visit any time. I'll be hurt if you don't. And I'll bring Kit over, like always."

So, it was settled that night. I was happy at the time. I couldn't imagine losing both my parents on the same day and going off to live in a house other than my own. But since then, I wish it had been settled the other way. I love my family, and I'm going to get to them as soon as I can. Or when I'm sixteen. Whichever comes first.

7

The two-toned green car was at Bella's that next Saturday morning when I went fishing. So I just walked on like I was minding my own business. Chief wasn't around and neither were the chickens or the guineas. I took that as a sign of drinking even though there weren't empty bottles sitting out. There were some cigarette butts in the lane and I picked them up because everybody knows that nicotine is poison to animals, and that chickens are crazy enough to eat anything. The fact that anybody would throw cigarette butts out where chickens could get them told me that whoever was driving that car was from a city. But I knew that, anyway. It was a city car. It's hard to mix up a city car with a country car.

So I put the butts in my jeans pocket and walked on. When I turned off into the pasture, I started knocking my stick against the ground to give out a warning to the snakes. I think I did hear a little rustling in the weeds once. But before I got very deep in the pasture, I sure enough heard a slapping sound in the distance. I stopped walking and listened. I heard it again. A lot of it. Slap, slap, slap was what it sounded like, and that's not a natural sound for a sunny morning out in the country. I'd never heard anything like it. And before I went any farther, I took a good look around.

Mrs. Burnett's house and garage were east on the top of the ridge at the end of the lane. The sun wasn't high enough to light the inside of the garage. It seemed like maybe her car was in there, but there was no other sign of life in that direction. In front of me, the pasture sloped down to a thicket of trees and tangles where backwater rose after big rains. It'd poured hard twice that week, so I was expecting the water to be over the banks in kind of a swamp. I usually fished a little west of the thicket, because it was a shorter walk and, even when it was dry, the thicket was the snakiest place around. However, past it were two fallen trees laid over in the water. They provided good cover for fish. And on dry days when I wasn't lucky in my usual spot and felt brave, I'd beat my way through the thicket with my snake stick and fish from one of those trees.

I felt like, standing there looking around and listening hard, that the slapping was coming from the thicket. And I didn't know what to do about that. It wasn't a human sound and it wasn't a cow sound and the creatures that lived in the backwater glided around silently— except for the frogs that would jump and scare the liver out of you. So, I was puzzled and curious. That's a combination that will often get you in trouble, but I know that better now than I did back then.

So I walked on, trying to make as much noise as I could to, maybe, scare off whatever it was making that slapping sound before it scared me off. But I didn't make one dent in the slapping. It just kept going on like a bunch of teachers spanking kids with ping-pong paddles. At some point, I realized that whatever was making the noise wasn't going to pay much attention to me. I could probably just get right up on it. And that's what I did.

It turned out to be a bunch of carp running up next to each other! There must have been fifty pairs of them! And they were chasing around in water that couldn't have been a foot deep. They were sparkling where the sun hit their wet scales and sparkling even when they were in shadows. But in some places they were also kicking up mud and silt. I'd never seen anything like it. And I stood on a little raised spot and just watched them. The best I could figure, somebody had poisoned the bayou and was running the fish crazy. Sometimes Uncle Russ put a telephone line in the water and brought up fish by the bunch to the surface. And Uncle Joe claimed he could get fish to the top of the water with a weed that made them drunk. So the theory about somebody doing something to make the fish crazy was, I thought, a good guess.

There was no getting them to stop. And fishing wasn't even an option because they'd run the other fish off. Nobody, not even me, will eat a boney old carp. So I watched them for a while because I was so surprised, and then I walked back through the pasture and up the lane toward Bella's cabin. By that time, the sun was pretty high in the sky, and Chief and the chickens and guineas were out and so was Bella. The car was gone, and she was sitting on the porch next to a post with her legs dangling over the edge and her hair unclasped hanging part way over her face. I had never seen her hair down like that before and she made quite a pretty picture sitting there.

She raised her head and smiled at me. Her eyes looked a little tired, but the rest of her looked just sort of lazy and relaxed.

I said, "The fish are crazy today. I couldn't get a line in the water."

She said, "What are you talking about, Kit?"

I told her about how crazy the fish were. And when I got through, she said, "Come up here and sit by me." She patted the porch with the palm of her hand. I'd already set my gear down, so I hopped right up. She hung her arm around my shoulder and said, "Kit, those fish were spawning."

I said, "What's that?"

"Well, it's how they make babies." She touched my hair with her fingers.

I liked her fingers in my hair. I wanted her to keep her hand there. It gave me some relief, and I hadn't even known I'd needed any. But I knew I was supposed to be thinking about fish making babies, so I turned my mind back onto them. I had seen dogs and cats and cattle, but they get on top of each other, and the fish were more side by side. I must have looked like I didn't believe Bella, because she added, "Fish don't have any arms or legs, so they have to do it the best they can."

I said, "Are you sure?" She took her fingers away.

"Pretty much." She nodded and winked. And then she said, "I've got something to show you. Come on." With that, she slid off the porch, shook her hair and headed off around the side of the house. I, of course, followed her.

There was a bunch of scrawny elm trees on Uncle Joe's property close to the lane toward Mrs. Burnett's house and the bayou. Uncle Joe's chicken house was in those trees. Next to it was a low fence and inside it was sort of a shack about three feet high with an opening in the front and a tin roof on the top. When Uncle Joe had a setting hen, that's where he put her with a pan of drinking water.

Bella put her fingers through the fence wire and squatted down. She said, "See her, Kit?"

There was a white hen sitting on a nest in the little shack. She cocked her head, looked at us with one eye, and then turned her head toward the back of the shack.

Bella said, "She's got eight chicks."

I said, "Can I see 'em?"

Bella got up and unbent a little wire that was holding the fence together. Then she put a hand on my shoulder and guided me in. The chicken made kind of a growl. That's not a good description, but it wasn't a normal chicken sound, although I had heard chickens make it before. It was a "leave me alone" sound. But Bella didn't pay it any mind. She just reached in and put a hand under the chicken and raised her gently. I saw three little heads and beaks. Their eyes were closed to little wrinkles, but their feathers were already dry.

I was thrilled to see them. I had seen baby chickens all my life, but no matter how many times you see a little baby animal, it's like the first time, because they are tender and cute even if they're ugly. It's like they have some hope for their lives, and they don't have any fear.

After we looked at the chicks, we went back up to the cabin and Bella asked me inside. Of course, that's exactly what I'd been wanting. I was curious to see both what Bella had brought with her and how the inside was different without Uncle Joe there. And when I first stepped in the door, I'm sure my eyes got wide because the biggest difference was that there was a bathroom beyond the kitchen on the back wall of the cabin. That had been a space for wood when Uncle Joe was alive. But I just skimmed my eyes over the bathroom door, the tub, and commode inside like they were no big deal. Nobody wants other people to think their relatives didn't have plumbing.

I looked toward the refrigerator instead and I remembered when Uncle Joe had first gotten electricity. Daddy and Mama took me to the cabin to see it. I was too little to realize it then, but I know now, electricity is a big thing for somebody in the country to get. Whenever that happens, neighbors go to visit to let people show it off and to talk about how good it makes everything look. But as I remember it, Uncle Joe didn't like his. He said the light was too bright at night. I was used to electricity. And I always felt a little scared in a room where coal oil lamps made things shadowy in the corners. But Uncle Joe got the refrigerator shortly after he got electricity, and he liked it a lot. He said the refrigerator made getting electricity worth it.

And I saw first thing that the refrigerator Bella was using was Uncle Joe's. I was sort of shocked. I don't know what I thought had happened to his refrigerator because Uncle Joe didn't have any wife or children to carry things off, but I didn't expect it to still be there. I opened my mouth to say something about that, but closed it again, and decided to look around more before I said anything one way or the other.

The rest of the kitchen was different. Not the sink, or the pump, but the table was different. Uncle Joe had had a round one, but Bella's was a rectangle, longer down the sides than at the ends. She had salt and pepper shakers and a little bottle of vinegar, but no table cloth. Uncle Joe hadn't had a table cloth either, but, for some reason, it bothered me that Bella didn't have one. It seemed like she should have. We had one at home, even with Mama gone. But Bella's table-top was clean, so I could tell she didn't just eat and make a mess and not wipe it off. I decided not to worry about the table cloth, and I was glad she had salt.

There weren't any curtains on the window, but I knew that from outside and I figured she hadn't had time to pick those out since women can be fussy about what they put on their windows. There was, how-ever, a calendar tacked to the wall over the sink, and on it was a real pretty woman holding up a jar of something like she was petting its top. I was trying to figure out what was in the jar when Bella said, "I've got some groceries in. Want some peanut butter?"

Peanut butter was (and still is) my favorite food and it was a good way not to think about the new bathroom, so I said, "Yes, ma'am."

Bella laughed. She said, "Don't call me ma'am, Kit. That makes me feel old."

Well, I don't generally like people laughing at me, but I was getting used to Bella doing that, and it was beginning to seem real friendly, not like she was making fun. And to tell you the truth, I wasn't used to being around a lot of laughter, and it made me feel good. There's just so much grief a person can take. So I slid into a chair and put my hands in my lap. (By that time, I had figured out that what was in the jar the calendar woman was holding was store-bought jelly.)

Bella fixed up two peanut butter sandwiches and she put them both on plates. That seemed pretty important to me at the time. Mama used to put food on plates, but Daddy never did by himself. If he made a sandwich, he just ate it out of his hand.

Before Bella sat down, she said, "Kit, do you drink coffee? I've got to make my milk last to next weekend."

I said, "Sure," even though I hadn't ever drunk any coffee in my life.

There was a pan on the stove, and Bella turned a knob and said, "Let's give it a minute to heat up."

I said, "Sure," again, just like coffee was a normal drink for a kid and like everybody cooked it in a pan rather than in a pot.

"Do you take yours black, or do you want milk and sugar?"

I said, "Sugar," because I had heard coffee could be bitter and because I didn't want to use up any milk.

Bella got a bowl of sugar out of the cabinet and set it on the table right in front of me. Then she set the plates on the table, too. While we were waiting for the coffee to heat up, I said, "That's my Uncle Joe's refrigerator."

Bella looked puzzled. Then she said, "It came with the house."

"This is his house," I replied, although calling the place a house seemed odd.

Bella looked out the window before she said anything else. When she finally looked back into the room, she said, "I think the coffee's warm," and then she took cups and saucers out of the cabinet, set the cups in the sink, and poured the coffee into them in there. When she finally sat down, she handed me a spoon for my sugar and said, "Where does your uncle live now?"

"Not anywhere. He's dead."

"Lord, Kit. Is everybody you know dead?"

That was an unexpected question and it sort of took me back. I did know a lot of dead people for still being a kid. And I realized then I was always afraid of knowing more. I said, "Not everybody, just Mama and Uncle Joe," and hoped I'd still be able to eat my peanut butter sandwich.

Bella nodded like she was considering what I said. Then she asked, "Did he have TB, too?" because I'd told her what Mama had died of when I'd told her she was dead.

"No, he was killed in a knife fight."

Bella nodded like she was trying to imagine that, so I told her the whole story. I'll set it down here the next time I get to write.

8

Uncle Joe was bad to drink. He couldn't help it. That was just the way he was. But it got him in a lot of trouble, and he couldn't hardly keep a job. At least that's what the grown-ups said about the job. I don't know that for sure, except he was almost always at home when Mama and I visited during the day. But I knew first hand about the trouble because Mama and Daddy would go get him from the jail in the middle of the night, and they'd take me with them because you can't just leave a little child at home asleep by itself.

So they would wrap me in a quilt and we'd go off to the jail. The jail wasn't very big. The two cells were right out in the room with the counter, the desk, and the cabinets, and you could talk to people locked up while somebody else signed papers or talked to the sheriff or his deputy. There was even a little bench visitors could sit on. While Daddy signed papers, Mama would sit on the bench and hold me in the quilt. If Uncle Joe happened to be locked in the closest cell where you didn't have to yell, we'd talk to him on the other side of the bars. Mama would talk to whoever else was in that cell, too, because she was friendly to whoever would be friendly to her.

Mama was already dead the night Uncle Joe was killed in the knife fight. But Daddy got me and my quilt off the couch as usual, and I thought we were going to the jail. I slept with my head on Daddy's thigh on the way. But when we stopped, I woke up and I saw lights on a sign. That made me know we weren't at the jail at all. Daddy said, "Kit, stay in the truck. Don't get out. I'm telling you."

I always obeyed Daddy, particularly when he said, "I'm telling you." But I rolled the window down and I listened to every word. That wasn't hard because people were talking in loud voices and Daddy was mad. There were eight or ten men standing over a body out in front of a building that was painted white. I could tell the color in the dark because there was a good bit of light from the sign and from another one over the building door, and the cars and trucks around had their lights on, too.

Daddy kept asking what happened. But there was a lot of head shaking and then everybody who'd been talking got quiet. That made Daddy even madder. He pushed a man. And then somebody grabbed him by the arm and said, "Let it be, Jack." Daddy hauled off and socked him. Then two men grabbed Daddy's arms so he couldn't sock that man again. And another man pushed the socked man away from Daddy over into a darker place next to a truck.

Daddy yelled, "You could have called a —— ambulance." He used a cuss word in there, but I won't write it down because a lot of people don't approve of "taking the Lord's name in vain," and, in case some- body actually reads this like I hope, I don't want anybody not to like Daddy. He had every reason in the world to cuss.

Anyway, there were a lot of sharp-sounding reactions to what Daddy said. He wasn't the only cusser there. And everybody talked over each other. But in the end, it just got real quiet and still. Then men started walking off, one by one, or sometimes in pairs. And the two men who were holding Daddy let him go. Pretty soon, there was just Daddy, another man, and Uncle Joe in the dirt at their feet. People were backing their cars and trucks up and turning them around, so just the light from the sign and the one over the door were still on. Those lights made Daddy's head and shoulders look yellow, but the rest of everything was in the shadows. I thought about getting out of the truck then, but remembered what Daddy had said and figured it'd be a terrible time to cross him. Pretty soon, another car came up and the sheriff got out. I recognized him because I knew him. Sheriff Hawkins. The sheriff, the other man, and Daddy stood there talking for quite a while.

Then the ambulance came. It had a light on the top, but the siren wasn't on and it wasn't speeding. I guess everybody knew Uncle Joe was dead and nobody was in much of a rush and didn't want to wake people up in the middle of the night. Although, if the truth be known, we were pretty far out in the country and there wasn't anybody to wake up except the corn.

9

Grandma, Granddaddy, my aunts and uncles, and some of my great ones, came for Uncle Joe's funeral. I was relieved to see them. We'd only gone to visit them once since Mama had died, and Daddy had cried all the way home and Uncle Joe had driven us back. Uncle Joe wasn't the best driver in the world, and I think maybe we didn't go again because Daddy thought we'd be safer if we stayed home.

Everybody, it seemed, knew Uncle Joe was going to get killed sooner or later, so nobody was surprised. But they were as upset as Daddy was about how he got killed. Granddaddy and Uncle Dennis were sick by the time they got to the house for the funeral and they had to drink coffee. But Uncle Mark, Aunt Rosa, and Aunt Lou were all fired up. They had a lot to say about nobody helping Uncle Joe when he was down and bleeding. But Grandma was even quieter than usual, and in the kitchen before we went to the funeral home, she asked me to sit on her lap. I did, and she put her arms around me and put her cheek next to my hair. It was the best hug I'd gotten since Mama had died, and I could've stayed right there snuggled against Grandma and not moved all morning long.

There weren't very many people other than ours at the funeral home, because, I guess, Uncle Joe didn't have many friends. But there was a reporter. He was a tall, lanky man and he had on a shirt that was wrinkled and stained under the arms. He asked Daddy for what he called a statement.

Daddy said, "They let him bleed to death in the dirt like a dog. Print that."

The reporter put his fingers in his shirt pocket, pulled out a pack of Pall Malls and knocked one out. Then he said, "Now, Crockett, you don't want to say that in the paper. You'll just make enemies."

"Then make up something, Charlie. The whole county likes lies anyway."

"Let me read what I've got so far," the reporter said. He held up a little notebook and read a bunch of words I couldn't follow. When he got through reading, Aunt Rosa, who had been standing there the whole time, said, "You didn't say a word about his murderer."

The reporter lit his cigarette and took a long drag. Then he said, "Well, now, ma'am, Frank Still is behind bars and he's going to get a fair trial. I've written a whole article on him. But this one is just about the victim."

Aunt Rosa said, "He wasn't a victim." She had her hand on my shoulder and she gripped it so hard it made me stand straight up on my toes. I think she realized she was hurting me, and she let me go.

The reporter held up his hand and his cigarette. You could see to-bacco stains on the insides of his fingers. He said, "Now I can't win for losing. You say he's been murdered. And Crockett here tells me they let him bleed to death. But you also say he isn't a victim. Which is it? I'm getting confused."

Aunt Rosa and Daddy looked at each other and Aunt Rosa's eyes went slitty. Finally, Daddy said, "Charlie, you're going to write what you want to anyway. But my wife's family would appreciate it if you'd say something nice about Joe. They'll keep your article until it's yellow and ragged at the folds. He had a lot of good points. He shouldn't have died the way he did. Everybody knows that, or they ought to."

"I understand that. I do." The reporter looked at Aunt Rosa. "I'm sorry for your loss, ma'am. I really am." He touched his hat. Aunt Rosa's eyes relaxed, but her lips stayed puckered and she shook her head.

The service, itself, was just like Mama's as far as I could tell. It was run by a preacher, even though Uncle Joe just sat on the porch on Sunday mornings and never went to church a day in his life. So it was another case of the preacher having the last say. But when it was through, I knew Uncle Joe was dead and wasn't coming back, just like I knew Mama was dead and wasn't coming back after hers. I think that must be the real purpose of a funeral, to make you know that the person is dead. When you don't get to go to one, then the person still seems alive and you keep looking for her and thinking she'll appear all whole and happy just around the next corner. So, funerals have their bad points and their good points both. Which wins out just depends on the way you look at them.

They buried Uncle Joe next to Mama. Grandma hadn't wanted Mama to be all alone without any of her people, so that seemed like a good solution. And Daddy wanted him nearby, too. They had been friends from way back in the Army. In fact, that's how they'd gotten to know each other, and, I think, had something to do with how Daddy met Mama.

As I've said, Uncle Joe didn't have a wife or children, but three ladies showed up at the funeral and cried hard, and they all went to the cemetery. I had never seen any of them before and the whole family talked about them later. Two of them were white. The other one was some kind of Indian that didn't look like us. Grandma said she looked like a Creek. I asked her how she could tell. She said Creeks are thicker than we are and a little on the short side.

Our family stayed for dinner. Daddy was glad to be with all of them and didn't cry at all after they got Uncle Joe buried. The men sat on the porch and smoked and drank, and Grandma and Aunt Lou cooked. Aunt Rosa trimmed the ends of my hair. Then we played Chinese checkers in the living room on the coffee table.

While we were doing that, Aunt Rosa said, "Maybe we should start writing each other letters."

I said, "I don't have any paper."

"There's no paper around here at all?" is what she said next.

"There's some in the desk, but it doesn't have any lines." I moved a marble over six other ones. It was a really long move for me.

"Do you have a ruler?"

We did. It was Mama's sewing kit. I hadn't touched it since she'd died, but I knew where it was. I said, "Yes."

"Well, do you think you could you draw lines on the paper with the ruler?"

It was a good solution. But I hadn't thought of it, and everybody was always saying I'm smart. So I was embarrassed. And I decided right then I would write Aunt Rosa a lot to show her I'm not really as stupid as I sounded.

10

From that point on, Aunt Rosa and I have been writing back and forth. (Some of her letters were stolen and I will tell how that happened later on.) One of her favorite subjects is canning. Mama didn't like to can, but Aunt Rosa does. And any time she puts something up she tells me how much sugar she put in it and how many cans it all made and, mostly, how hot it got in the kitchen. She's got a thermometer that hangs on her window, and she reads that and writes me the temperature. She got the thermometer from the Calumet Baking Powder Company. She asked them for it and they sent it to her in the mail.

Aunt Rosa likes to send away for all sorts of gifts, and sometimes those gifts are for me. I get them from different companies that make different things, like soap and chocolate drinks, and they give me something to look forward to and hope for. It's odd how just the littlest thing, like a plastic ring or a badge, can give a person something to go on, like gasoline does in a car.

Another thing Aunt Rosa likes to write letters about is television. She and Uncle Mark have the first television in the whole family and everybody goes over there and watches. It's real interesting, much more so than canning. They have comedy programs and news programs and singing programs mostly. Aunt Rosa's favorite is "I Love Lucy," but she thinks I would like "The Mickey Mouse Club." I think I would like it, too, and she has sent me a picture of Annette Funicello with Mouseketeer ears on. She writes about how cute Annette is and I know the whole country agrees, because even here at The Ashley Lordard Children's Home (where there isn't a TV) we know about Annette. She's everywhere, just like Davy Crockett used to be.

Another one of Aunt Rosa's favorite topics is appliances. She and Grandma and Aunt Lou all want new washing machines that jiggle and spin, rather than what they've got now, which is the kind where you have to feed the clothes through rollers in order to wring them out. I can understand that, because washing is such a pain that Mama got to where she couldn't do it and Daddy had to take ours to a colored woman. Wash is too much hard lifting for anybody who's not strong.

There are other things I think Aunt Rosa would write about and things I would write to her. But our letters are read, so we have to be very careful. I didn't even write her about when they cut off my hair. That was as soon as I got here, and I put up a fight, but they did it anyway. I was pretty mad about it, but one of the other Indians here told me, "Hair grows back. That's the best way to think about it."

Aunt Rosa and Uncle Mark come to visit me here once every six months and get a report from Mr. Hodges, the Director. I don't know what's said because the report is always given in Mr. Hodge's office with the door shut. But when they come out, he's always smiley and talking about what progress "we've" made. Mr. Hodges always talks like that. When I first heard him, I thought "we" meant a bunch of people, but since then I've figured out that "we" means me, Kit Crockett. I don't know why he doesn't say "she" because even I know about plurals and know they refer to more than one person. But that's the way he talks, and that's the way he talks when we are alone. He says, "Kit, we won't tell anybody about this or we'll have our letters taken away." Since they're my letters, not his or ours, I know he's misusing the English language. "Misusing the English language" is my teacher, Miss Reynolds's, favorite phrase. I bet she says it six times a day. And she expects me to never misuse the English language because I'm supposed to be intelligent. But Mr. Hodges misuses it all the time and nobody says anything. (Does that make him dumb? That's a question I'd like somebody to answer.)

11

But I've misused the English language by getting away from what I'm trying to lay out for my proof here. Back to the summer when Bella was in Uncle Joe's cabin, the next time I went to visit her was on a Friday we had off from school. By that time, I felt like I was getting to know Bella pretty well and we were turning into regular friends. I know that sounds strange, considering the difference between our ages. I had just turned 9 and she was 28. But Bella was the easiest person to talk to I knew and she acted interested in everything I had to say, and in what I was feeling, too. She asked questions in a way that made you think about new ideas and said things that made you see them in a whole different light. So since she was so good at finding out about me, I asked her about the cars.

At the time, she was taking down the wash and I was putting it in the basket. She tucked a clothes pin in her sling and said, "Well, Kit, they're my boyfriends, I guess you might say."

"Have you got two of them?" Two seemed odd because when the

older girls talked about boyfriends on the bus they usually had their minds set on just one.

"Well, I suppose I do." She handed me a towel.

"Which one do you like best?"

"Hum, that's a good question." She took down another towel and also a wash rag. Then she said, "Neither, if the truth be known."

"Why do you go with them?"

Bella snapped three pins off the line real quick. Then she said, "Kit, you won't understand this yet, but they pay the bills."

I did understand that. Mama used to talk a lot about bills. But I didn't say anything for a while after that because I was turning things over in my mind. From the way Bella said the part about the bills and the part about not liking either one, it sounded like she wasn't about to marry one car or the other. All of a sudden the cars seemed not that big of a problem.

I said, "Did you ever marry anybody?"

"I did once. Here, I'll trade you the sling for the basket."

We made that switch and went in the house. Bella put the basket on a kitchen chair. Then she picked it back up and said, "Let's go in there. It'll be easier." She nodded toward the bedroom.

I sat down on the bed and just looked around. The bed was made out of iron or brass or some metal and had a little table and lamp beside it. There was also a dressing table, a chest, and a metal rack for hanging clothes. The rack was next to the front window, and I knew that when Bella was in bed she moved the rack over to block the view from the road. I had noticed that from the outside, and it seemed to happen most when one of the cars was around, even during the daytime.

Bella started putting clothes in the chest. I said, "Did he die?"

She turned around. "Who?"

"Your husband?"

"No. He's still alive. We divorced."

I had never known an actual divorced person before. But I did know from going down to the jail that not everybody had happy marriages. Some of the men were in for hitting their wives. And when they were let out, they got a warning from Sheriff Hawkins. But their wives were always there to take them home, even if they'd signed papers to put them in. Mama always tried to distract me when that was going on, and later Daddy said things like, "Read your book, Kit," even though it was usually in the middle of the night, and one time I didn't even have a book with me.

But, anyway, divorce was something nobody I knew did, no matter how many fights they had. So that Bella was divorced seemed shocking to me. I put both my hands between my legs and squeezed them together. I must of looked funny because Bella said, "Does that bother you, Kit?"

That was a good question. I didn't know the answer. Or, really, I knew it, but didn't want to say it. Bella must have read that on my face because she moved the basket to the floor and sat down next to me on the side of the bed. She rubbed my back with her hand. She said, "He was a lot older than me, Kit. I liked him at first because he reminded me of my father. But he was jealous and mean. So we went separate ways."

Bella kept rubbing my back in a circular motion and I think that she knew I was still upset about what she had said because she didn't say anything after that. She just rubbed real softly. And then I didn't say anything more because I didn't want her to stop. I just wanted the room to stay exactly the way it was, with light coming through the window, and a green and red loop rug on the floor over the boards, and the chest all solid with a picture of a snowy mountain over it.

After a while, Bella said, "Are you all right, Kit?" and she stopped rubbing and folded her hands in her lap.

I said, "I'm okay. Did he hurt you?" I looked up at her and I could see a little twitch in her cheek right at the corner of her mouth.

She put her fingers together on the front of her blouse and tapped herself on the chest. "Inside, Kit. He hurt me in here the most."

Well, I couldn't take the thought of Bella being hurt and I slid my arm around her waist and started crying pretty hard. She put her hand on the side of my head and she pressed me to the side of her breast and we just stayed like that for a long time rocking a little. I didn't want to stop crying because I didn't want her to let me go, but as I think back on it now, if I'm honest, I was really crying for myself and for all the hurt I had penned up inside of me.

12

The next day, the Ford was there when I went fishing, so I stayed on the bayou until after lunch and ate my sandwich down there. I stayed even after the fish had totally stopped biting and I'd run out of any real reason to be there. I finally figured if the Ford was still parked when I walked back, that was just something I couldn't do anything about, and as I closed up my gear and gathered my stringer in, I debated with myself whether or not I should knock on the door and give Bella her fish in front of that man.

I was still debating that when I hit the lane and saw the Ford was gone. That erased my worry just like it had been words written on a blackboard. I hurried a little on down the lane and I went on up to Bella's door and called in the screen. She came out of the bathroom and greeted me like she was truly happy to see me, and I think she was.

I'd caught several fish and we cleaned the ones for her together out by the pump. The two-toned car man was coming that evening, and Bella was going to fry the fish up for him and save whatever food he brought her for another day. That two-toned car was a DeSoto and the man's name was Marvin. Bella told me about Marvin while we chopped off the heads and gutted. He was an insurance sales-man who traveled all over selling policies door to door, and she met him when he came to the door of the house where she was working keeping children. This was a big house owned by some rich people in New Orleans. Bella described it in a lot of detail. It had outside porches on the top and the bottom floors both and those porches went all along the front of the house and had iron fences. I could sort of figure out what the iron fences looked like, but she described the inside of the house, too, and the furniture, and she used a bunch of words I had never heard before and haven't heard since, so I still can't picture the rooms in my mind.

I was really more interested in the children than the house anyway, and when we went to the kitchen I asked about them.

Bella said, "The boy's name was Jonathan and the girl was Priscilla."

I said, "Priscilla isn't a very pretty name."

"Well, it wouldn't be my choice either." Bella threw some salt in the bowl with the fish. "But she was a sweet little girl and I loved her."

That was really not what I was expecting Bella to say and it didn't make me feel too good right in the pit of my stomach. I didn't know what to say, and I suddenly wanted to get out of there and get away. I told Bella, "I better be going. Daddy might get in early today."

Bella closed the refrigerator door and looked at me and smiled sort of slowly. She said, "Don't be jealous, Kit. Priscilla can't hold a candle to you." Then she tugged my ponytail just a little bit and said, "Get on out of here. I've got things to do before Marvin rolls in."

I was glad to get out of there for once, and I did take some com-fort in Bella saying Priscilla couldn't hold a candle to me, but I had a little ache in my heart that made me feel like a hole had opened up in my chest. I didn't like that feeling, and I didn't want to think about

Priscilla or the time Bella lived in New Orleans, so I listened to the weeds. As there was a wind coming up, it made everything around seem like it was rustling and bustling to get somewhere, and I just hoped that somewhere wasn't out in the lane and the everything around wasn't snakes and skunks.

13

Daddy did get in early. Rain followed the wind and drove everybody out of the fields. I fried up the fish and we boiled potatoes from the cellar. After we ate, Daddy started listening to a baseball game, so when I finished the dishes I went in the living room with him and played dominoes by myself. That's not so hard to do, because you just lean on one elbow or the other and stretch your neck a little and keep two columns of scores. Dominoes is mostly just the luck of the draw, so cheating yourself isn't really much fun. I won the first game from myself by 35 points.

During my second game, it started raining in St. Louis. They delayed the ball game and started talking baseball statistics over the air. Daddy was interested in batting averages and RBIs, but beyond that he didn't go much for the math of the game, and after a while he turned the radio down, got another beer, and sat down on the couch close to where I was playing.

He said, "Are you winning?"

I said, "Yep. Hard not to."

He took a long gulp of beer and started watching me play.

I said, "We could play a game if you want to."

He shook his head. Then he said, "It's sort of lonely out here in the country."

I think that was the first thing Daddy had ever said to me about how he felt about anything. I was surprised and stopped playing. I said, "It was better when Mama was here."

He took a longer swig of beer then, and looked so sad that I wanted to get up and hug him. But Daddy wasn't a hugger. He'd just squirm. So I said, "I've made friends with the woman who moved into Uncle Joe's cabin. Her name is Bella."

Daddy smiled. "Good for you, Kit. I hear tell she's pretty."

"She has two boyfriends," I said real quickly. I didn't totally realize it at the time, but I didn't want Daddy setting his eye on Bella.

"Two? That's a little excessive."

I wasn't exactly sure back then what "excessive" meant, but it did seem odd if you didn't know the details, and I wasn't going to tell them.

"Have you met them?" he asked.

"No, I've just seen their cars. One drives a Ford and the other one drives a DeSoto."

Daddy nodded and then he put his beer bottle in the palm of his hand and rubbed the bottom of it like he was trying to produce a genie. He said, "Now, Kit, when either one of them comes, I want you to trot on home. Grown people like to have their time together alone, and Bella might not want to hurt your feelings."

"Oh, I know that. She scoots me right out of the cabin before they ever get there." I said that like it happened all the time, which was an exaggeration, but not a lie, because she'd done it just that afternoon and I planned for her to do it again on a regular basis.

Daddy up-ended his beer, and then he said, "How would you feel about moving to town?"

Well, I was surprised by that suggestion and not at all pleased. First, I was surprised because Daddy had never mentioned anything like that before. And I wasn't pleased because I had finally made a friend and I didn't want to lose her. I said, "I like it out here. The town kids are snobby."

Daddy leaned back into the couch and rubbed a hand over his hair and down the back of his neck. He said, "I remember that." He had been raised in a small town in Georgia. I never heard him talk much about growing up except to say that he had learned that he didn't like reading early on in school and that being the preacher's kid was a hard business all the way around. I started to ask him what he remembered, but it stopped raining in St. Louis and Daddy went to the kitchen to get another beer to finish out the game with. He did say when he sat back down that he'd feel too confined in town anyway.

I went back to playing dominoes, but I've wished several times since that night that we had finished that conversation. Mr. Hodges is a preacher's kid, too. He didn't tell me that as a secret, he said it in assembly. In fact, he's said it more than once. He gives us talks every morning before school. Those talks are on a whole bunch of subjects like honesty, hard work, Christianity, cleanliness, respecting your elders, original sin, and the evils of Communism. But, somehow, Mr. Hodges works into whatever he's talking about the fact that his father was a preacher and respected by everybody in Pine Bluff, Arkansas.

He was doing that when I first got here, so I don't know anything about when it started, but I do know that, for as long as I've been here, which is going on two years now, he talks about his daddy more and more. This week alone, he's mentioned him twice, and it's only Thursday. I don't know if he'll do it tomorrow, but if he does, that'll be in over half the talks this week. I think that's kind of strange, since every kid here is away from their daddy or their daddy is dead, and a lot of us are awful lonesome. You'd think he wouldn't mention his daddy so often, because I know what it does to me is make me miss mine even more and keep him in my mind for most of the day.

14

The next time I was at Bella's, she had the radio on and we listened to music in the kitchen and went through the Sears and Roebuck catalogue. Looking at the Sears and Roebuck was one of my favorite things to do. I did it all the time, and it turned out Bella liked doing it, too. We started in the toy section and looked at all the toys for babies first, and then we looked at toys for kids my age, and then we looked at bicycles. I had my heart set on getting a red one for Christmas. That was several months away, but part of the fun about Christmas is planning for it and wishing and hoping and dropping hints. And the Sears and Roebuck catalogue is perfect for that because you can just thumb through it and look at pictures and naturally bring up the subject of whatever you're looking at.

So we looked at bikes for a long time, and then we looked at ladies' shoes, dresses, and underwear. Bella said that she wished she had more shoes, that when she got rich she'd have shoes in every color and with heels of every height. I had never seen Bella wear any shoes except flat slippers, but she had long legs and they were shaped just like the legs of the women in the Sears and Roebuck.

Bella did own a lot of dresses. She had a whole rack of them and they were pretty. She had them in every color, had them in solids, had them with little pictures on them, and had them speckled with flowers. She had one or two striped dresses, but I think she really looked best in the flowered ones. One I remember especially had little blue flowers all over it. She called them "de-li-cate," and at the time I thought that was the name of the flower, because flowers have all sorts of strange names. But I realized later that Bella was talking about how small and gentle-looking the flowers were and that she had said "delicate" with a funny accent just to be playful.

We had moved on to the pictures of the ladies' underwear and were poring over them when I first heard the guineas screech. I looked up, because for some reason I always think I can hear better with my head up rather than down. Bella said, "What do you think of this brassiere, Kit?" and then she said, "What's wrong?"

I said, "There may be a snake around. Listen."

A guinea screeched again. Bella got up, turned off the radio, and walked to the door. She stood at the screen for a minute, and then went out it. I just stayed where I was because I try to avoid snakes at all costs. But I listened, and heard Bella say, "Good afternoon, Mrs. Burnett."

I got out of my chair then. When you're out in the country you want to see everybody you can, and I knew Mrs. Burnett, but not well. She was one of those skinny, flat-chested older women. She wore her hair in a net, her hose were dark, and her shoes were black lace-ups without any heels. Mrs. Burnett had a long beak of a nose, and her eyebrows grew together over its top. That day she had on a dark dress but no apron over it. She was standing out in the lane right in front of the cabin when I came out the door.

She said, "Karen, I didn't expect to see you here."

I said, "Hi." I didn't expect to see her either, but I didn't say that because grown-ups can say all sorts of things that children can't get away with.

She said, "Don't you think you ought to be getting home?"

Bella said, "Mrs. Burnett, I invited Kit to come."

That wasn't true. I had dropped in after fishing. And it was the first lie I ever heard Bella say. It sort of tickled me. Then Bella said, "Would you like to come in? We were just looking at the Sears and Roebuck."

Mrs. Burnett shook her head. She said, "I'd like to have a word with you."

Bella said, "Kit, why don't you go back on in the house. I think my neighbor wants us to have an adult conversation." Then she shook her hair.

I went back in and watched out the screen door. Bella walked out into the lane to Mrs. Burnett, who took a step back and looked up at me. Bella looked up at me, too. She shook her hair again, and I stepped back away from the door and slid into a chair at the table. The Sears and Roebuck was lying open and I stared at the pages. They had those brassieres on them, and I didn't need one yet, so I turned the pages and looked at cut off legs, garter belts, and hose.

I don't know how long I looked at those legs and the things you put on them, but eventually Bella came back in. She was red in the face and her hands were sort of trembling. I said, "What'd she do to you?"

Bella shook her hair again and went to the cabinet and took out a bottle of liquor and a glass. She opened the bottle and poured herself a drink. While she did it, her hand was trembling and the bottle made a little tapping sound against the rim of the glass. She said, "You better get on home, Kit."

I said, "It's not late."

She turned around then and leaned against the sink. She took a sip of her liquor.

I said, "Don't you want any ice?"

When I said that, Bella's face softened and she smiled a little smile that I'd seen before, but not often. It was just in her eyes and at the tips of her lips where they came together. She said, "Come here, Kit," and held out her hand with the palm up. I got up and went to her and put my arms around her waist. My head came up to under her breasts and she smelled like some kind of perfume and liquor all at the same time. She kissed my hair and said, "I don't think anybody understands me except you."

I remember a tingle went all the way through my body. But the next thing I remember I was in the middle of the road walking home. And I didn't realize until I was all the way there that I had forgotten to bring my fish and my gear with me. I turned around to go back to get them, but I stopped in my tracks and thought better of it. Going back didn't seem like the right thing to do. Like it was almost dangerous.

So instead, I went on in the house and got some sausage patties out of the freezer. I put them on a plate to thaw and then I got a box of Daddy's frontiersmen out from under the bed and took them to the front porch. I got lost playing with them until Daddy's truck pulled in.

I felt sick that night and didn't eat any supper. But when I woke up the next morning I felt a lot better. It was Sunday and Daddy and I did the same thing we always did on Sunday morning, except I didn't have to get the frontiersmen out because they already were. That afternoon, I helped Daddy in the garden instead of going fishing. He needed the help because it was that time of year when everything needs tending in a garden. We cut a mess of lettuce and pulled some green onions and Daddy made wilted lettuce for supper. Daddy always made the lettuce because he was afraid I'd burn myself pouring the grease.

15

By then the days were longer, and there was a good bit of light in the afternoons when I got home after school. But I didn't go fishing for a while. I did my homework and if I didn't have too much, I read a Nancy Drew novel in the porch swing while I waited for Daddy to come home at dusk. Along about that next Thursday, I was deep in one of those books when Randy started barking. I looked around, and walking across the yard was Bella. She smiled and waved. That threw me a little. I was surprised to see her. She'd never come before. But I was also glad of it. I called out, "What are you doing here?"

She called back, "Can't a person go visiting?" Then she waved my fishing pole in the air like it was some kind of magic wand.

I told Randy to be quiet and stay. I left my book on the swing and went to meet Bella and hugged her. She had on one of her dresses with flowers and her hair was pulled back on both sides with barrettes. When I stepped back, I said, "You look pretty."

She held my fishing pole out. "You won't be able to go fishing this weekend without this."

I said, "Did you happen to put my worms in the refrigerator?"

She laughed. "Did you think I was going to keep grimy old worms in my refrigerator? That's disgusting."

I don't know what we talked about after that. But I got happier and happier to see her, and felt flattered that she'd made the effort to come see me like I made the effort to go see her. That said more than anything that it wasn't a one-sided friendship. I wanted her to stay and come in the house, but she came only as far as the old capped well out in the yard and she left before Daddy got home.

When I went fishing on Saturday, after the car (the Ford) was gone, I stopped off at her house on my way back just like always. We cleaned the fish and went to the hillside behind the cabin to pick wild flowers. I had spent my morning practicing how I was going to ask Bella what Mrs. Burnett had said, and I had tried out all sorts of casual ways, but when the time came I just blurted, "What did mean ole Mrs. Burnett say to you the other day? I want to know."

Bella was bent over gathering flowers and she turned her head and looked up at me without standing up. She said, "Among other things, she doesn't like Marvin and Stan."

I had never heard the Ford's name before, but I knew who she was talking about. I said, "Does she know them?"

Bella kept on picking flowers. She said, "No. But she doesn't like the idea of them."

Mrs. Burnett didn't have friends in two different cars going down to her house. People hardly visited her at all. I knew that because I walked the lane all the time and new tire tracks are real noticeable things. I said, "She's jealous."

Bella picked a flower stem with a lot of blue little heads bobbing on it. She said, "I think you're right about that."

"Don't let her bother you." I picked a yellow flower.

"I'm not. But Marvin is bringing some curtains tonight. I think that old woman is stealing around outside my house."

I had never heard the word "stealing" used like that, and I misunderstood. I said, "What'd she steal off you?"

Bella laughed. "Kit, I don't have anything left to steal. I mean she's sneaking."

Well, I understood about sneaking. And I said, "What you need is a dog."

Bella stopped picking flowers then. She sat down on the slope and patted the ground beside her. I sat down, too, and handed my flowers to her to put in her basket. She said, "I don't like dogs, Kit."

There were a couple of kids at school who didn't like dogs, and both of them had been bitten when they were little. I said, "Did one bite you?"

She said, "Yes, you've seen the scar."

I hadn't seen any scars on Bella. I didn't know what she was talking about. But I didn't want to say that, so I said, "Oh, yeah, I forgot. Was it a big dog?"

"Well, at the time he seemed big. But I was little, so it's hard to tell how big he really was. But he took a hunk out of me. And I've never gotten over it."

"You didn't seem too scared of Randy."

"I was. That's why I didn't go on up to the porch."

I said, "Randy won't hurt you. He'll bark and bark until you tell him not to. But unless there's somebody around to protect him, he just stays near the house and raises Cain. He got sprayed by a skunk once."

Bella laughed again. "Well, I can't take Randy off you. So, I'll have to make do with guineas and curtains."

That struck me as funny. I started giggling. Then Bella started giggling, and we rolled around on the hillside and giggled and giggled and hugged each other. The grass wasn't short, but it wasn't tall either. It was a soft mat, and the sun was shining, and the temperature was just right. It was a perfect day, and I never will forget it as long as I live, because I'll tell you there is some meanness in the world. But there's some goodness, too. And sometimes it's hard to tell the difference between the two, and I'm not saying I've even got it straight in my mind. But I am saying that no matter what anybody says, Bella loved me. Maybe she shouldn't have, but she did. And I can tell the difference between love and hate. I sure can. I've had a lot of practice at that.

16

My teacher, Miss Reynolds, is always, like I said before, talking about the misuse of the English language. If any of the kids around here were in good enough moods to make fun of a teacher, we'd make fun of her for that. But most of us are pretty blue, so we just pick on each other. But this morning when she said that for the third time, I finally just blurted out in class, "Is this place a boarding school or a prison? What's the correct usage?"

Talk about everything coming to a halt on a dime. The room got so quiet that the only thing you could hear was Janie Johnson's wheezing. Miss Reynolds had a pointer in her hand, and she stuck it straight out at me. She said, "Karen Crockett, come up here."

I went. It wasn't a choice situation. I blanked out while she was disciplining me, but I will tell you why I asked that question other than just because I couldn't take it any longer. About two weeks ago, we got a couple of new students. They're obviously Indians, and look like sisters. Both are darker than me, but the one in my grade is a little darker than the other one. They're called Linda and Susan, but those probably aren't their real names. Nobody knows what their real names are because they don't talk the English language, and the teachers and Mr. Hodges won't let them talk whatever language they know. The first day they were here, they sat next to each other at lunch, which is the only time they could because one of them is in the fifth grade and the other one is with me in the sixth. They were talking their language to each other, and Mrs. Lathrop, the fifth grade teacher, went over to them and grabbed hers by the shoulder, and said, "Come with me." The girl shook her head, and wrenched her shoulder away. Well, that made Mrs. Lathrop so mad she nearly had a cow. She started talking real fast and firm and then she picked up the girl's tray and she marched off with it over to another table where nobody at all was sitting. She said, "You are to eat over here from now on."

The girl, the one they call Susan, just sat where she was and big tears came up in her eyes and rolled down her cheeks. Her sister put her arm around her shoulder and said something real loud in their language.

Well, Miss Reynolds got into it then. She said, "Girls, don't touch each other." That was to both of them, not to all of us in general. But I put my hands to my sides real quick, because you can't ever tell when that kind of order will spread to everyone else. But the two girls didn't do anything, except the one in my grade, "Linda," she started crying, too, and her sister started hugging on her, so then the hugging was going both ways.

I couldn't stand seeing that. And it was the kind of situation where I keep my eyes on the teachers to try to be ahead of what they do next. And Mrs. Lathrop and Miss Reynolds, they looked at each other from across the cafeteria, which was silent except for the crying. Not even saying a word to each other, they moved together like pinchers straight toward the sisters. Mrs. Lathrop jerked the one in her room up and made her climb over the bench. Miss Reynolds tried to get ours up, but she's bigger and put up a fight. There was some screaming and hitting, and let me tell you it went both ways, even though Miss Reynolds later said we all knew she wouldn't hit a student except on the bottom. That was a total lie because practically the whole school saw the fight. But Miss Reynolds now says that almost as often as she talks about the misuse of the English language, like if she says it often enough we'll all believe it. Some people might, but not me. I've seen people lie before, like that old, white-haired preacher, Rev. Cunningham, who lied and lied and lied. Just because you say something over and over again doesn't make it true.

Anyway, I've been trying to be nice to the girl in our grade because she's an Indian and having a hard time. But I still don't know her tribe. We've got a Comanche here, and they call her Caroline. She just goes along with them on the name thing because it's so much easier. And we've also got a Chickasaw in our grade, and she's like me, she doesn't even speak Chickasaw and she's called by her real name, which is Lana. (Lana is who told me not to worry about my hair.) Anyway, Caroline and Lana and I talked about the new Indians on the playground, but we couldn't figure out what they are. Lana asks questions like a white person, and is taller than either Caroline or me, and gives off an air of being superior when she wants to. So she asked Miss Reynolds what tribe they are, and she told her not to worry about that. They're just like everybody else and we should treat them that way.

So, it's an unsolved mystery who they really are, but we know they aren't Comanche, Chickasaw, or Cherokee, and I don't think they're Creek because they're both pretty skinny and getting skinnier by the day. But, whoever they are, they're in the same boat as the rest of us, only worse, because they either can't talk English or won't. Which is a good question, because they could be like Grandma, and acting like they don't speak English because they don't want to talk to whoever is irritating them. But I'm going to find out which it is, because I know what the people in this place are up to, and Susan and Linda are going to need all the help they can get. I couldn't save their hair. That was already chopped off before I'd ever seen then. That's the first thing they do to you here. But it's not the last by a long shot.

17

I got so upset about the mystery Indians again that I got off the path of the story I was telling about Miss Reynolds and me. So back to that, after I went to the front of the room for asking the boarding school or prison question, Miss Reynolds marched me over to Mr. Hodges's office and told him what I'd done. He acted all concerned and like what I had said was a serious misbehavior instead of a question that nobody had even tried to answer. But he also acted all kindly, which is exactly the way he acts whenever the teachers are around and whenever we are alone together unless he thinks he's not going to get what he wants, in which case he gets red in the face and trembles with anger.

After Miss Reynolds got through saying her mind, Mr. Hodges told her to go back to her class. Then he told Mrs. Williams, his secretary, that we were in a disciplinary situation and were not to be disturbed. I knew what that meant, so my mouth got real dry, which is the way it always gets when Mr. Hodges and I are alone together.

I just went off in my mind again. But afterwards, Mr. Hodges gave me one of Aunt Rosa's letters. I think he'd had it for about four days, because the postmark is several days too old, and because I hadn't seen him since the middle of last week. He didn't send me back to class, he sent me to the dormitory to brush my teeth.

After I finished with that, I laid down on my bed and stared at the ceiling. But the letter was in my pocket and I could feel it under the material. It was something to live for, and nobody else was around, so I could read it all alone. That's the best way to read a letter both in terms of enjoyment and because you can read it over and over without anybody realizing how homesick you are. I shouldn't really care about people knowing that because we're every one homesick for somebody. But I do. I'm afraid if anybody finds out how I feel inside I could crack open like an egg where the little chick just has enough strength to peck through, but not enough to unfold itself or even get its head in an up-right position.

So I won't write about that anymore and say instead that Aunt Rosa's letter is real chatty. She starts out about the weather, which had been rainy for three days, but then she gets to the interesting part, which is that she's taken a job at J.C. Penney's. I didn't even know she was thinking about that, and she said she didn't tell me because she wanted it to be a surprise. I've read that part over several times, and I think maybe she believes that in her heart, but I also think maybe she was afraid she wouldn't get the job and didn't want to say anything just in case.

Her job is in Ladies'. At first when I read that it didn't make much sense, but my only experience with a department store is the Sears and Roebuck catalogue. The first thing she said about Ladies' is that her boss is a young man about half her age who took college classes at Northeastern and that he's real nice, but she thinks he's embarrassed about working in a department that sells women's dresses. He tries to stand off across the aisle in Men's as much as he can.

After that, she wrote about what television shows she's watched since she last wrote. "Gunsmoke" is now her favorite, and she told me all about what Matt Dillon was up to. But she also said that she had watched a "Special" that wasn't like anything she had ever seen and she thought I would've enjoyed it. It was "Peter Pan," and I know the story.

I think I would have liked the special, too, because there's something about going off into a strange Never Never Land that I completely understand. I do that here at Ashley Lordard a lot, and I think I did it even before I got here. I can't describe exactly where I am then and it's not always the same place. And, unfortunately, it's not where Wendy and the Lost Boys are because there are no pirates and no fairies and no Indians. So I can't tell you about it or what's there, but I can tell you this: Sometimes when I get back from there I know what has happened someplace else, or I know what is getting ready to happen here at Ashley Lordard, or I can hear a voice from somebody else who's not in the room.

I know that sounds strange and I don't know exactly how to explain it without sounding crazy, except to give an example. Most of the time the examples are little bitty things that if I told to anybody else they would say I was making them up and I wouldn't be able to prove otherwise. But this one was public, and there's no way to dispute it, so I don't mind giving it as an example, and people can think what they want. Although, the people who know about it don't know what to think, and neither do I.

It happened last fall. I was sitting in Miss Reynolds's class, which is where I'm sitting every morning during the week, and it was just about 10 more minutes until we had morning recess. So while Miss Reynolds was having people stand up and read out loud, I just went off somewhere in my head. And all of a sudden I had a terrible feeling rush over me. It wasn't like a panic feeling, it was more of a deep feeling of being sad. Only, I didn't recognize that at first because I'm not really used to feeling much of anything at all. But this just hit me like I was being tackled, and I started crying out loud, wailing, really, and heaving up and down at my desk. I was embarrassed, but I couldn't stop, and Miss Reynolds came over to me and she put her hands all over my back and shoulders, but I still couldn't stop. So she helped me get out of my desk and she took me out into the hall. She was real nice for Miss Reynolds and I think she must have been as startled as I was because she looked white and pasty and had a wrinkly forehead and her eyes were squinty. She finally took me to my dormitory room and she asked the cleaning inspector, Mrs. Ritter, to look after me.

Mrs. Ritter is nicer than almost anybody here. She's one of those stout older women, but she's not like the rest of them, because she's a real comfort and she's not always acting like we're criminals. She just charts our cleaning jobs as done or not, and if they're not she gently reminds us or helps us get started. And sometimes if somebody is particularly blue, she tucks a little present under their pillow. It's usually a little piece of candy or sometimes a picture she has cut out of a magazine.

So Mrs. Ritter stopped marking on her chart and she just let me lie on my bed and she patted my hair and rubbed my back. And then when I felt better I rolled over and she asked me what was wrong. I said, "Somebody died."

She said, "Who?"

I said, "I don't know. But I know the feeling."

Mrs. Ritter could've acted like I was crazy or told me I wasn't being a Christian, but she didn't. She said, "We need to find out who. I'll call your family. Do you have their telephone numbers?"

I have all my family's telephone numbers in a little book in my closet, so I got them, and Mrs. Ritter told me to go on and get in my closet and she'd be back after a while. Now, I've mentioned my closet before, but I haven't really explained it, so I'll do that now. There are nine girls to a room here, and we all have our own closets in a line down the wall of the room opposite the heads of our beds. They are really the only nice thing we have and the only private place that belongs just to us and to nobody else. Most of us sit in our closets at night, especially when we're upset or when we just want to be alone. Nobody here thinks anything about that, it's considered normal and I do it all the time. It's where I do all my writing and where I am right now.

Anyway, I was in my closet for some time and really worn out, so I fell asleep and I woke up to somebody shaking my arm. It was Mrs. Williams, the secretary, and she was on the floor on her knees. Mrs. Ritter was standing behind her. I was groggy and sat up and said, "What is it?"

Mrs. Williams said, "Karen, your grandfather has died."

I took a deep breath and tried to let that sink in. Then I said, "When?"

Mrs. Williams looked up at Mrs. Ritter. Mrs. Ritter said, "This morning."

Then Mrs. Williams said, "If the court will send somebody to escort you, we're going to let you go to the funeral."

18

I didn't go to the funeral. I don't know who decided that or why. It could have been because the funeral was in the morning and they couldn't get me there in time, or it could be that somebody decided I'd been to too many funerals already for somebody my age, or maybe it was because they only let me out for a short time and somebody had sense enough to figure out that spending that time in church rather than really being with my family wasn't such a good idea.

Anyway, I got there after the funeral was over. And I did get to go see my grandmother and the rest of my family, except for Daddy, who (it hurts to say this) is in jail. They wouldn't let him out.

An off-duty policeman took me to my grandparents' farm, and when I got there, Grandma came out on the porch, and there were a lot of people with her, standing behind her, my aunts and uncles and some people I didn't even know. I had been in the car with the policeman for two hours and he hadn't said a word to me. But after he turned off the engine and looked at the people on the front porch, he turned around and looked at me. He said, "You ain't a nigger, are you?"

I shot him a mean look and said, "That's a misuse of the English language."

He said, "Huh?"

I said, "We're Indians."

He said, "Indians? Ain't many of them left. You got two hours." Then he looked at his watch and said, "Ya better get on with it."

I got out of the car real fast. And I stood out in the dirt until he backed up and drove off. Fortunately, it had rained and there wasn't a lot of dust, so the car didn't kick any up. But then I turned and looked at my family on the porch. They hadn't moved really. And they looked like total strangers to me. I thought, Who are these people?

But then Aunt Rosa broke loose from the pack and she came running toward me with her arms open, waving her hands and smiling and crying at the same time. The rest of them followed her, and before I knew it they were all swarming over me, even people I had never met before in my life.

They took me inside in sort of a wave of motion, and then they sat me down at the table, and the men went out the back door and took the other children with them. The women fed me. Mostly it was Aunt Lou and some grown cousins who were dishing up the food, because Grandma wasn't feeling too good and Aunt Rosa was sitting right beside me. There were other women there, too, and they ran food in and out to the men, but they all got introduced at one time or another. It turned out a lot of them were also Mama's cousins and aunts. They every one were pretty, and they ranged in shades from fullblood looking to almost white.

After I got plenty to eat and started in on a piece of cherry pie, Aunt Rosa said, "Kit, tell us how you knew about Daddy," and the room got quiet.

I pretended like I was chewing my food real good because that gave me time to think and because not chewing good is one of my faults they're trying to get corrected here at Ashley Lordard. But they just sat there and looked around, down, or off in different directions without talking. I ran out of food to chew and had to swallow. Finally, I said, "I didn't know it was him. I just knew somebody had died."

Aunt Rosa said, "How did you know that?"

I ate another bite of pie, and some of Mama's cousins started moving around a little like they weren't really listening, but I could tell they were still ready to hang on every word. I said, "I don't know."

Aunt Lou said, "It doesn't matter," and she shot Aunt Rosa a look.

Aunt Rosa shot her one back, and then she said, "No it doesn't, but we're just curious. Some people have distance sight."

I had never heard of that at the time. But I knew animals know things people don't and people know things animals don't, so it didn't seem impossible and it had happened to me. I shrugged, and ate another bite of pie. Then everybody started moving again and the subject was dropped.

It was a wonderful two hours. All the women hugged on me, and Uncle Mark and Uncle Dennis came back into the room and they ruffled my hair. And a man cousin of Mama's introduced himself and said I looked just like her. That made me feel more proud than sad, and I was surprised about that. Mostly people don't mention Mama to me, and I had thought talking about her would feel awful, but it didn't feel bad. That's not to say I didn't miss her, but being with her family, which is really my family, too, made me feel like she was still with me. That whoever we are is spread out all over our kin and we have pieces of each other in us, and that's true even if some of us are dead and some of us are living.

The other kids were outside playing. And one of Mama's cousins asked if I wanted to play with them, too. But I'd never seen most of them before, and I wanted to be as near my grandmother and aunts as I could be, even though Grandma wasn't like her usual self. She hugged me real hard and kissed me on the forehead and told me not to worry about my hair. Just like Lana, she said it would grow back. Then she left the kitchen to lie down. Aunt Lou said she hadn't had any sleep and was just worn out.

Unfortunately, the policeman came back right on time and I had to leave. Grandma had already left the room by then, but everybody else cried, including me. I was worn out, too, but afraid to go to sleep in the car with a strange policeman, so all the way back to Ashley Lordard I kept myself awake by thinking about whether or not I should have come at all. The school limits our visits so we'll adjust. And in a way they might be right because it might have been easier not to go. It wouldn't have caused so many tears, and I wouldn't have felt so bad afterwards. But on the other side is the fact that sometimes you have to have good things to remember just to get through the days and the nights.

19

The summer before Bella was in the cabin I went to the bayou every day, even when it was too hot for the fish to be biting and too hot to eat them fried if they were. But I didn't want Bella to get tired of me, so the summer she was there some days I didn't go down the lane at all. I took care of the garden and read. Daddy worked all day in other peoples' fields, driving a tractor or thrasher or whatever, depending on the cycle of the crops. That's hard work, even sitting, because those big machines aren't easy rides, and all day long of that will make even a strong man hurt in his sides. So, some mornings I spent in the garden alone, and if I didn't go fishing, I went out there again in the late afternoon and picked vegetables for supper. I spent the hot middle of the day reading. Reading is something I love to do and also it gave me something new to talk about with Bella.

The bookmobile arrived at the intersection of our road and the highway every Thursday morning at 9:30 just like clockwork, and I waited for it, rain or shine, because missing it was about the worst thing that could happen to ruin a week. I was caught up with the

Nancy Drews because I had read most of them already, and I asked the bookmobile lady, Miss Francis, what else I could read. She said, "Here, try Dr. Dolittle," and handed me a little book that she said was written in England. I read a few pages, and it looked pretty interesting, so I asked if there were any more of them. They did come in a series, but some were checked out. So I just got the first three. Then, I asked Miss Francis if she had any books for adults.

She laughed and said, "Half a bus full." She waved her hand toward the left side of the bookmobile. Then she said, "But you're too young for them."

I said, "I'm asking for my Daddy."

She said, "Oh. What's he interested in?"

Well, I wasn't really thinking about getting books for Daddy. He didn't read anything he didn't have to. I was thinking about getting books for Bella, so I had gotten myself into a trap. I didn't know how to get out, so I said, "Baseball."

Miss Francis went down the side of the bus, and came back with a book with a green cover and a batter on it. She said, "I have this. It's a novel, but it's all about baseball. And it's good. A lot of people have read it."

The name of it was The Natural, and when Miss Francis stamped its card, she said, "Now, Kit. This is an adult book. When you get old enough to read those, I'll let you know, and we'll pick out some that you'll like. You wouldn't like this very much even if you did read it."

I knew Miss Francis was trying to keep me from even peeking in the book, but I didn't care because I wasn't going to read a book about baseball even if it was written for children.

While I was walking back down the road with three books about a man who talks to animals and understands what they say back and a book about baseball that Daddy would never read, I got to thinking that I really didn't know what kind of books Bella liked. I'd only seen her read magazines and the Sears and Roebuck catalogue.

20

That afternoon I went visiting without my pole because it was too hot for the fish to be biting. I took <u>The Story of Dr. Dolittle</u> with me. The first thing I noticed when I got close to the cabin was that Chief and the chickens and guineas weren't anywhere to be seen. That was often true on weekend mornings when there was a car pulled up in the front yard, but I had never seen it happen in the middle of the week and I got a tight feeling in my chest. I stopped in my tracks and listened and looked. I didn't hear anything unusual. The front door was open a little and the curtains closed as they usually were during the heat of the day.

I kept walking and started looking in the dust of the ruts for tracks. It was clear a car had been there since I had last stopped by, which was Tuesday. I figured it had probably been there the night before. There weren't any chicken tracks on top of the tire tracks and it was hard to believe that the chickens had been cooped up for two days. Thinking about that, I had a sudden feeling of panic that Bella had left. But then almost immediately, I heard Chief crow. I was relieved because the thought of Bella just disappearing was too bad for me to bear.

I felt like Chief knew I was there and was calling for help. So the first thing I did was walk over to the chicken house and open the little door in the bottom where the chickens and guineas went in and out. Man, they came out like they were running to a parade, only they ran in all different directions rather than in the same way. And a bunch of them looked back at me like I had the feed. But I just had Dr. Dolittle and my snake stick and I lifted both of them in the air so they could see they were mistaken about what I was carrying.

The cabin was just northwest of the chicken house. There weren't any windows on the side facing me, so I couldn't peek in. I'd have to walk up onto the porch and knock on the door to see if anybody was home. And I was on the way to the house in grass that was pretty tall when I stepped on a snake.

That just scared the liver out of me. I dropped my book and took my stick into both hands and beat at the grass as hard as I could. The snake slithered away. But I chased him and got some licks in before he totally disappeared into the weeds. I don't normally go after snakes, but you always have to be sure a snake isn't a cottonmouth. They run in pairs, and if it is a cottonmouth, there's usually another one around somewhere. You're not safe until you find it also and kill them both. But that was just a chicken snake. A big one, though, and slow. He'd probably just eaten. And when I determined what he was, I just stood there breathing hard. Panting really, because I was scared and needed to get a better grip on myself.

After that, I picked up Dr. Dolittle and walked on around to the front of the house. I sat the book down on the porch, but kept my stick in my hand and knocked on the door. On the second knock, I heard Bella call my name. I went in then and right through the kitchen to the bedroom door. I took it all in. There were clothes on the rug and a sheet draped over the end of the bed. A fan that was sitting on top of the dresser was turned on and rotating. Bella was folded up into a ball on her side holding a pillow. She didn't look too good to me. In fact, she looked terrible. Her hair hadn't been brushed, and her face was a funny color and puffed out under her eyes. And she had makeup on, which wasn't normal in itself, but it was even worse because the makeup was either on crooked to begin with or smeared. I said, "Are you sick?"

Bella said, "Sort of."

I said, "Do you want a glass of water?"

She said, "That's an idea."

So I turned back to the kitchen, left my stick on the table, and got Bella some water. I sat on the side of the bed while she drank it.

Bella didn't have on any clothes except a slip. It was silk with lace on top, but it had a stain on the front that wasn't too pretty. The stain was over her left breast and beneath it her nipple was sticking out. Her other nipple was sticking out, too. She said, "Kit, why don't you get my toothpaste. I'll brush my teeth with my finger and the rest of this water."

So I went and did that and sat back down on the bed. When she was finished with her teeth, I said, "Are you having a hard time walking?"

She shook her head. "No, I'm just lazy. What time is it?"

I looked at the clock on the table beside her bed. "1:30."

"Whew," Bella said. "It's too hot to start the day now. Can you get me a clean slip out of that second drawer?" She pointed to the chest and sat up higher.

I found a whole pile of slips and took the top one. When I handed it to Bella, she took the one she was wearing off over the top of her head, wadded it up, and threw it over the foot of the bed so that it hit the floor. Then she picked up a powder box off her end table and padded powder around on her neck, breasts, and stomach. She handed me the puff and asked me to come on up on the other side of the bed and powder her shoulders and back. When I did, I saw that scar she had talked about. It was on her side, just over her hipbone. The powder was lighter than her skin all over her body, because, as I have said, Bella was dark. She was darker on the parts that got exposed to the sun than on the rest, but she wasn't a totally white lady, and I liked that about her.

When I got her all powdered up, I handed her back the puff, and she lifted up my shirt and dabbed powder on my chest between where my breasts were going to be. The powder smelled soft and delicious. She said, "Take your shirt off." So I did.

I said, "There was a snake just outside your house."

She said, "Turn around and I'll powder your back."

I did, and she said the powder was lilac. When she got me all powdered up, she patted the bed, and said, "Lie down and tell me all about the snake. What kind was it?"

21

That afternoon on my way home I was a long way down the road before I remembered I had left Dr. Dolittle on Bella's front porch. I turned around to go back, but it was too far and I didn't think it was going to rain, so I decided I'd call her when I got home and tell her where the book was and ask her to bring it in. But by the time I got all the way home, I realized I still didn't know Bella's last name, so it was going to be hard to call her. I thought for a minute I would ask Daddy if he had heard her name, but I decided pretty quickly that wasn't a good idea. We ate fried bologna and tomatoes for supper and they made my stomach hurt. Daddy said they had probably caused me acid indigestion and he gave me another glass of milk to settle my stomach and put me in his bed so he could listen to the radio in the living room like he did every night. I didn't feel like reading. And, anyway, I didn't want to read the Dr. Dolittle books out of order.

I felt fine when I woke up and went back early the next morning to get my book. Everything was just totally normal at Bella's. Chief and the chickens were out pecking around like they should've been and

Bella was hoeing in her garden. I fell into pulling weeds and we talked about all sorts of things, but mainly about her plans to get a television set. She thought Marvin was going to buy her one, he had been hinting about it. Or, rather, she had been hinting to Marvin and he had been hinting back that he was thinking about it. I was glad to hear that because I didn't want her to get bored and leave the cabin. We worked and plotted together about how to get a television out of Marvin. Of course, I had some interest in getting the television, too. Everybody likes TV, and Daddy was still having to pay off the money he owed because of Mama dying, so we couldn't get one.

But Marvin bought Bella an air conditioner instead. On Sunday morning, it was sitting in the side window of her bedroom. I heard it before I noticed it, but it was in clear sight as I walked toward the cabin. Marvin's car was still there, so I went on fishing and stayed long enough that it was a pretty good bet that he was gone. When I came back by, Bella was over toward the chicken house, spreading some corn. It was too early in the afternoon to be feeding chickens, and so the first thing I said after we greeted each other was, "How come you're feeding the chickens?"

She said, "I'm looking for my little guinea. Have you seen her?"

I looked around. And, as I had my catch dangling off the end of my snake stick, it swung around when I did. I hit Bella in the side with six catfish. She said, "Good God, Kit. Watch those fish."

I said, "I'm so sorry!"

She shook her head and said, "Don't worry, I can change. But have you seen that guinea?"

"I don't think so. Not in a while," I said, and I got to thinking back to Thursday when I let the chickens out of the house. I couldn't remember whether or not the guineas had come out, too. They had gotten so used to me that they didn't squawk when they saw me and I had gotten to where I didn't pay them any mind, either.

Bella held her dress out, examining the fish goop. "I guess a fox or a hawk got her. Come on. I'll show you what Marvin came in with."

Bella had a pan on the porch reserved for my catch. I set the fish in it and she pumped in some water. We left the fish on the porch when we went inside. It was cool in the kitchen. I haven't been in many air-conditioned places, and I think that must have been the first air conditioning I'd ever been in.

It was weird. First, it wasn't hot. That made it unnatural for summer. Then, there was, as I've said, the noise. It drowned out everything. All the natural sounds from outside that you usually could still hear inside even with the curtains or shades drawn to keep the sun out, they all were muffled. That bothered me. It was like being deaf. So, there on that first day of air conditioning inside Bella's house, I didn't know if I was going to like it or not.

Bella took her dress off over her head, and when she left for the bathroom, I inspected the new machine. It blew cool air right out the front through little vents at the top. It had push buttons on it where you could choose between cool, very cool, and cold. Very cool was pushed in, and that's what it felt like with the wind blowing in my face. The air conditioner box itself was mostly brown. I liked the cool, but decided that the way I was feeling about air conditioning was probably the way Uncle Joe had felt about electricity. Bella came back in the room without me hearing her. She hugged me from behind, smelling like powder. She said, "It's not a TV. Are you disappointed?"

I turned around and hugged her. I said, "No. I'm happy."

22

I like writing about some of those days with Bella, but they also make me sad. And what's going on here at Ashley Lordard is really what I'm trying to get down and what I hope somebody reads. But even if nobody ever does, writing is a good way to figure things out. There are a lot of things that need figuring out here. Like who the new girls are, and how to avoid Mr. Hodges entirely.

His lecture this morning was about how we all need to be baptized to show we've been saved. I sat with Mary Anne and Bonnie on the left side of the auditorium, which is the girls' side. Mary Anne believes every single word Mr. Hodges says, and she tortures herself with them. By lunchtime, she had worked herself into a knot, and she was sitting right across from me. She said, "My grandma said I was baptized as a baby. I don't think he thinks that counts."

One of the other girls said, "It doesn't. You have to accept Jesus. Little babies can't do that."

"Then if you die as a baby, what does that mean?" Mary Anne was really fretting by then. I could tell by the tips of her ears. They were pink as could be. She's white, so she gets to wear her hair the way she wants to, which is pulled back so you can see her ears, which are pretty big.

Bonnie said, "I think they go to Heaven." She's smart but doesn't act like she knows everything, which is something I like about her.

Another girl, Joyce, turned her thumb down and made a jabbing motion. I didn't get into the conversation. It seemed like useless speculation to me, and Mr. Hodges hadn't said one word about babies. He had talked about children, which everybody knows are not the same as babies. He had talked some, too, about Eve, and how sinful she was. I listened pretty close to that part because everybody wants to know what's sinful and what's not, and sometimes that's confusing.

The new Indian girl in my grade ("Linda") was sitting one girl down from Mary Anne and heard the entire lunch conversation. So far, she hasn't said a word, so nobody knows for sure if she can talk English. But I got a clue to that mystery when Mary Anne said, "I think if you just accept Jesus, he looks out after you, and that would go for the parents of dead babies."

It took me a minute to figure out that what Mary Anne was trying to say was that Jesus wouldn't let a baby of parents who had accepted him go to Hell even if the baby died before being really baptized. At least, I think that's what she was getting at. But the most interesting thing was that I caught the look on "Linda's" face, and I could tell that she was as confused as I was. That means, I think, that she understood what Mary Anne was saying and that it didn't match what Mr. Hodges was talking about. If that's true, then she understands English, but just won't speak it unless she wants to. Like Grandma. It also means that she's been around Christians enough to figure out that they just make up what they want to believe, no matter whether it's logical or not.

I've read that last paragraph back over about three times and I'm not sure I'm making myself clear. But it doesn't matter. If there's anything I've learned here, it's that you can't argue with Christianity. That just makes people crazy. I don't want to make anybody crazy because I want to get out of here.

After lunch we do more lessons and then after them we do chores. Today we washed windows. And Caroline and I got to wash them together. That's sort of unusual because even though nobody has said so, we can tell the teachers and Mr. Hodges really don't want the Indians here to pair off. They either think we'll be a bad influence on each other or are trying to turn us white by keeping us apart. I haven't quite figured out which it is yet, because they're sneaky and won't come out and say. They just say things like, "Karen, why don't you and Joyce mop that floor," when Caroline or Lana already has a mop in her hands.

Anyway, I told Caroline about the look on "Linda's" face, and she said she figures the sisters can understand English, and she thinks they're Civilized Indians. She said that with a smirk, then she poked me. This is our joke, and it shows you just how dumb the teachers and Mr. Hodges are. I was afraid of Caroline when I first met her, although she turned out to be the sweetest person here. My family thinks most Wild Indians are dangerous, and the Comanche are just about as wild as Indians get. Caroline heard about Civilized Indians from her family, and she says they're just as bad as white people. That you can't tell the difference between a Cherokee and a white, except maybe for the smell. So the dumb part is, of course, that the teachers and Mr. Hodges don't know how different Indians feel about each other and don't realize we have to learn about each other like we have to learn to multiply and divide. We're not natural allies, but we're sure getting to be that way.

But back to the mystery Indians. I think Caroline is right. It seems to me if they were reservation Indians and their parents died or got sent to prison, they'd have the rest of their family living close around them and they wouldn't have to come here. But Caroline says that's not entirely right. They could be sent off to a government boarding school if the whites found out and were able to grab them. But she also says some of those schools are on reservations and most of the others she thinks are just for Indians, and don't allow whites. I don't know anything about other boarding schools or reservations, either, except that we've got one over in North Carolina. I've never been over there. My family walked the Trail of Tears and we are not reservation Indians. We are Indians who get along with white people. More or less.

But as I was saying, that would make "Linda" and "Susan" either Choctaw or Seminole because Lana says they're not Chickasaw and I think they're too skinny to be Creek. The only illogical thing about Caroline's theory is that she's a Wild Indian and she's here, not in a reservation school or a government boarding school just for Indians. I don't know why. She'd never said and there's no way to ask her because she has a hard time even answering the teachers' questions when she has to.

Miss Reynolds keeps working on Caroline to get her to answer like the white kids do. But most of the kids, even the whites (except Tessy), understand that asking questions isn't always polite. And we sure don't ask each other questions about our real lives unless we're picking at each other's scabs because we're bored or just can't stand being here without acting mean to get punished so we can cry and have someone to blame it on.

But Tessy is really mean a lot of the time, and last December she got on to Caroline real bad about Santa Claus. She kept asking Caroline if she believed in him and did he come to Comanches? Caroline wouldn't say yes and she wouldn't say no, and that just made Tessy even worse. It was just total and complete meanness on her part because nobody in the sixth grade, Indian or white, believes in Santa Claus, and he's a sore subject here where some kids don't even get presents from home, let alone get to go there for Christmas.

Tessy kept on and on even after I told her to lay off, so I finally just socked her. I didn't like hearing about Santa myself, so it wasn't totally a good neighbor fight. But I did do it mostly for Caroline and I knew exactly what my punishment was going to be before I ever made a fist. And, sure enough, Miss Reynolds marched me right off to Mr. Hodges.

It was at the end of the classes, right before the chores. And a lot days that's when Mrs. Williams goes home, and sure enough when we got to Mr. Hodges's office, Mrs. Williams was standing up behind her desk, stuffing things into her purse. I always hate to see that because that means there are two locked doors between Mr. Hodges's office and the hallway, not just the usual one.

Mrs. Williams left and Mr. Hodges told Miss Reynolds he'd take care of our discipline, and she could go on to her chores. All of the teachers have duties after classes just like we do. Miss Reynolds oversees the sewing and mending, and I guess that's where she went off to. Anyway, Mr. Hodges locked the door behind her, put a hand on my back to guide me into his office, and then he locked that door, too.

Usually, I just put up with Mr. Hodges and go off somewhere in my mind, but I was mad at Tessy and too upset just to open up and let him put his snake in my mouth. So I said I wasn't going to do it.

He said, "Yes, you are."

I said, "Not on your life."

He said, "Don't threaten me. You'll do as you're told." He was getting red in the face. He'd already started unbuckling his pants.

He kept one hand on my shoulder while he got out his snake and he was shaking all over. I twisted away and got out of his grip. I tried the doorknob, but it wouldn't turn. It was stupid of me, but you just sort of hope the lock hasn't caught. He jerked me around by my neck and he had his snake in his other hand. It was red and angry, too, and he kept pulling at it, like he couldn't get it under control. He had a hold of my neck and my hair and he kept trying to get my head in the right place and make me open my mouth. But I wouldn't do it. I stomped on his shoe and I kicked him in the shin. We had an out and out fight, and while we were fighting, he messed all over himself.

When that happened, it made him start screaming that I was dirty and that he was going to teach me not to tempt adults into abominations. (I don't know if I spelled that right. That's the way it sounds.) But he had to let go of me, and I was relieved about that. I backed up against the door while he wiped all his man stuff onto both of his hands. Then he came toward me and put his dirty hands on my head and started mumbling and jumbling about how he was baptizing me in the name of the Father and the Son and the Holy Ghost. Then he tried to push me down real hard toward the floor. I guess he was trying to make me kneel the way people do when they pray. But I held onto his trousers trying to keep my knees from getting busted against the linoleum. That broke my fall. My left knee hit the floor pretty hard, but my right knee didn't.

I was determined not to cry if it was the last thing I ever did. And he just stood still a long time with his hands on my head. I didn't move either, except to grit my teeth to keep from crying or yelling. Somebody might have heard me and tried to help, but he also might have broken my neck before they got to me. Then, he started moving his fingers. They were sticking to my hair and it started pulling. I said, "Ouch, you're hurting me," but I didn't yell it.

He took a breath so deep it sounded like a gulp. Then he said, "We have to do something about your hair, Karen. Get up." He pulled his pants up some.

I did what he told me to do and he said, "Sit in that chair," and started wiping his hands and snake off with a towel he keeps in his desk drawer. He had a spot of his man stuff on his pants, and he said, "Now, what am I going to do about this?" He looked at me.

By that time, I was seated. I said, "Spit on it."

He flushed red again just for a second and squinted his left eye. I could tell he thought I was being smart, but I was really just trying to help so I could get out of there. And I think he saw that, because he calmed down more and stuffed everything back in his pants real careful, trying not to get any more sticky stuff on the outside. Then he said, "Karen, I want you to sit right there and don't move. I'm going to get some water for your hair. Don't get out of that chair." He got the key out of his pocket, went out the door, and locked it. By that time I was numb and couldn't even believe what had happened.

I don't know how long he was gone, but when he came back, he had a towel and a thermos of water. He said, "I'm going to clean your hair, Karen. Don't move."

I can't remember exactly what I said, but while he went over my hair with the water he started talking. Only it wasn't his normal talking and it wasn't his mean talking. It was really pretty decent and not angry at all. He said he wanted me to like men and that was really what he was trying to get me to do. He said he knew I got off to a bad start, but that wasn't my fault because I hadn't been raised in a Christian family or gone to church like everybody else. So I was at a disadvantage. It was to be expected that I could easily be led astray by an Eve, but that Jesus would redeem me if I would accept him. He said that's what Jesus Christ is for, to redeem us from our sins.

By that time, my head was pretty wet, but it felt like the sticky stuff was gone. And Mr. Hodges put the thermos down and dried my hair with the other end of the towel. Then he got down on his knees right in front of me. He took my right hand in both of his and looked me directly in the eye. He said, "Karen, I want you to think of me as your father. I'm here to give you guidance and I really do love you. Just like our heavenly Father loves us both. You believe me, don't you?"

I knew what I was supposed to say, so I said, "Sure."

He said, "We can't ever tell the other children or the teachers what we do here together. They would get jealous, and that wouldn't be good for the school."

I said, "I know."

That seemed to satisfy him. And he went to his drawer and got one of Aunt Rosa's letters. Then he wrote a note and handed it to me on top of the letter. He said, "That's a pass to go to your room and read your letter instead of doing your chores."

I said, "Thank you."

He said, "Thank you, Karen. You're a nice girl. We'll get you straightened out."

23

I'm ready to get to the part of my story that's about how I got put here in Ashley Lordard in the first place. I've told you Daddy carved frontiersmen. I can't safely go back and check if I've already said that he carved them from the wood of black gum trees, but he did. During some stages of the carving he set up a vise on the side of the porch to hold his wood while he worked. He had chisels and gouges and knives of all shapes and sizes, and the frontiersmen had enough details that you could see their eyes and noses and ears. They all were dressed in buckskins, and some had little knives at their waists. The hardest part of one to get right was the rifle because it stuck out, and I saw Daddy give up on more than one because the rifle broke or got carved crooked. I had to be careful of the rifle on the finished ones, too. I only broke one, and that was in the fall before Mama died. She said, "Don't worry. Your daddy already knows things don't always turn out the way we want."

Early in the summer, after Marvin bought the air conditioner, but before the first trial, one Sunday morning Daddy and I were out on the porch, him carving and me laying on my stomach lining the frontiersmen up to shoot a bear. The bear was an old baseball that was brown with dirt, but it looked more like a bear than anything else around, and it worked fine for my purposes. But while I was setting the shoot up, a chip hit the porch close to my head. I looked up. Daddy was sitting on his chair, cross-legged like a girl, with his tongue in the corner of his mouth and a large knife in his hand. He was studying his wood hard. It wasn't anything yet. I kept looking at him. I could tell he was up to something different.

I said, "What are you making?"

"Don't know for sure. Maybe an Indian."

"A Cherokee?"

"Plains Indian."

"How come?"

"How come what?"

"Why not a Cherokee?"

"I was thinking about making a big headdress."

I went back to playing with the baseball bear and the men. But I thought about that, and it sounded good to me. If he made a Wild Indian, I could play frontiersmen and Indians. But if he made a Cherokee, well, obviously, I couldn't have anybody shoot him.

I don't know how long I played there with Daddy carving, but the morning passed some, and he put his knife and wood down and got up and stretched. He said, "Your uncle Mark's coming over here tonight. We're meeting him at the Dusty Roads for supper."

I was caught by total surprise. Aunt Rosa was writing me letters a couple of times a week and she hadn't said anything about that. I said, "Are you sure?"

He leaned on his arm against one of the porch posts. "Nothing's ever sure. But I think so."

"How come?"

"The trial of the man who killed your uncle Joe finally starts tomorrow."

"Can I go?"

"A courthouse's no place for little girls."

"Is Aunt Rosa coming?"

"Don't know. Hasn't she said anything about it in those letters?"

I shook my head. And I felt disappointed that I was going to miss something as interesting as a trial and also uneasy because Aunt Rosa hadn't even told me anything about it. But I was glad to be going out for supper and glad to be seeing Uncle Mark. I had told Bella I would visit that afternoon, but I stayed at home instead and held tools for Daddy because he wanted to tune up the truck before we went over there.

When we got to the Dusty Roads, Uncle Mark wasn't in the same booth we always sat in when Mama was dying. He was in one in the far back corner. He looked a little fatter since the last time I had seen him, and he had on short sleeves and was smoking a cigarette. He got up, slapped Daddy on the arm, and said, "Sure glad to see ya, Jack." Daddy gave him the same greeting, and then Uncle Mark said, "Give me a big ole hug, Kit," and he bent down and I did. Then I just looked around.

Uncle Mark is a pretty smart man, and as soon as we sat down he said, "I'm sure you're wondering why your aunt Rosa isn't with me." It was a statement rather than a question, and I didn't say anything, just looked at him. He went on, "She wanted to come. So did Lou and Dennis. But Dennis misses too much work as it is. And Lou, well, you know she's not big on sitting out in public, fanning herself in a room full of people."

I knew that to be true, so I nodded. But I did notice that Aunt Lou wasn't really the question.

Uncle Mark knew that, too, and he raised a hand to the waitress and said, "Two three-twos and a lemonade." Then he went on. "Your aunt Rosa was going to surprise you, but we've had a little problem at home."

That scared me a little. I said, "What?"

"Your grandmother had a dizzy spell."

Daddy said, "Is she out of the hospital yet?"

My uncle shook his head.

I must have looked puzzled. Uncle Mark added, "Not this one. The hospital at home."

But that wasn't what I was puzzled about. I said, "Did you know about Grandma?" and looked at Daddy.

"Mark called yesterday evening when you were cleaning fish. I decided to let him tell it."

I didn't know about any diseases except TB, so I didn't know what to ask except "Is she gonna die?"

Uncle Mark said, "No, no. The doctor says it's her blood pressure. They're gonna get it under control. I probably oughta do something about mine, too. Rosa's convinced these are part of my problem." He held his cigarette up like it was a pencil. "But the damn things are sure hard to quit." He took another puff and stumped the cigarette out.

After that, we ordered food and they got to talking about the trial. I didn't know as much about trials then as I do now, so it may be that I'm using what I learned in the second trial to explain about this one. But I don't really know about that, and never will. There are pieces of information I'm missing, and others I think are turned around in the wrong holes. It's sort of like a jigsaw puzzle where most of the picture is put together, but one corner or maybe the top or bottom is still not worked out. In a jigsaw you always have faith that all the pieces are there and colored on the right side to make the picture, but I'm not sure that's true of my memory. In fact, I'm almost sure it's not. I'm certain I now have pieces from other puzzles, and I bet some of mine are lost, and not just under the table.

Anyway, what I remember is that Daddy and Uncle Mark both thought that the trial took too long to happen. Uncle Joe had been dead a year, and for a lot of that time Frank Still had been out of jail walking around, going to his job over at the mill just like he never killed anyone in his life, let alone committed a murder.

They went on back and forth through the whole meal, but they talked in low voices and Uncle Mark kept an eye on the rest of the place. I watched his eyes and turned around two or three times to see who walked in. Daddy did the same, and each time he nodded, telling Uncle Mark it was okay to keep talking.

My uncle was of the opinion that Frank Still would get convicted. But Daddy said he didn't think there was a chance in hell of that. His point was that there were too many men standing around watching Uncle Joe die. They'd all need to be convicted and they weren't going to put each other in jail. Daddy said good men standing around and not doing anything allows meanness to grow like weeds in a garden. Uncle Mark agreed with that, but he kept arguing that it was cold blooded murder to cut up a man as drunk as Uncle Joe was, and that we didn't fight the war to allow that kind of injustice to go on in our own country. He didn't think we were living in Germany.

Even I knew we weren't living in Germany. But I kept quiet and ate my French fries, and learned that Daddy had met Uncle Joe in the war. They lived together in a hole in the ground for a long time during a battle called the Bulge, and it was like living in hell. Uncle Mark said that in the middle of their argument. Then he looked me in the eye and waved his fork. He said, "Kit, your daddy is a war hero. Tougher than a goddamn oak tree. So was Joe, for that matter, just weak to drink. But he came by that naturally. Me, I just sat out the war driving officers around. But your daddy and Joe saw some real fighting. The worst there was."

Daddy said, "That's enough of that." Then he burped. "Ruined my digestion."

They went back to talking about the trial. Uncle Mark said he was there to sit in the courtroom to remind the judge and everybody else that Uncle Joe had a family who loved him. Daddy said nobody would know Mark was Joe's family because he didn't look a thing like him. They talked back and forth about how to best handle that, and Daddy said that when we got home he'd call Charlie Simmons and tell him. Charlie Simmons was the newspaper reporter who'd been around when Uncle Joe died. We left with them agreeing that we'd meet the next night, have dinner again, and hear all about what happened.

24

The next morning, I went to Bella's to tell her the news. Even from a distance down the road, I saw she was sitting on a kitchen chair on her porch like she was waiting for me. I liked that, naturally, and I waved. But she didn't wave back. She just sat there and stared like she was mad. I decided before I got to the porch that whatever she was mad about, I could make her glad with the interesting news about the trial. And I started our conversation while I was still in the front yard. I said, "You'll never guess what's happening."

She said, "Why don't you tell me?" Only she said it in sort of a mean way.

"Uncle Joe's murderer's trial starts today. Uncle Mark came over for it. We went out to dinner last night."

Bella ran her hand through her hair and cocked her head at an angle. She said, "I see. You could have told somebody."

I realized then I was in trouble for not coming to see her the day before because I'd said I would. That surprised me. I'd never seen Bella get mad. But it also made me feel like she really cared about me or she wouldn't have gotten her feelings hurt. So I told her that Daddy had asked me to help him get the truck running good, and that it was an important trip, and that I couldn't let him down. It was an exaggeration, maybe a white lie. But I did it as much to make Bella feel better as I did to get out of trouble.

Bella licked her lips like she was thinking about if it was a good excuse or not. And she must have decided to give me a pass, because the next thing she said was, "Do you want some sweet tea?"

I did, and she said, "Stay here. I'll get it." She went inside the door, which she'd started keeping closed because of the air conditioner, and she came back with two glasses of tea. She handed me one and sat down on the porch beside me instead of back in the chair. I knew by that more than by anything else that she liked me again, and I told her about everything that was said during the dinner. I added my own feelings because she liked to know what I felt about everything. She didn't ask too many questions, so I told her some details that I thought might make the story more interesting. They didn't really happen, but they could have, and they weren't big lies, just little white ones. But I didn't tell her about Daddy being a war hero. I needed to think that over some more, and I didn't want Bella and Daddy to become friends. The truth was, and I'm ashamed of it, I would've rather Daddy be lonely than me.

The next night, we ate in the same booth at the Dusty Roads, only this time Mr. Simmons, the reporter, ate with us. There was a lot of talk about selecting the jury. That's a hard thing to do in a county where everybody knows everybody else, but that's a good example of what I'm saying about not really knowing if I knew that during the first trial or not. Uncle Mark was worried the jury would be bought. But Daddy kept saying nobody was going to have to waste their money buying the jury. They whole town was guilty of not caring about Uncle Joe. They thought he was just a drunk Indian, no matter what he had done in the war.

Mr. Simmons drank his beers and ate dinner smoking and writing notes on a pad next to his plate. But they had all agreed even before the first beer that the whole conversation was off the record. Mr. Simmons said he was taking notes for background. I think, though, he was just a nervous man and taking notes kept him busy like smoking gave Uncle Mark something to do. Daddy never showed his nerves any way at all. But he had them, and they would explode.

Bella was nicer when I got there on Tuesday morning. She was in her garden on the east side of the chicken house. It had a fence around it that was about two feet high. Bella knew chickens can fly higher than two feet, but she also knew most of them are lazy and won't often try. The fence was made out of barbed wire and sticks. As I think back on it now, I realize that Bella wasn't strong enough to dig postholes, and that may be the reason the fence was so skimpy. We'd grown Uncle Joe's vegetables for him, so the fence wasn't already there when Bella moved in.

Bella's tomatoes were ripening behind ours, but she was proud of them. She showed me some beautiful ones before I told her about the jury being selected. I didn't add in any extra things because I don't do that very often, and Bella seemed to understand that juries can be bought and that people in small towns stick together.

I did leave out the part about Uncle Joe being a drunk. I didn't think Bella would really mind if he was, but I know it's not a nice thing to say about a person. So I didn't tell Bella about Uncle Joe except that he'd been in the war and had done well while he was there. But I will say here just for the record that Uncle Joe was always good to me. He never said or did a mean thing, and my mother loved him a lot, and she wouldn't have if he'd been mean.

Anyway, the visit with Bella went well and she was back to her old self again. So I think I told about the right things, and, of course, I showed up like I said I would. I wanted Bella to know I was someone she could count on. I felt bad I had let her down, but I think I made it up to her and our fight was totally in the past.

The trial only lasted one more day. And not really a full one. Uncle Mark came to our house in mid-afternoon of the next day while I was reading one of the Dr. Dolittle books on the porch. He got out of his car shaking his head, and I could tell from that he had bad news. When he got to the porch, he rubbed the back of his neck and said, "Don't guess Jack's around anywhere?"

"He's turning stubble for Mr. Surry."

"Where's Surry's?"

"No one place really. He's got a lot of land."

"Well, Kit, I guess you can tell I wouldn't be here this time of day if the news was good. They let that son of a bitch off with time served."

"How come?"

"They said it was self-defense."

I said, "Was it?"

"Frank Still didn't have a cut on him."

"So what does that mean?"

Uncle Mark took his handkerchief out of his pocket and wiped his face with it. He said, "Can I have a drink of water?"

I got him a glass of water and got one for myself. Then Uncle Mark sat down on the side of the porch like Bella and he talked. He didn't talk the same way she did because she always kept her eyes and attention right on me. Uncle Mark talked more to the air. He rambled on for a good while, and some of it I don't think made sense to even him. But his drift was that Uncle Joe made people uncomfortable. He had done a lot of fighting and killing in the war, and people had a hard time accepting that from an Indian. It scared them. He also said there wasn't anything that made most white people more self-righteous than a drunk. Then he said that self-righteousness is just another form of hate, one that's taught in church.

I didn't even really know what self-righteousness was at the time. I don't believe I had ever heard the word, so I couldn't even think about that. So I settled on the part of what Uncle Mark was saying that I knew something about, white people and Indians. Unless they were trying to teach me something particular that Indians have to know, my family didn't talk about being Indians any more than white people sit around talking about being white. People are just who they are without thinking about it unless they have a reason to.

And while Uncle Mark was rambling on trying to make sense of the trial, I decided I wouldn't have ever even noticed Uncle Joe was an Indian or thought about it except that one night in the jail when we were sitting outside the cell on the little bench, one of the other prisoners called him Chief Cheap Whiskey. Uncle Joe didn't pay him any mind, but Daddy, who was at the counter waiting for the deputy to return, came over to the cell, crooked his finger at the man and smiled. Then when the man came over to the bars, Daddy reached out and grabbed him by the collar and banged his head against the bars about three times. After that, he let him go, and the man slid to the floor. Daddy walked back to the counter and stood there like he was before. Mama got up and we went outside. But all the way home in the truck, Uncle Joe kept chuckling and telling Daddy he'd sure suckered that white son of a bitch.

Uncle Mark talked about how the trial turned out through another glass of water. Then he said he wouldn't be around for supper, he was going home to explain to everybody. He told me to tell Daddy everything he said and to tell him to buy a paper. Daddy didn't like reading, but he brought home two or three papers a week just to keep up with things like the price people were getting for corn. I read them from front to back. So I told Uncle Mark I'd take care of that.

25

One day, a couple of weeks after Frank Still's trial was over, I found Bella standing in the ruts in front of the cabin with her fists on her hips. Her hair looked like it either hadn't been brushed or she'd been running her hands through it. I knew right away there was something wrong, and when I got up to her, worry showed in her eyes. She said, "That other guinea's gone."

I had my fishing pole and my bait with me and I had been planning on fishing for supper, but I could see I needed to be guinea searching instead. I said, "Does she have a hideout?" because sometimes chickens turn funny and start going off to special, strange places. Usually, with chickens, you can track them. Sometimes they're dying, but most of the time they're just nesting.

Bella said, "Not that I know of."

I said, "Have you looked under the house?"

"That's the first place I looked. But she's not under there, unless she's up in the flooring."

I wasn't sure what "up in the flooring" meant. So I tried to remember if any of Uncle Joe's chickens had nested under the cabin. That can be quite a problem if there's not a stop put to it, so he probably would have mentioned it. But I couldn't recall that he ever had. So I figured maybe the guinea wasn't under the cabin unless they did something stupid putting the new bathroom in. I said, "Did you look under the bathroom part of the house?"

She said, "I looked under the porch. You can see clear to the back."

What she was talking about is that the cabin was set up on sandstones to keep it off the ground. I don't know anything about house building, or why they didn't set it on a foundation, but that's how it was built and being set on the stones helped keep the snakes out. However, once Uncle Joe did kill a snake in his kitchen. He chopped him in two with his hoe. But that snake had probably come in the front door because, up to then, Uncle Joe had had a habit of propping that door open. He skinned that snake and ate him and let me play with his rattlers. He said snake tastes like chicken thighs.

But I'm a little off the track here. I was writing about guineas. They can fly, of course, whereas snakes can't. And I thought it was possible that whoever put the bathroom in had left an opening up off the ground that the guinea was nesting in.

I told that to Bella, and we went around to the back of the cabin and I crawled in under it and checked under the bathroom. Whoever had added it had nailed together some boards to cover the pipes where they came through the flooring down into the ground. That was like a box set up in under there, but it was a tight box, and there weren't any spaces between the boards that a bird could wiggle into and build a nest behind. So that theory was wrong.

After that, Bella and I sat down on the hillside and she told me everywhere she had looked for her guinea. Mostly, that was just pretty close around the cabin, chicken house, and garden. Bella wasn't much of an adventurer. She had never once gone fishing with me. But she had checked inside Uncle Joe's old outhouse, and she said that was the first and last time she was opening that door.

I said, "When was the last time you saw her?"

"I don't know. A couple of days ago. I'm not a person who counts my chickens every day."

I laughed at that because Daddy often said that some people count their chickens every day and that those people are probably counting yours, too. But I didn't tell Bella that. I said, "Can you remember hearing her?"

"Yes, I can. She screeched at Marvin."

That meant the guinea had been there on the weekend and it was only Tuesday. I said, "That's not long. Maybe she's not really gone for good."

Bella pulled up a weed with a flower on it. She said, "Kit, does it strike you as odd that both the guineas are gone, but none of the chickens are?"

I thought about that. And I couldn't think of any animal that had a taste for guineas, but not for chickens. Foxes and wolves and hawks go for either one. I said, "Well, you just said you don't count your chickens every day. Maybe some of them are gone, too."

Bella said, "I suppose. But what if somebody is watching me and they're killing the guineas?"

I said, "Don't people keep guineas mostly for snakes, not to eat?"

"Some people eat them. But I got them because I can't have a dog around me."

I didn't know what to say. People killing your guineas to eat seemed far-fetched.

"What if some of the townspeople want to watch me? Or, maybe, Mrs. Burnett?"

"You mean somebody would want to steal up on you without you knowing it?"

Bella nodded, and she studied her flower like she was thinking deep. I picked a flower, too. And my mind settled on her theory and turned it over. But I decided it was more likely that the guinea had taken a powder. Birds have minds of their own.

Bella hadn't wanted me to leave her to go fishing, so I didn't bring in any meat. That evening, Daddy and I ate bacon sandwiches. But they were good and he made wilted lettuce and we had ripe tomatoes to go with them, so we weren't hurting for food. In the middle of the meal, I asked him, "Do you know anything about guineas?"

He said, "What do you want to know?"

"Are they like chickens?"

"You've seen guineas, Kit." He helped himself to more lettuce.

"I'm asking for Bella," I said. "Hers have gone missing."

Daddy took a long drink of sweet tea. Then he said, "I never raised guineas, myself. They scream like machine guns. But I think they're bad to go off and nest. Hers are females, aren't they?"

"How do you tell?"

"I don't know. They all look the same to me. But there's no reason to keep a male. He won't give eggs. And I think they're hard on roosters."

I chewed on that. Nesting was the best theory. Bella could worry about things that weren't real. She had, earlier in the summer, found a spider that didn't look quite right to her. She smashed him, of course. But when I got to her house, before we could do anything, I had to look under everything, in every hidey hole, and behind the refrigerator, stove, and hot water tank, all just for poisonous spiders. I didn't turn up a single one, but I didn't mind hunting them either. I don't want to be around a fiddleback spider myself, and I liked doing things for Bella. I was glad she had a need for me. I don't think you can really love somebody and not need them and want them to need you. We aren't like silos out in the fields, we're more like fences connected to each other. We have to have our own posts in the ground to keep from sagging, but a line of fence just standing out alone doesn't keep anything in or anything out.

Anyway, the next day, I told Bella what Daddy said about guineas being bad to nest. We decided to go out searching for the big one, and Bella changed into long-legged pants. Now, I had seen her in shorts. In fact, she wore them pretty often once it got hot. But she usually wore dresses and I didn't even realize she had any pants. However, I may have seen them when I was looking for the spiders and just not noticed them. They were folded in her drawer, not hanging on the rack.

We decided not to search in the road north toward my house. I walked that road all the time. If there were a guinea nesting in the weeds beside it, I probably would've at least heard its rustling. Also, the wheat had been harvested and the fields both north and west of Bella's had been planted in new crops that weren't high. There was no place in them for a guinea to hide. So, we went east toward the bayou, as that was pasture and a wild place, and, also, familiar to me. We both, of course, had snake sticks, and we used them against the weeds.

We were not very far off the ruts into the pasture when I heard Bella grunt. I had been looking at the ground and was about fifteen or twenty feet from her. But I could sense at a distance any change in Bella's movement or mood, and I have pretty good ears. I looked up. Mrs. Burnett was standing northeast of us.

Bella seemed sort of frozen. So, I said in a loud voice, "Hi, Mrs. Burnett. We're looking for Bella's guinea."

Mrs. Burnett said, "Come here, Karen." And she shot Bella a look like a schoolteacher.

I went. It wasn't a choice situation. But Bella, who I thought would come with me, just stood still in the pasture.

When I got up to Mrs. Burnett, the first thing I noticed was that she smelled awful. She was not using any deodorant or perfume, and the day was as hot as a firecracker. I stepped back. But she grabbed my arm. She said, "Children don't call adults by their Christian names." Her eyebrows were thick over her nose. Above them were wrinkles. She smelled like she'd been eating dead things.

I was in a trap I knew I couldn't get out of myself. I looked toward Bella to rescue me. And she came through. She said, "I told Kit to call me by my first name. My husband ran off with another woman and his name is painful to me."

Mrs. Burnett let go of my arm. But she glared at Bella. She said, "You're a Jezebel. Only worse."

Bella said, "We do the best we can, Mrs. Burnett. How has your day been?"

Mrs. Burnett said, "At least I'm not going to hell." Then she said, "Get off my land."

I staggered back. I had never felt that much hatred. It stung like a hot wind blowing dust.

Bella said, "We will. Come here, Kit." And she held out her hand real gentle and made a motion for me to come to her.

I backed away from Mrs. Burnett until I was well out of her reach. Then I turned and walked toward Bella, hitting my snake stick against the ground. Bella turned toward the lane and walked ahead of me. I could tell by the way she walked that she was trembling on her front side. But the back side that she showed to Mrs. Burnett and me, well, it was graceful, and she held her head high.

26

I always waited for the bookmobile behind an oak tree at the edge of the gravel where it pulled in off the highway. The highway was a state road, and all sorts of people drove it, so there was no use just standing out beside it in the broad daylight, attracting trouble that might be traveling east or west. The tree was big enough to hide me, and Miss Francis knew to stop even if it looked like there was nobody there. The oak had two large roots that I fit right between, and it was really a comfortable place for reading, even though I was limited to books I had already read because, obviously, I was waiting for the new books to arrive.

I always let Miss Francis pull the bookmobile to a complete stop and honk the horn before I got up, dusted my rear off, and headed on in. Usually, I was the only person at that stop, and that was true on the Thursday after Mrs. Burnett ran Bella and me off her place.

I had paced my Dr. Dolittles by reading other books in between them so the series would last. I was finished with the last one and I was looking for a new series to start. But my main concern was finding out who Jezebel was. Bella was too upset by Mrs. Burnett's meanness to do anything except shut the door hard behind us, get a drink of whiskey, and lie down on the bed. I rubbed her back for a long time, and tried to give her some comfort, but I knew not to ask any questions.

I didn't ask Daddy, either. It was clear to me that Jezebel wasn't a very nice thing to be called, and I didn't want him to get any wrong ideas about Bella. It was also clear to me then, and still is now, that no matter what anybody says, Mrs. Burnett was rotten in her very heart. There's a lot of wrong done in the world, everybody commits it, but some wrong comes from love and need and some comes from hate and jealousy. There's a difference between those two kinds of wrongs that a lot of people can't see.

But Miss Francis was the perfect person to ask about Jezebel. She knew everything in books, and she was helpful. (The librarian here at Ashley Lordard doesn't like for anybody to read the books. Miss Francis wanted people to read.) So once she put the borrowing cards back in the books I was returning, I said, "I'm thinking about reading about Jezebel."

Miss Francis blinked hard several times. Her eyes were a little buggy, so it was easy to notice that. She said, "Jezebel, really?"

I nodded. "Really. You got any books on her?"

"Just one."

"Is it checked out?"

"No, it's not. But you probably have a copy at home."

We didn't hardly have any books at home except almanacs. I said, "What's its name?"

Well, you probably know the answer to that, and I guess I should pretend I did, too, or maybe not even put this part in here for anybody to read because a lot of people think reading the Bible is something you should do every day like brushing your teeth. And that, somehow, you get good by reading the Bible. I know now from personal experience that's not true, but back then I'd never even opened a Bible or been around people who did, except for Aunt Jean. So Miss Francis's answer came as a surprise to me. I said, "Is that the only one? Nothing else?"

I wound up getting a whole bunch of books about the Hardy Boys. But as soon as I hit the front door of the house, I started searching for a Bible. Now, I'm not a sneaky person. Daddy taught me to respect other people's property, so normally when I was home all day alone I didn't go through his stuff. And I don't think he went through mine. But I broke our rule and searched high and low for a Bible. I knew there had to be one somewhere because Daddy's daddy was a preacher and they were in all the classrooms at school and teachers sometimes read from them at assemblies. So I figured if I looked everywhere I'd find one. And I did. We had a desk in the living room that had several drawers, and in one of those drawers, under some papers, was a Bible.

Well, finding the Bible was just the first part of the problem solved. It's a very big book and has thin pages. I've seen Bibles since that have a list of names in the back and pages where those people are mentioned, but as my luck would have it, that wasn't the case with Daddy's copy. It did, however, have at the top of the pages a few words, like "The test of leprosy," and "Spies sent to Canaan," that tell you the general subject the writing's about. Finally, after I had very carefully licked my thumb and gone through page after page without tearing a single one, I came upon the name Jezebel at the top of a page in Kings.

I read that whole part. And it didn't make any sense to me. That is, except for one line, and that caught my attention like a bass jumping out of water. It was, "And of Jezebel the Lord also said, 'The dogs shall eat Jezebel within the bounds of Jezreel.'" I, to this day, don't know where Jezreel is, but I knew instantly that line was a bad omen. A feeling of dread crept over me that was the worst I've ever had, and that includes when Granddaddy died. That sentence told me right then, right there, that Bella was going to die a violent death, and that there was nothing I could do to stop it.

I would tell you that I was panic-stricken, and I guess I was. But I wasn't panic-stricken like I was running around with my jeans on fire.

I was more panic-stricken deep in my heart. I was too scared to move for a long time, and my mind went off somewhere else. The next thing I remember, Daddy was home and I was in the front swing and I hadn't even started dinner.

He said, "Kit, what are you doing?"

I said, "Nothing."

He said, "It looks like you're reading the Bible." And his head tilted over to the side and his eyes squeezed up.

I said, "Miss Francis suggested it."

"Who's Miss Francis?"

"The bookmobile lady. I told you about her."

"Oh, yeah. I forgot. How far along is supper?"

The lie came out quick. I said, "I was waiting on you to get home to make wilted lettuce."

He said, "Did you catch anything?"

I hadn't gone fishing all week. Bella just wanted us to visit in the house and I didn't want to run into Mrs. Burnett. I said, "The fish still aren't biting. It's too hot."

Now, it's true that fish mostly don't bite in hot weather, so Daddy believed me. He said, "What's our alternative for meat?"

I said, "Country ham."

He said, "That'll do. Put that Bible away and get to chopping onions," and he left to clean up.

Daddy wasn't a big talker by any means and he didn't much tell me what to do. But I guess he could see I wasn't myself that night at dinner. And he started talking in a way I'd never heard him talk before. He said, "Kit, I don't want you reading the Bible. You can when you're older if you want to. But it's not something for children to be reading by themselves. It's got too many things in it that are confusing, and they're used all the time in ways that are just twisted. Do you understand what I'm saying to you?"

I said, "Some of the parts are scary."

"That's right. They are. They're used to frighten people. And I suspect they were written for that purpose, too. If I thought the Bible would be a comfort to you, I wouldn't care if you read it. But it's not a comfort to people. It causes more torment than any one thing I've ever seen, except war. And people put a lot of energy into trying to understand it that they should be putting into things worthwhile, like working and loving and being thankful we've got beds to sleep in and food to eat and that nobody's trying to kill us on a daily basis."

I enjoyed Daddy talking to me. And I wasn't about to read the Bible any more. But just to keep the conversation going, because talking was a comfort, I said, "The other kids read it all the time."

Daddy forked a big slice of tomato and put it on his plate. "I'm sure they do. And their parents take them to church. But we're not church-going people."

I said, "Why?"

Daddy sighed. Then he said, "Kit, when I was your age, I went to church every time the doors opened. Had to. Daddy was the preacher. But he was a hard man when he didn't have to be. He condemned people to Hell for being sprinkled rather than dunked in water for their baptism, and for dancing, and for card playing and just for trying to have a good time. People would worry over those things, and they'd come to our house and sit in the living room, or at the kitchen table, with their hats all twisted in their hands, just tormented about nothing. Kit, nobody knows what God's going to do. Not even preachers. But preachers like to have the upper hand by pretending they've got inside information. And they like to see people squirm and cry if they don't follow in just exactly the way they want them to. My Daddy wasn't trying to save anybody's soul, although he claimed to be doing that every day. He was just trying to have power over people. That's all it amounted to."

Daddy didn't say any more after that, and I already had so much to think about that I didn't ask him anything. We just finished the rest of the meal in silence, and for once I didn't mind. But I've thought about what Daddy said again and again. He nailed Rev. Cunningham and

Mr. Hodges both, even though Mr. Hodges isn't a real preacher, just a big Christian. I think they're the same kind of men as my father's father and more interested in power and in getting their way than in helping anybody. And it is of considerable interest to me how they can both be men who a lot of people look up to and are running around scot-free while Daddy is locked up and in a real pickle.

27

Caroline found out what tribe the new girls belong to! They're Choctaws from Mississippi. They talk English as well as the rest of us. The one in my class hadn't said a word of English to anyone other than Caroline, but at recess, Caroline got her to slip off into the woods, and Lana and I met up with them in a hole in a cane thicket that was made by kids who came before us and that we keep up to have some privacy.

The first thing Lana asked her was, "What's your real name?"

And she said, "Linda."

We were surprised. So I said, "Is your sister really named Susan?"

She nodded. "We couldn't hide our names with all that social work information."

We all knew what that meant and I felt stupid for not figuring that out earlier. They have big folders on us they call case histories. What they really are is the dirt on us and our families that they're using to keep us here. I've seen my folder a lot of times. Not in it, but the folder itself. Mr. Hodges keeps mine on his desk sometimes. I don't know if he keeps anybody else's on his desk, too. Mine is the only one I've seen. But he could. There's no telling what he'll do.

We told Linda our names and tribes, and then we got to telling her all the stuff she needs to know to survive. I'm sure every school has those kinds of rules, who you can't cross and who you can trust, and who's nice and who's not. Lana and Caroline did most of the talking because I just sort of went off in my head. Not like I usually do, but remembering actual stuff about my main social worker, Mary Jayne.

Mary Jayne was real nice and had long gray hair and big blue eyes. Sometimes her hands shook, but not because she was nervous. I think because some people are just like that, or they have something go wrong with them and they get like that. I know it's off the point, but things do go wrong with people, and if we can just overlook that or help them out, it's better for them and for us, too. I didn't trust Mary Jayne at first. But she tried to help me. And I bet that if I could see inside my folder, I'd find out the information they're using to keep me here was written by Rev. Cunningham, not by her.

When my mind drifted back to the conversation with Linda, Lana was talking about how mean Tessy is. Caroline is too nice to say that sort of thing, but I chimed in. I told Linda about the fight Tessy and I had, and I confessed to socking her. I didn't tell it for recognition. Caroline had already thanked me. But the way she thanked me was odd, and I'm still chewing on it. She hugged me and said, "Kit, don't do anything else to get sent to Mr. Hodges. He's mean."

As I said before, Mr. Hodges acts like he's the big Christian example for everyone to follow. But what Caroline said made me wonder if he's mean to her, too. I've been trying to think of a way to ask her about that, but I haven't come up with a good solution. Even if Caroline was white, I don't think I could ask her how she knows Mr. Hodges is mean. There are just some things you can't ask people about.

Actually, there are a lot of things you can't ask people about around here. The main rule is don't ask anybody about their family. But you also can't ask people why they are here or when they're getting out. I wondered if Caroline and Lana had mentioned those rules to Linda while I was thinking about Mary Jayne, but nobody ever says those rules out loud, so they probably didn't, and when my mind got back on the present I changed the subject. I said, "Another thing you need to know is that they think Indians are dirty." I wasn't sure they thought that, but I was almost sure. I told her, "We're only assigned to the cleaning squads."

Lana said, "You're right. I never realized that." And she looked like somebody had just pinched her bottom. Then anger came up in her eyes. Caroline reached out and put her hand on her arm. She just held it there until the anger went away. She let go and Lana shook her head and made sort of a grunting noise.

The way the squads work here is that every child is assigned to at least one, but sometimes to more. There's boys' work and girls' work. The boys do most of the heavy outside work, like mowing the lawns, tending the fields, cleaning up after winter, and window washing outside, high up. They also dig the septic tanks, which is, I'll tell you, a never-ending chore. They keep the boys on the other side of the campus except if they have work over here. So, I don't know the details of their assignments, just what I see them do.

But on the girls' side, I've got a good fix on everything. The assignments get made mostly depending on what grade you are in. A lot of the high school girls do the looking after the little ones. I had somebody who looked after me the first year I was here. That was two years ago and her name was Evelyn. She was sort of nice, but you could tell she didn't want to spend her time with a kid, which was all right because I didn't want to spend my time with her, either. Mostly, when we were together we just read. She read fashion and hair magazines and I read books. Then Evelyn disappeared. And I don't know what happened to her, but that's just the way it is around here. People appear and disappear.

I didn't tell Linda that. You don't talk about that either because there's always the hope that some new person will get attached to you, and you don't want to say anything that will keep them away. At least, I always hope somebody will get attached to me. But a lot of the girls here have already given up. You can see it in their eyes and their shoulders. But not me. I'm not going to be that fence standing alone out in the field, so I don't give up hope. That would be against my nature. I am descended from people who survived the Trail of Tears. Aunt Rosa keeps reminding me of that in letters. So I'll just put one foot in front of the other until I get to where I have to go. It doesn't make any difference if they are driving me to it. Those that gave up hope and stopped on the road died in the snow.

But back to my point about the chores. The high school girls also do the mending, most of the letter writing and cooking and the hair cutting. Mending and cooking are things that obviously need to be done anywhere there are people. And hair cutting is something they do to the white girls, too, although they don't have to wear theirs as short as we do. But the letter writing is a special project set up by Mr. Hodges. He says we live on donations, and we have to get them. Sometimes, the younger girls write short little thank you notes. I've done it, but not much because I'm usually cleaning. The longer letters always get written by the big girls. They have books of letters they copy them from. Each letter is numbered and Mrs. Williams keeps track of what letters have gone to which donors, so that the same donor doesn't get the same letter twice from two different girls. That would look too fakey. The letters have to sound sincere.

In the fourth, fifth, and sixth grades, we mostly do cleaning and help with table setting, dish washing, and gardening chores. As I think I've mentioned before, Mrs. Ritter is the official cleaning woman, but the kids do the work. And what I'm saying about the Indians is that, although the white girls have to clean, too, they get to do other chores. For instance, the girls do the garden and flowerbed weeding, and I'd like to do that and am good at it. But I didn't once get that assignment last spring. And so far this spring, not a single Indian girl has gotten to do garden work of any kind. I've been watching and keeping count.

That's not hard to do because the number is zero. It's April, a lot of the garden is in.

They do let me read to the little kids. I'm the youngest girl here that gets to do that. I have a good voice and know a lot of words, and I don't mind little kids. I wouldn't want to be around them all the time, but I know how they feel and know that a good story read well will take their minds off their worries for a few minutes or an hour. I've started practicing my reading a lot so I can do more of it. It beats mopping floors.

But I didn't tell Linda that part, either. I didn't want to be bragging. And shortly after I told her about the Indians getting only cleaning assignments, the bell rang for recess to be over and we had to split up so that when we came out of the woods we'd look like we had been different places. You don't have to be a genius to know that white people don't want to see a bunch of Indians come out of the woods together. I haven't seen much TV, but I've seen a little, and I know what happens to Indians that come out of hiding all of a sudden. Bang, bang, they get killed.

The one thing I didn't get to tell Linda that I wanted to is about sitting in your closet. I know she's seen girls do that every night and knows about it. But there are all sorts of closet rules. Like, it's fine to be in yours whenever you want to. But don't go in anybody else's uninvited, no matter what. And also you get to keep whatever you want in your closet, but you need to find the hidey hole. I think there's at least one in every closet and I guess the school people know it and just overlook it. But just to be sure, everybody acts like they don't have anything important or valuable in theirs. I've got some of the little trinkets Aunt Rosa has sent to me in mine, and every now and then I'll say something like "I have one of those in my hole," depending on whatever it is someone is showing off. But it's never anything worth anything because no one wants anybody rummaging around.

But, really, there are hardly any thieves around here, unless you count Mr. Hodges and the other people running this place who are stealing our lives. But the girls don't steal, and that's sort of against human nature. I think the reason for it is that if something went missing everyone would be forced to open up their hidey holes for inspection. And even if they're empty, they are the only secret parts of our beings. We want to protect them more than we want anything that belongs to anybody else. I may be wrong, but that's my theory.

28

I didn't go fishing again until Saturday. By then, I really needed to catch some, and I'd sort of convinced myself that Mrs. Burnett didn't mean for <u>me</u> to never come on her property again. And that was the only way to get to the bayou. So, I walked past Bella's, noticed Marvin's car there, and figured that, at least inside the cabin, everything was okay. Then I walked through Mrs. Burnett's pasture just like nothing had ever happened. Or really, that's what I tried to look like on the outside. On the inside, I was shaking.

Once I got to the bayou, I picked out a shady place where a tree curved over the water. The bayou is sometimes green, sometimes brown, and sometimes blue, but on that day it was blue, and there were little silver spots dancing on the surface where the sunlight broke through the leaves onto the water. I settled in, and pretty quickly a catfish started gumming my bait. I let him gum and felt sure that I'd have dinner on my stringer in a few minutes.

While the catfish and I played with one another, I got to thinking about Marvin's DeSoto. Usually, Stan's Ford was at Bella's at least one morning a weekend. But it seemed to me that lately I'd seen only the DeSoto. That sort of bothered me. I didn't mind Marvin, but I preferred Bella to have two boyfriends to one, and I decided to ask her about Stan on my way back. About the time I got that settled in my mind, that catfish took my bobber all the way under and held it. I jerked my pole to the right, and he took the bait lower. That started a tug of war. The catfish was so strong that I had to steady myself with my leg against the trunk of the tree. My pole bent and I hoped to goodness the fish didn't break it.

And he didn't. But when I drew him out of the water, my pole was bent double and the catfish was bigger than any fish I'd ever caught. He was so close to the ground that his tail hit it with a whapping sound. I got in front of him and pulled him along on his belly farther away from the bank so he wouldn't flip and flop back into the water. Finally, he just lay in the weeds, glared at me and gulped. He was colored strange, not mud or blue, and I couldn't tell what kind he was. Not any I'd ever caught before. But whatever kind, a catfish that size can be a considerable problem, more so than a bass or any fish other than a gar. And that's because a catfish will cut you in a heartbeat and they'll cut you deep. I knew that it'd be too dangerous to try to get my hook out of his mouth. So I pulled my pole around so the line was tight, and I wound that line around the trunk of a little tree nearby. That gave me two hands to work with.

My stringer was looped in my belt. I got it undone and came on the fish from behind until I straddled him. Then when he took one of those gulps, I poked the metal end of the stringer through his gills. He started fighting and flopping then, and he caught the inside of my left leg with his fin. The blood was instant and so was the pain. Catfish have some kind of poison on their fins that make their cuts sting like the dickens. I cussed and backed off and looked at my leg. The blood was already into my sneaker. I had to stop fighting with the fish and do something about the wound.

At first, I thought I would use my bait sack to wipe off my leg, as it was really an old Gold Medal flour sack. I went back to the bank to get it and my snake stick. But there were just too many old dried worm guts on it. So I took my shirt off and wiped my leg with it. Then, I dipped my shirt in the water, wrung it out, and cleaned off my leg again. The cut was curved and deep into my calf. There wasn't anything out there at the bayou that I could use to stop the bleeding entirely, so I cut my shirt with my pocket knife, tore off a strip, and cleaned my leg with bayou water again. Then I wrapped that strip around my calf tight. But I still had the catfish to deal with.

When I got back to him, he wasn't gulping as much as he had been, and I could tell the sun was doing some of the work for me. Still, a catfish can trick you into thinking he's dying when really he's just resting up to fight you. But the tip of my stringer was hanging out of his lips, so I looked him square in the eye, creeped slowly up to him, and pulled it gently. He started flopping again, but I had him. I pulled that stringer another two feet through his gill and looped it into the ring.

Then I sat down and thought on the situation. I had a cut leg and a catfish longer than my arm that refused to die. If I carried him in the usual way, I knew he'd cut me again. So I cut my line and tied it to my pole, and I wound the stringer around the snake stick and tied it tight with three different knots. Then I squatted down in front of the fish, with my back to him, my pole and bait sack in one hand, and my stick on my shoulder. I spread my feet and struggled up. When I got my balance and looked around, the fish's tail seemed only about six inches off the ground. I tilted the stick to a different angle, but that brought the catfish too close to my back where he could cut me again in a place I couldn't reach.

So I squatted back down, dropped the pole and sack, and took the stick off my shoulder and searched around for what I needed. I found it back toward the bank. It was a stone big enough it took two hands to lift, but it was still small enough to carry. I lugged it to where the catfish was lying in the weeds. Then I lifted it as high as I could and brought it down on his head. That put a stop to everything. I didn't want to do it. But I did. And I am telling this story because it's true and took up that morning, and also because I want whoever reads this, if somebody ever does, to understand that most of us, if we don't have rotten hearts, just do the best we can. Crushing that creature's head wasn't kind, and now I sure wish I hadn't caught that fish. But I did, and I had to do something with it. I had to. And the strange thing is that today when I put my finger on the curved scar on the inside of my leg where the catfish cut me, I can feel that fish living as a part of me. My left leg wouldn't be mine without that scar and the catfish in it.

But back to that day, Bella must have seen me walking the lane with the bloody shirt around my leg, my pole and snake stick across my shoulders steadied by both arms, and that huge fish making me tilt to one side. Before I even got to the cabin she flew off the porch and ran to me with her arms wide. The first thing she did was take the snake stick and my pole off my shoulders and throw them and the fish down in the rut. Then, she grabbed me to her and held me real tight. I said, "I'm okay, but don't throw my fish away."

She said, "He's a monster."

I said, "I had to crush his head."

She said, "Your leg. He cut you."

I looked down then. My leg, both of them really, were streaked with dirt and water and blood. I said, "I'm dirty. But I need my fish."

She said, "Okay. We'll get your fish, but you're coming with me." She picked the snake stick up with both hands because the fish was too big to just use one. Then she said, "Get in front, I want to see how bad you're hurt."

So, I grabbed my pole and we walked to the cabin that way. I went in first and Bella came behind me with the snake stick and fish. She dumped the fish in the sink and ran water over it. Its tail stuck out because it was too big to go in, but she turned to me and said, "See, your fish is taken care of. Now, we're taking care of you." She grabbed me by the shoulder and marched me to the bathroom. In there, she got down on her knees, turned on the tub water, and let it run over her hand until it got to the temperature she wanted. Then she unwrapped the bloody rag on my leg and untied my shoes. She said, "Take your shorts and panties off." I put my hand on her shoulder, and she removed my shoes and then I undressed myself, one leg at a time.

I think that was what Mrs. Burnett saw: Bella down on her knees and me standing there by the tub getting undressed right next to her, with my hand on her shoulder and hers on my waist steadying me. I don't know for sure, but I guess Bella must have left the door open when she came in with the fish. I really can't remember and I wasn't paying any attention to the porch or the door, but the bathroom was right across from them on the other side of the kitchen. With the door open, anybody could see what was going on in there. But, like I said, I don't know for sure. However, that's what people asked me about, and I can't think of any other time that Bella and I were in the bathroom like that together. I'm not saying we weren't. I just can't remember one way or another. But I do remember Bella helping me get clean that day and taking care of me. I remember how tender she was.

29

The next day, Sunday, was the day it all happened. There were people who said that if Daddy had taken me to church like he was supposed to none of it would have ever come about. But I don't think that's true. Uncle Russ wasn't in church that Sunday, and nobody said anything about that.

Daddy and I were on the front porch. He was carving a second Wild Indian when Uncle Russ came in hauling a flatbed trailer behind his truck. It had a mower of some kind on it. I don't know what kind of mower it was because I never worked in the fields and it's not important, but it's a detail I can remember and I've told Mr. Hodges this part of the story over and over. I don't mind saying it because it doesn't make anybody look bad.

Uncle Russ came up to the porch and was friendly like he always was. Then he asked Daddy to come look at his mower and Daddy went with him out to the trailer. They talked out there and Daddy got close up to the machine. Then they walked off to the garage, which is where the tools were kept.

Well, it was about 11:00 by then, and I could tell that Uncle Russ and Daddy were going to get into working on that mower. And it was sort of lonely up on the porch by myself with just wooden men and a dirty baseball to play with, so when they got back from the garage I told Daddy that I was going fishing. He said, "Okay, but we've still got plenty of fish." Then he told Uncle Russ about the giant catfish. I stayed around for the telling because no one walks off in the middle of a story about their own fish. And Uncle Russ asked me some questions about how I hauled the fish in and I showed him my leg where it was bandaged.

I admit I was pretty proud and it all made a good story. By that time it was a real mystery what kind of fish I had caught. Daddy had taken a picture, but it was still in the camera and he told Uncle Russ that he'd never seen a fish like it. He called it a monster, which is the same thing Bella had said. But I told Uncle Russ that she had started out a handsome fish, just big and strange, and looked bad mostly because I had to bash her head in. By then we had skinned and gutted the fish and frozen some of her, so we knew she was carrying eggs and knew she wasn't a him. Anyway, when the fish talk died down, I got my snake stick and some bait and walked on down the road.

Stan's car was at Bella's. I had thought she'd be alone by that late, but I was glad to see the Ford rather than the DeSoto, so I thought it was going to be a pretty good day. (When I tell Mr. Hodges the story I leave this part out even though I remember feeling that way. I know better than to let on to him that I cared who spent the night at Bella's. He'd have a cow or a hissy fit, and it'd just make everything worse.)

I had left everything except my fish and snake stick at Bella's the day before. And she had it sitting out for me next to her front steps. I picked it all up and went on to the bayou. The water was browner that day than blue, and I caught a bunch of little fish that I threw back because they weren't worth keeping. But to tell the entire truth about this part, I was just fishing with little bits of bacon and bread. I've seen catfish bite on everything under the sun, but usually they like big, dirty bait, and I really wasn't in the mood for another fight with a fish. I just wanted to fish a little, maybe catch enough for Bella to eat that night and visit with her. I sure didn't want to take a chance on catching that giant fish's brother or daddy or granddaddy.

And I didn't. I just sat on the bank and watched my bobber dip and shake, and watched, too, the birds flying in and out of the trees. A red winged blackbird was sitting across the bayou from me and he was whistling to his partners on either side. They have territories they guard, and that kind of whistling back and forth is common. But there came a time when the whistling died down and a big crow flew into a dead tree on the bank opposite me. It was right after that crow landed that I heard the first shot.

It was a deer rifle. I know that now because everybody knows it, but I knew it then, too. I know what they sound like. And I knew, also, instantly, what it meant. I knew that in every way you can know anything. I knew it in my head and I knew it in my heart. But just on a practical level I knew there was no good reason to be shooting deer in July.

I don't remember exactly what I did then. I do remember hearing a second shot. That shot I had no explanation for.

They say they found me sitting on the bank of the bayou, just frozen. Not fishing. Not even with my pole in the water. Just sitting, looking straight ahead. I don't remember that. I do remember feeling that I was never going to get off that bank. That I wouldn't leave it no matter what. So when they came for me, I put up a fight. I do remember kicking and screaming. Because I knew, without anybody having to tell me, that my whole life had been stolen from me, but that it wasn't over. And I do remember thinking both then and later that I would have been better off if I had drowned myself in the bayou.

30

The next place I remember being was at Uncle Russ's preacher's house. That's Rev. Cunningham, the old white-haired preacher I mentioned earlier. His living room had doilies in it. His wife was wringing her hands. His chair scratched the backs of my legs.

There was a lot of commotion. Cars driving up. People coming in and out. I sat and watched them. Then Dr. Fletcher came. He told everybody to leave the living room and they did. Then he put his hand on my shoulder and said, "Kit, I'm going to look at your wound." I didn't know what he meant. Then he pointed to my leg. I turned it out so he could see it. He set down his black bag and got down on the floor on his knees. He undid the bandage, folded it over itself so the bloody part was inside, and cleaned my cut. He had to get up and get some water to do that, and somebody, I think, gave him a rag. I was afraid he was going to put some Mercurochrome on me, but he didn't. He did put on some gauze and new tape. Then he said, "It's been an awful day," or something like that.

I said, "I want to see my daddy."

Dr. Fletcher had been on his knees again since getting the bowl of water and rag. He sat down full, with his bottom on the floor and one knee up and the other down. He looked at the space between his legs. He said, "I don't know if they're going to let you do that or not."

I said, "Did he get shot?"

"No. It's just for observation."

I didn't know what that meant. But I was afraid to ask. Instead, I said, "When can I see him?"

Dr. Fletcher put a hand on the floor and got up. I didn't look up at him. I looked at his doctoring bag. He put a hand on my shoulder and said, "I'll try to find out. I'll leave some gauze and tape if the Cunninghams don't have any. That wound needs to be cleaned every day." Then he left.

I don't remember who came in next. Or when. But, finally, Uncle Russ came. By that time, I was in a bedroom with light colored furniture in it. There was a dresser, mirror, bed, and two chairs, one straight-backed for the dresser and an arm chair with a little table beside it. I was in the arm chair, and I remember feeling glad Uncle Russ didn't bring Aunt Jean with him.

He sat down on the straight chair, and as soon as he did I could tell he was tortured. His hair was all tangled and his eyes were puffy like he had been drinking hard or crying. He put his face in his hands and rubbed it. Then he shook his head several times. Finally, he said, "Are you doing any better?"

I didn't know exactly what he was saying. The last time I could remember seeing him, we were talking about my fish. I said, "Where's Daddy?"

"Sheriff Hawkins has got him in the hospital."

"Is he hurt?" I asked.

Uncle Russ blew air out of his mouth real hard. Then he stared at a picture over the bed. It was of a river and some trees.

I said, "He's not hurt, is he?"

Uncle Russ shook his head. "No. Nobody's touched him." Then

he looked at me. "Kit, Jack's my best friend. I'm on his side. You're going to need to help me help him."

I said, "What about Bella?"

Uncle Russ's face turned red. He waved a hand. He said, "Kit, I can't discuss her. There are some people who are going to come talk to you about her. You just tell them the truth, and we'll get your daddy out of as much of this mess as we can."

I said, "What people?"

"I don't know. People from the state or somewhere. I don't know how all of this works."

I said, "Is Bella alive?" I knew the answer to that before I asked it. But nobody had said she was dead and that's something that somehow just needs to be said about people, whether they're alive or they're dead. I would've liked it better if Bella had not been dead, to say the least, but I knew she was, and I knew everything was ruined, but nobody had said it yet.

Uncle Russ shook his head. I started screaming.

31

There are some pieces missing after that. But at some point, I realized I was living in the bedroom with the light colored furniture in it. People came in and out, brought me food, changed my bandage, made me go to the table, or took me to the bathroom and made me stay in there and use it or bathe. But mostly I looked out the windows. Out the west one was the driveway and a garage. The garage was painted white, and the doors were pulled back against the sides. They stayed open all the time. There was also a bush under that window. I don't know what kind.

Out the other window was the backyard and the clothesline. Beyond them was a fence and a field. Sometimes, there were cows in that field. I decided later they belonged to somebody else because the Cunninghams didn't know much about anything except living in a house and going to church. There were also big trees in that field. I never went out there, but I'm almost sure they were pecans. That window also overlooked the back door.

Most people went in and out that door. But when my aunts visited, they must have stopped the car in the pull-in at the front of the house and come in the front door. They took me by surprise. Mrs. Cunningham knocked on my door and then opened it. She said, "Karen, your aunts are here."

I was sitting in that arm chair. I don't think I was doing anything. I can't remember. I just turned around and looked at her.

Then she stepped aside and Aunt Rosa and Aunt Lou came into the room. They both hugged me. Aunt Lou sat down on the side of the bed. Aunt Rosa sat in the straight-backed chair. They talked, but I couldn't hear them. I just knew they were talking because their mouths were moving.

After some time, Aunt Lou put her hand inside her handbag, which was large, and she pulled out one of the frontiersmen. I reached for him and put him right up against my heart. Then suddenly I could hear them. And I must have started crying, because Aunt Rosa put her hand in her bag and pulled out a handkerchief. She wiped my cheeks and made me blow my nose. Then Aunt Lou left the room. She came back with some toilet paper and both my aunts wiped their faces and blew their noses.

I asked how Grandma and Granddaddy were. Aunt Rosa said that they were worried, but that they knew I was strong. Aunt Lou said that Grandma wanted me to know that our people walked the Trail of Tears. We all were strong enough to survive anything anybody threw at us.

That confused me. Nobody had thrown anything at me that I could remember and I didn't, at that time, know what the Trail of Tears was. I could only tell by the name that it was a sad occasion. But I did figure it was something having to do with being a Cherokee, so that comforted me.

They talked some more. I began to think they had been there before. But I couldn't remember those visits. When they got up to leave, I held the frontiersman closer because I didn't want them to take him back. Aunt Rosa must have known what I was worried about and she said, "Kit, Jack sent that to you. Nobody's going to take it away."

I said, "Where is Daddy?"

"He's down at the jail. Sheriff Hawkins is looking after him," Aunt Lou said.

"Can I see him?"

Aunt Rosa knelt down next to my chair. She said, "Not yet, Kit. You have to talk to the social worker before they'll let you do that."

I didn't know what a social worker was at the time. I didn't say anything. Aunt Rosa said, "You might as well get it over with. Then they'll let you see Jack."

Aunt Lou sat back down on the bed. She said, "Do you think you're ready to do that?"

Well, I was ready to see Daddy. And I was ready to get away from that room. And I knew my aunts were trying to help me. I said, "Can you take me to see Daddy now?"

Aunt Lou's eyes teared up. And she and Aunt Rosa looked at each other. Then they both rubbed my arms and one of them said, "We're gonna take you as soon as we can. Will you talk to the social worker?" I said, "I guess so," and they hugged me again and again. Then they left me there with the frontiersman.

32

Sometimes when Rev. Cunningham wasn't home for supper, Mrs. Cunningham let me eat in my room or we ate in the kitchen together. But if he was home, we all had to eat in the dining room. The day my aunts came, he was home for supper. There was a big plate of fried chicken on the table, and a bowl of hominy and a bowl of beans. I don't know what month it was, but it was still hot, and Mrs. Cunningham was sweating. She had rings on her dress under her arms. I remember noticing that, and wondering if she had been like that all summer. I was glad to be noticing anything.

Rev. Cunningham said a long prayer. I knew to sit still and pretend to listen, so I thought about Mrs. Cunningham's sweat. I hoped it hadn't gotten in the chicken because I felt like I could eat some of that chicken. I wasn't very hungry, but I was a little. I don't think I had eaten for a long time.

The prayer went on and on, but finally Rev. Cunningham said, "You may eat now, Karen," and he stuck his fork in a breast. Mrs. Cunningham said, "Have a piece of chicken, Karen." I took a drumstick with my fingers. After that, she spooned out the hominy and beans onto my plate and hers. Rev. Cunningham got his own.

They talked between themselves for a while, saying things about people I didn't know. I picked at the crust of my chicken and ate it in little bites. It was pretty good, and at one point my stomach growled. Rev. and Mrs. Cunningham looked at each other and smiled. I said, "Excuse me." Mrs. Cunningham said, "That's okay, Karen. It means you're hungry."

I ate a whole drumstick and a little bit of hominy. About the time I had eaten as much as I could, Rev. Cunningham said, "I understand your aunts came by."

I said, "Yes, sir."

He said, "Are they churchgoing people?"

I remembered the night in the hospital when Aunt Rosa had lied to him about going to church. I said, "Yes, sir."

He said, "What denomination?"

I said, "Nomination?"

"De-nomination. What church?"

"The one in their town" was my answer.

Rev. Cunningham said, "That's what I thought. Do they drink liquor?"

I couldn't remember if my aunts drank or not, but I knew the right answer. I said, "No, sir."

He said, "Not even a little?"

I said, "No, sir."

"They told my wife that you'll talk to the social worker" is what he said next.

I looked at Mrs. Cunningham. It seemed like he was talking about her like she was a stranger or not really there and able to talk for herself. I guess I just imagined that, but that's the way it seemed. I said, "Yes, sir."

Then he said, "Marjorie, I want you to leave Karen and me alone for a while. I want to minister to her."

Mrs. Cunningham got up and left the room. There was still some food on her plate that she left behind. I put my hands in my lap and Rev. Cunningham put his elbows on the table, clasped his fingers together, and started talking. I don't pretend to remember everything he said. I didn't understand some of it. But a lot of it was about doing wrong and about Jesus washing away our sins. Rev. Cunningham said that I had sinned a great deal for a child my age, but that I could go with him to the river and confess in front of the congregation and it would take those sins off of my soul. I don't think I knew at the time what a congregation was. But he also said that it would make me feel a lot better.

I could hardly feel anything at all, good or bad. And I didn't see how going to the river with him was going to make anything better, or make anything that had happened any different. But Rev. Cunningham seemed to want an answer about that. So I said, "I'll have to ask my daddy."

Well, this might sound like I'm making this up, but he got mad at that. And he picked up his fork and started waving it around without anything on it. His face turned red and he said a lot of things, but they all amounted to the fact that he didn't think that it was necessary that I talk to Daddy. Daddy didn't have any moral authority. Rev. Cunningham said "moral authority" several times, although I'm still not sure what that means. Then he said Daddy was in prison for killing two people and he didn't show any remorse at all.

I know I probably should have stuck with Rev. Cunningham's points about moral authority and going to the river and said "yes" and "no" because clearly that's what he wanted. But when he said the last thing about Daddy, it was the first time that I realized that he had killed two people, not one. So, I said, "Who did he kill?"

Rev. Cunningham looked at me like I was crazy. Then he said, "He killed that wicked woman and Irene Burnett!"

At first, I didn't know who Irene Burnett was. I tried to think of girls at school named Irene and didn't come up with a single one.

Then I realized that Mrs. Burnett had a first name. I know that sounds dumb, but I didn't think about adults having first names unless I was kin to them or knew them real well. I said, "He killed Mrs. Burnett?"

And I must have smiled. Because Rev. Cunningham got a wilder look on his face and his eyes got real big. He dropped his fork to his plate. And then he leaned forward in his seat, reached out across the table, and slapped me. I was so stunned I couldn't even feel how bad it hurt at first. Then he said, "That'll wipe that smile off your face." The whole side of my face was numb, but then it started stinging like I'd run into a bunch of bees. I started crying real hard. Rev. Cunningham got up and left the table so fast the table cloth moved and knocked over his ice tea.

I just sat there and cried. Then after a while, Mrs. Cunningham came back in the dining room. She was a fright. I wouldn't have described her that way at the time, but that's a word I've picked up here at Ashley Lordard. And it's useful. It means somebody isn't normal in the face, and their hair is out of place, and there's a wild look in their eye. That's what she was like. But she was gentle with me, and she said, "Let's get you to bed early tonight, Karen. I'll run your bath water. You get your pajamas. Don't worry about the tea."

33

This is something that I didn't know before, but found out while I was living at the Cunninghams', and that is that objects are just as powerful as people. Even with Rev. Cunningham slapping me, from the day I got that frontiersman, I started feeling better. He wasn't one of Daddy's newest frontiersmen, or even one of his best ones, but he was familiar and he seemed like a friend to me. He was the only frontiersman that Daddy had carved that didn't have a rifle on him, and after I'd had him for a few days I realized that wasn't by accident. Somebody had picked out that particular frontiersman as the one I could have. Maybe that somebody was Daddy, but with what Rev. Cunningham said about him not having any remorse, I figured it was probably someone else who did the picking. But not my aunts, either. One of the Christmases I can remember when we went to Grandma and Granddaddy's before Mama got real sick, everybody shot rifles, even the women. Nobody in our family had anything against guns. Everybody just tried to be respectful of them and shoot well.

The frontiersman was a real friend to me. I could feel Daddy in him, but I could feel other things, too. I felt like he was sturdy and could endure. I also felt that he knew what I was going through and had come there to help me. He was somebody to talk to, and sometimes it seemed like he talked back. He said things like, "Kit, beyond those trees there's a clearing." I looked square at him a lot, when before I had mostly looked out the windows. But sometimes I watched him out of the sides of my eyes, and when I did, sometimes I could see him move. I know that people say pieces of wood don't move by themselves, and I suppose that's logical, but I still think to this day that frontiersman moved when he thought I wasn't looking at him. And sometimes we played a game where I looked off and tried to catch him moving out of the sides of my eyes and he tried not to get caught. Mostly he won, but sometimes, as I have said, I won and I saw him move.

I didn't take the frontiersman with me to see the social worker. I had decided that social workers were not anybody to share much with, and I knew, too, that Mrs. Cunningham didn't need to know much about the frontiersman. Wherever she was in my room, he stood still just like a block of wood and I was careful not to pay any attention to him. So when I got in the church woman's car with Mrs. Cunningham, the frontiersman was safe in my room on the table beside the arm chair. I had pointed him looking out the side window so he could see the car drive in when we got back.

The first social worker I talked to was not Mary Jayne. It was some man and he had a bunch of papers that he asked me questions from and then marked down my answers in little boxes. I know that went on for some time because by the day I saw him I was getting back a sense of time passing. That, in itself, made me feel better, even though I don't think people realize that knowing time passing is a good thing because they don't know what it's like not knowing it's passing. I'm not sure this will make any sense to anybody unless they've been through a patch where they've lost time. I suspect a lot of people haven't. But I don't know for sure.

After I answered that social worker's questions, he got up and came back in with Mary Jayne. I've already said that she had gray hair and blue eyes, and I noticed the gray hair right off, but the blue eyes I didn't notice until I had talked to her several times. I did notice first thing though that Mary Jayne was a big woman, and I put her in that category of stout older women, even though she didn't have her hair up in a bun or caged by a hairnet. But I turned out to be wrong about putting her in that category. Mary Jayne was younger than she looked. I think that gray hair threw me off.

Mary Jayne told me to call her by her first names. She said her last name was too hard to pronounce and then she said it for me. She was right, and I can't even spell it. She also told me about herself. She said she was 36 years old and had a husband and two children. She had been raised in the next county over and still lived there in a house next door to her mother and father. Her husband ran the mail. Then she said, "Tell me a little bit about yourself."

I said that I had passed the third grade and that I liked to read. She asked me what I liked to read and I told her. She had read the Nancy Drew books and the Hardy Boys ones, too, but she hadn't read the Dr. Dolittles. She had never even heard about him. I told her he talked to animals and told her about Polynesia, Jip, Dab-Dab, and the pushmi-pullyu. She acted like she was interested in them and asked me all sorts of questions, especially about the pushmi-pullyu. I acted like I was interested in them, too, because I figured they would keep her off the subject of what she was really interested in and eat up our time. That worked. When I left that first day we had just covered Dr. Dolittle.

That night Rev. Cunningham was home for supper again. Ever since the night he slapped me, he had been gone at suppertime and Mrs. Cunningham had been especially hard on her hands, wringing them, it seemed to me, all the time. We were in the dining room again, and about midway through the dinner, Rev. Cunningham said, "So I hear you visited with the social worker today."

I thought he'd be happy about that, so I said, "She's a nice lady," and tried to leave the impression that talking to the social worker was at the top of my list of things I wanted to do.

But he said, "Social workers have a warped view of God's world."

Mrs. Cunningham stopped eating. Her eyes got wide and she put her hands in her lap. I knew what she was doing with them. But I wasn't quite sure what Rev. Cunningham was saying. Although I did know what warped looked like. Daddy kept an old canoe in one of our out buildings. It was warped and it wouldn't sit right in the water. So, I figured Rev. Cunningham was sort of saying that Mary Jayne wouldn't sit right in the water if she ever got in.

Then he started talking about original sin and how all of us come into the world sinful and then get tempted into more sin and have to do all sorts of things to get the sin off of us. I knew he was back talking about getting in the river, but just wasn't going to say it straight out. That was the first time I had heard about original sin, so I didn't understand it like I do now with Mr. Hodges harping on it. But I was getting the general drift, and so was Mrs. Cunningham. She got up from the table.

That made me nervous, of course, because I was afraid he would slap me again. So I said, "Can I have another glass of milk?"

Rev. Cunningham acted confused by that request. He looked around like Mrs. Cunningham was standing right behind him and would get the milk. But she was nowhere to be seen. So he scooted back his chair and left the room. He came back with Mrs. Cunningham, who was carrying the milk in an entirely different glass. They both sat down and we didn't talk about any more sin that night.

34

My whole reason for talking to the social worker was to get to see Daddy, and after I realized Rev. Cunningham didn't like the social worker, I didn't know what to do. So the frontiersman and I talked about that. He thought I should avoid letting Rev. Cunningham know anything at all about what was going on in my mind. He said I was like an animal being tracked, and I had to throw the preacher off my scent. I thought that was some of the best advice I had gotten in a long time. I decided not to say a word to either of the Cunninghams about going to see Daddy, and to wait and bring the subject up with Mary Jayne the next time I saw her.

That was the following Tuesday. She started out asking how things had been going for me, so I didn't waste any time. I said, "I want to see my father."

She took a deep breath. Then she said, "Tell me about that."

"About what?" I said.

"About wanting to see your father."

I must have looked at her like she was an idiot. That's what she sounded like to me. I said, "Do you see your father?" I knew she did. She lived next door to him.

She said she did see her father, and that she was glad I wanted to see mine. She said she didn't mean to make it sound like wanting to see your father was unusual. She just wanted me to talk a little bit about how I felt about my father.

I said, "I love him."

She nodded like I was supposed to say something else, but I felt like we were having a stupid conversation. I waited her out, and finally she said that she was there to help me get to see my father, but that I would have to do it with supervision because he was being held in the jail.

I said, "It would be hard to have a private conversation with anybody in that jail."

She looked startled at that, and said, "Have you been in the jail?"

I said, "Lots of times."

She said, "Could you tell me a little bit about that?"

Well, I could tell I was dealing with a person who didn't want to have a conversation between two people. She wanted to find out what I was thinking, and not really tell me what she was thinking back. However, that didn't make any difference to me because I didn't really care what she was thinking unless it had to do with seeing Daddy. So, I told her about going to get Uncle Joe out of jail. Mary Jayne thought that was real interesting, and said so.

When I finished, I said, "So when do I get to see Daddy?"

She said, "Kit, before we let you see your father, the district attorney wants you to answer some questions about what happened. It would be best, I think, if I asked the questions for him, and you just tell me what you can remember and want to."

She sort of lost me there. So I said, "Okay."

When I said that, she got a notebook out of a big bag on the floor that was beside her chair. And she took a pen out of there, too. When she held the pen up it was the first time that I noticed that her hands were shaking just a little. At the time, I thought she was nervous about the questions she was going to ask me. And she may have been. But I noticed later her hands shook a little all the time.

She said, "Now, just tell me what you want to. You don't have to make anything up in order to have an answer. Just whatever is true is what I want you to say."

I nodded.

She said, "Okay, the first question is, could you tell me a little bit about what your father is like as a father?"

I had no idea what that question meant. I'm surprised I can even remember it as well as I do because usually it's particularly hard to remember things that don't make much sense. But I remember that question and I remember my answer to it. I said, "He's a good father," although I wasn't too sure about that at the time because killing Bella was definitely not a good thing to do.

Mary Jayne seemed to think about my answer for a minute and she wrote it down. Then she said, "Did he ever hit you or your mother?"

I said, "No."

"He never even spanked you?"

Well, I knew that it's unusual for a father not to spank his children. The kids at my school got spanked at home when they were bad. But the truth was that Daddy never had spanked me, and I had never really thought about that before. That made him different from other fathers. I said, "He told me what to do and I did it. He didn't have any reason to spank me," and that was true.

"Did he ever hit your mother?"

I thought that was a dumb question. I said, "Why would he do that?"

She said, "I just have to ask." Then she said, "Were you ever afraid of your father, Kit?"

I said, "All kids are afraid of their fathers."

"What were the kinds of things your father did to make you afraid of him? You don't have to tell me anything you don't want to."

I thought, Well, why are you asking so many questions then? But I said, "Nothing really. He was just quiet. He was unhappy."

"And why would that be?"

I didn't want to say. And she should have known anyway. Tears came up in my eyes. And Mary Jayne got a little excited about that. She pulled out a Kleenex from that big bag and said, "Just cry when you want to."

And I did. I just cried and cried thinking about Mama dying. And, maybe, thinking about Bella dying, too. I don't know. It was all jumbled up together. And Mary Jayne tried to put her arms around me, but I wouldn't let her. After that, our time ran out and the church lady gave Mrs. Cunningham and me a ride back to the house. I felt drained from the crying and frustrated because I still didn't have anybody nailed down on when I was going to see Daddy.

35

A couple of days later, I got a letter from Aunt Rosa. She said that a date for Daddy's trial had been set in October and she wanted me to write her and tell her how things were going. Aunt Rosa had been writing me letters about three times a week, but some of them, the ones I got when I first started living with the Cunninghams, I had never even opened. But I had saved them, and when I got that letter, I went back and opened the ones I hadn't opened before, and I reread the ones I had opened. I realized that I hadn't written Aunt Rosa back even once. So I asked Mrs. Cunningham for some paper and an envelope and a pencil, and I sat at the dressing table and wrote Aunt Rosa a letter. I told her mainly that they wouldn't let me see Daddy and that I wanted to.

I thought long and hard about who I should give the letter to and I talked to the frontiersman about it. I needed a stamp and I didn't have one. I didn't even have three cents to buy a stamp with or anywhere to buy it. And I wasn't sure I could trust Mrs. Cunningham to mail the letter, and neither was the frontiersman. So I kept the letter until the next time I saw Mary Jayne. Her husband was a mail carrier. She knew that it is against the law to mess with the U.S. Mail.

Mary Jayne was happy to get the letter and she promised me she would mail it. In fact, she said she'd be honored to. I took that as a good sign and I answered her questions as well as I could to give something back to her for being so nice about the letter.

She wanted to know if I had ever seen Daddy be violent to anybody. So I told her about the night in the jail when he knocked the man's head against the bars and the night Uncle Joe was killed when he socked that man. She seemed to think that was interesting information, and asked me all sorts of questions about those times and even more questions about Uncle Joe. I answered them pretty well because I could remember Uncle Joe better than I could remember a lot of things that had happened after he died and, at the time, I didn't see any reason not to tell her about Uncle Joe and us getting him out of jail and Daddy defending him. It seemed nice for people to take up for their relatives. But I wish now, of course, that I hadn't said anything at all about any of that because they used it to help prove that I should go to Ashley Lordard. They said it just went to show that in Mama's family drunkenness and violence were normal things, and that children shouldn't be raised where they have to go to the jail to socialize with their relatives.

36

Here at Ashley Lordard, everything happens pretty much on a schedule. We get up at the same time every school morning, which is at 6:00 a.m. We make our beds, shower if it's a Monday, Wednesday, or Friday, dress, and go over to breakfast. Then we come back to our dorm rooms, round up our books and things, and go over to assembly and listen to Mr. Hodges talk about whatever he's got on his mind that morning. More often than not, he reads from the Bible and says a short sermon, or he gets to remembering his father and all the things he learned from him as a child that show he's better than us. But, sometimes, he lets a guest speaker talk instead. That's always like a cool breeze in summer.

Then all the rest of the morning we have classes, except for a 20 minute recess. We go to lunch at 11:30. That lasts for 30 minutes. Then we go back to classes until 2:00. Then we get 30 minutes of free time before we start chores. They last for two hours. At 4:30, we have homework time. At 5:30, we eat. We do more homework after that, or sit in our closets or do anything else we want until 8:30 when lights are out. After lights out, a lot of us get back in our closets. We all have flashlights. Batteries are highly prized, like gold. I spend most of the money that Aunt Rosa sends me to buy them, but other girls trade things for them, and the girls who have batteries sent to them from the outside world have more power than any of the rest of us. They are the battery queens.

Sometimes, I spend the whole night in my closet, not just the time I'm writing. I can sleep better in here than I can in my bed, and sleeping is a problem for me. Most of the time I can go to sleep at night and I can usually sleep in the early morning. But I wake up after I've been asleep for two or three hours, and I can't go back to sleep unless I get in my closet. Lately, I've just been staying awake until the 11:00 monitor comes around, and then I get up and go to my closet. I think I get more rest that way. I feel better anyway.

But I'm not the only girl here who can't sleep. Mary Anne wakes up about 4:00 every morning. If I've fallen asleep in my closet, she opens the door and wakes me up and I get in bed then. It's common knowledge that the monitors don't want girls sleeping all night in their closets.

I should say something about the monitors now that I've brought them up. They are high school girls who get us out of bed in the morning and make the 11:00 round at night. They don't like being monitors because they're grumpy about having to get up early enough to get us awake at 6:00. Sometimes, one will oversleep, and when that happens everything gets off to a bad start. Mr. Hodges isn't going to begin assembly late unless Jesus appears in the cafeteria for breakfast, so if the monitor overslept and we get off to a late start, it's hurry, hurry, hurry on everything until assembly. That makes a lot of us nervous, and lately Mary Anne has been getting us all up when the monitor is late.

I started having a problem sleeping at the Cunninghams' house. I'm not sure exactly when it started, probably in that time when I didn't know time was passing. I realized it after I got the frontiersman and started noticing things again. The first time I remember waking up, Rev. and Mrs. Cunningham were standing in my bedroom in their robes. The light was on. Rev. Cunningham's hair was standing up. Mrs. Cunningham's hair was in a net that looked like a shower cap. She tried to grab my arms, but I fell off the bed backwards trying to get away from her. I hit my head on the sill of the window that looked out over the backyard. That made me yell. I had blood in my hair that got on my hand. Rev. Cunningham went back to bed after that and Mrs. Cunningham brought me a wash rag to clean up. The rest of that night I couldn't sleep at all. But most nights weren't that bad.

The days at the Cunninghams' weren't tightly scheduled like the ones here. Rev. Cunningham didn't get up early. About 8:30, Mrs. Cunningham cooked breakfast, which we all ate at the kitchen table. Rev. Cunningham took the paper and he read it while he ate. Mrs. Cunningham read her daily devotional. When I got to where I could read again, I read the cereal box, because you can't hardly eat breakfast without reading. As for eating, I just ate little bites, the fat part of the bacon and the buttery inside of the toast.

Sometime in the middle of the morning, Rev. Cunningham always left in the car. If there was grocery shopping to be done, Mrs. Cunningham went with him, and so did I. I stayed in the car during the shopping, but Rev. Cunningham usually went to the drugstore next door. When Mrs. Cunningham was through with grocery shopping, she went to the drugstore and got Rev. Cunningham. Then we all went back to their house and he left again.

At first, I stayed in my room almost all of the time. But after I got to feeling better, I stayed on the front porch. I like front porches, and the Cunninghams' was nice. It had a brick wall around it, was shaded by trees, and had a swing that was more comfortable than any of the living room chairs. There wasn't anything to read in the house except the paper and religious stuff, but Miss Francis found out I was living there, and she started bringing me books. At first, I couldn't read anything as long as a book. The words wouldn't stick. But she kept bringing more books or renewing the ones I had, and after the frontiersman came, I

started reading for real again. Miss Francis came to the Cunninghams'
on Wednesdays.

Mrs. Cunningham was learning to drive. So sometimes in the afternoons, Rev. Cunningham would come home and she would drive
the car up and down the driveway and pull it into the garage to practice. There was a turnaround place in the front yard, and she'd pull in
and out of there and back up and do all the things that drivers do. The
only time Mrs. Cunningham seemed happy was when she was practicing her driving. After she did that, she could go for a couple of hours
without wringing her hands.

When the first of September came, a woman appeared at the house
with fourth-grade books. Her name was Miss Davis and I could tell
at first sight she was one of those young women who talk a lot and
wave their hands. But the first day, she just introduced herself and left
the books and some writing paper and pencils. She said she would
be coming on Tuesday mornings, Thursday mornings, and Friday afternoons. She handed me a sheet of things to read in the books and
a sheet of arithmetic problems. I didn't ask her why I couldn't go to
school. It was clear to me that I was being kept away from people, and
I didn't much mind that, to tell you the truth. I didn't want people
staring at me and I didn't want to answer any questions.

Before he slapped me, Rev. Cunningham was home most nights
to eat. But after that, he wasn't home as much in the evening. So, Mrs.
Cunningham and I ate alone and we listened to the radio. She liked
news programs, but she liked music, too. Her favorite kind was show
tunes. But she also liked Bing Crosby and Perry Como, and they both
had programs where people came to visit them and they sang together
and made jokes. But if Rev. Cunningham's car pulled in while we were
listening to music, Mrs. Cunningham changed the station to the news
or the weather real quick, and then sat back in her chair and did her
knitting. I think the first time that happened she was afraid I'd say
something because she looked at me with sort of a pleading look in her
eye. But, at the time, I wouldn't have said anything to anybody about

anything, so she didn't need to worry. After I got to feeling better, I enjoyed her changing the station when he drove in. It was a secret between us and, although we never said so, it made me know that she didn't like him any more than I did.

On Sundays, they went to church. And, for a while, they dropped me off at the home of an old woman who lived not far from them on the way there. The old woman (Mrs. Turner) was crippled with arthritis in her knees or hips and her daughter lived with her. The daughter was always asleep when I got there, and usually she stayed asleep all morning. So I helped the old woman if she wanted anything, which meant I mostly brought her cups of coffee and changed the radio channels. She went to church on the radio, and when one service was over she moved on to another. She didn't try to talk to me much, and I didn't try to talk to her. Even I knew you aren't supposed to talk during church. And I wasn't ever there very long, because a little after noon every Sunday some person or another brought Mrs. Cunningham back to the house to get me and then took us both on home. Mr. Cunningham never came back until after dinner was ready to be on the table. And sometimes he fussed about that. I could tell I had upset their Sunday routine.

Not the next Sunday after Rev. Cunningham slapped me, but the one after that, they took me to church. I don't know why they hadn't taken me before because it was clear that was the business they were in and it was a chore for them not to do it. But they didn't, and I have no explanation for that other than that they were keeping me away from people. When I finally went, I didn't sit out with the rest of the audience. I sat in a little chair across from the choir. It was in an empty space where there wasn't anything but my chair and where I couldn't be seen by anyone except the choir. It was an odd space and I felt like it had been emptied of its real purpose. That was a strong feeling, and I felt, too, like the space was glad to have somebody in it.

That first Sunday, I was already sitting in that space when the piano started and the choir came in and sat down. Uncle Russ's wife, Aunt Jean, was with them. She saw me sitting there and looked real close like she couldn't believe her eyes. Then she smiled a little smile. I waved my finger at her because I didn't feel like smiling and I wasn't even sure it was allowed in church if I felt like it.

After the service was over, I just stayed where I was, but the choir filed out and Rev. Cunningham left from behind his talking stand. It seemed like, just from listening, that the church was getting empty, but then I heard footsteps coming near and suddenly Uncle Russ was in the space with me. He picked me up and hugged me. I was so glad to see him that I just grabbed his neck and didn't want to let go. But he said, "Kit, let me get a good look at you." Then he put me down and looked me over.

He said, "Are they feeding you?"

I nodded. Then he said, "Well, it doesn't look like it. I'll have to take that up with Mrs. Cunningham."

I said, "She feeds me. I just haven't been hungry. Why do I have to keep living with them?"

He squatted so that he was on my level. It was strange seeing him in a jacket with a tie on and it looked like his neck was being squeezed. He said, "I took you there first because I didn't know what else to do. Everything was crazy. Then, you were in such bad shape that the judge didn't want you moved until somebody from the court could talk to you. I hear you're talking with the social worker now."

I said, "How did you know?"

"It's a small county, Kit. Everybody knows everything." Then he started whispering. "They're not going to put him under the jail for killing your friend. But they sure as hell might for killing Mrs. Burnett. I don't know why he did that, Kit, do you?"

"Cause she was mean" just flew out of my mouth.

Uncle Russ squinted. "What do you mean? Was she mean to you?"

"Yes. She threw me and Bella off her property."

"Have you told the social worker that?"

I shook my head.

"Kit, you ought to. We've got to establish some kind of good motive for that killing." I must have looked puzzled, because he added, "Jack won't say anything about it. Just that she needed it. And that's not helping his case at all. If you know anything that can help him, you need to tell the social worker. She's hooked right into the sheriff and the district attorney. Sheriff Hawkins in particular really likes your daddy. But the district attorney is being squeezed by the folks in this town who think they know what's right for everybody. And the Irene Burnett thing is hard to justify. Don't make stuff up, but if you can think of any good reason he might have had to kill her, let that social worker know it. You understand what I'm saying?"

I did understand what he was saying. And I knew why Daddy had killed Mrs. Burnett. Because of her rotten heart.

37

That first Sunday I went to church was a long day. The Cunninghams had been invited out to dinner and they took me with them. As soon as we were in the door, the people we were visiting complimented Rev. Cunningham on his sermon, so I realized they had heard it, even though I hadn't seen anybody in the church except the choir and Uncle Russ. The family, the Wallaces, had two children and I knew them. Becky was in my grade at school, and she was outgoing and tried to make friends with everybody. Her big brother, Billy, who was a year older, was thin and wore glasses. He wasn't as outgoing, but there wasn't anything wrong with him, and the three of us ate on a card table in the living room and then we played badminton outside.

The badminton was fun and felt like the first normal thing I had done in a long time. And Becky and Billy both were nice to me. They didn't say anything about me coming back to school and I didn't say anything about Miss Davis showing up at the house and giving me books. But before we left, Becky hugged me and told me not to pay any attention to what anybody said. Now that I'm older and know how girls do each other, I know that might sound like she was being catty. But I don't think Becky meant it that way. I think she was trying to be helpful, and that's how I took it. It also gave me another little piece of information about what was going on. It was while I was living at the Cunninghams' that I began to think of my life as a jigsaw puzzle, and started to look for pieces to fit together and also to figure out what pieces were missing for good.

Rev. Cunningham liked eating with the Wallaces. And all the way home, he talked about how much they liked his sermon. Mrs. Cunningham didn't say much except she agreed that it was good. If I had been in a better mood, I would've found that funny. The sermon had been about the meek inheriting the earth. Rev. Cunningham said about a thousand times that the meek were going to get what was left over after everybody else had been destroyed. I figured that meant Mrs. Cunningham was going to finally come into her own, and that she knew it and was looking forward to it.

We only had soup for supper that night and I finally got to go to my room and have some time by myself. I hadn't realized it, but being around people after being away from them for so long is tiring, and before I went to bed I just lay on top of the covers, rested, and held the frontiersman on my stomach and talked with him.

Neither one of us knew what to do about getting Daddy off for killing Mrs. Burnett. I could hardly remember anything about Mrs. Burnett except that she smelled bad, had one long eyebrow over her nose, and was hateful to Bella. I wanted to tell Mary Jayne how hateful Mrs. Burnett had been, and how Bella had just walked off holding her head high and swinging her hips. But I didn't think I could say Bella's name out loud, and the frontiersman just looked wooden and wasn't much help.

I got tired trying to think it all out, and got up and took a bath. Then I went to bed and to sleep without even reading. But in the middle of the night, something happened and Mrs. Cunningham came in and turned on the light. She didn't try to touch me, but she told me to get in the chair and she took the top sheet off my bed and put it on me there. Then she said maybe I could sleep better with the light on. I couldn't, and I stayed awake until the air started getting gray outside and the birds started singing. The next thing I knew, Mrs. Cunningham came in and shook me and told me I needed to get up and eat my lunch because I needed to go talk to the social worker.

I had been seeing Mary Jayne on Tuesday and Friday mornings, and I was as surprised and confused to be told I was going on Monday afternoon as I was to find out I had slept through the entire morning. I asked Mrs. Cunningham why we were going then, and she said they had to change my schedule because Miss Davis was coming on Tuesday mornings. Usually I probably wouldn't have cared one way or another, but that day I was tired and I hadn't figured out what I was going to say to Mary Jayne to get Daddy out of his jam. So the whole thing didn't sit well with me. When the church woman came to pick us up, I was in a bad mood.

Mary Jayne started out by asking me how I had been. I knew that looking like I was in a bad mood wasn't a good thing to do in front of a social worker, so I told her about the badminton and that it was fun. That was a regular thing for a child to be doing and I wanted her to know that I played well with other children. Playing well with other children, as all children know, is something adults are always on the lookout for and one of the ways they judge you.

Mary Jayne smiled while I told the badminton story, but she said, "You look tired."

I didn't know what to say, so I just shrugged my shoulders. Then she said, "Tell me about your sleep problems."

I knew then that Mrs. Cunningham had told her. I didn't look that much worse than usual. I said, "It's hard to sleep away from home."

Mary Jayne nodded. She said she had the same problem whenever she had to do it. That made me feel better, and I added, "I'm worried about Daddy."

Mary Jayne said, "Talk to me a little bit about that."

I thought, Here's my chance. I'll take it and see what happens. And I told her that I knew Daddy had killed Mrs. Burnett and that that was what everybody was mad about, but that Mrs. Burnett was mean to her neighbors and killed their guineas.

Mary Jayne's hands started trembling a little more than usual when I said the part about the guineas. And she looked puzzled and said, "Why do you think she would kill guineas?"

I said, "Do you live on a farm or in town?"

She lived in town, so I explained about the guineas being a warning system for snakes and other dangerous creatures. I told her that my friend had two guineas that went missing, but that all of the chickens seemed to be in place. That showed that someone had done something to the guineas, and there was only one reason to do that, which was to be able to sneak up on people and spy on them without them knowing it. I didn't call Bella by name because I couldn't stand to say her name out loud. If the truth be known, I still can't, but as you can see I've been able to write it for some time now.

Mary Jayne got quiet after that. I could tell she was trying to figure out in her head what to say next, and I was glad to see that because usually I was the one with that problem. When she finally said something, it was, "Can you tell me what you mean when you say Mrs. Burnett was mean to her neighbors?"

"Well, killing their poultry is mean," I said because it was obvious.

"How else was she mean?"

I knew that showing that Mrs. Burnett was mean was important and that she was already dead and nothing I said would bring her back or make her any deader. I said, "She was jealous of her neighbors." Mary Jayne took a deep breath and wrote that down. I added, "She didn't want them to have friends, and she would go onto other people's property but kick them off of hers."

Mary Jayne wrote that down, too, and then said, "Kit, it's important that you tell me everything you know about that."

I don't really know now how much of what I told Mary Jayne was true, how much I made up, and how much I just figured out from the information I had. Nobody tells a child much of anything directly, except to correct her behavior, so most children, I think, have to put two and two together. But I was trying to tell the truth, whatever that is, and tell it about Mrs. Burnett's rotten heart, which is, unfortunately, not something other people can see directly. But I knew that Mrs. Burnett had one, and that Bella didn't and neither did Daddy.

So this is what I told Mary Jayne: Mrs. Burnett hated people and tried to cause trouble. She stole around and spied and talked ugly to people for doing things in their own homes that weren't any of her business. She was ugly to me and she was ugly to my friend, and if Daddy killed her, which I wasn't sure he did because nobody would let me talk to him, but if he really did kill her, she deserved it.

Mary Jayne turned sort of white when I said all of that, but she was pale anyway and that white hair didn't help. And for a little while she didn't say anything. Then she said, "Kit, did Mrs. Burnett see you and Bella in the bathroom together?"

I wasn't expecting that question at the time, although I got used to it later. So it surprised me. I said, "Doing what?"

Mary Jayne blushed to the roots of her white hair, and seeing her do that made me feel like I was turning hot from the inside. I had never had that feeling before and I didn't know what to call it then. But since then I've heard sermons on it, and I feel that way again sometimes after I've been with Mr. Hodges alone. But I don't feel that way all the time then. Sometimes I just feel nothing at all. But other times, I feel hot. And I now know that the name for that heat is shame.

38

I'm in a bad way today. Something terrible happened, and I don't know what to do. It's Saturday and Mr. Hodges isn't usually here on the weekends, but he showed up this morning while I was with Lana, Tessy, and Janice throwing an old tennis ball. Janice was doing most of the talking. She's a year older than the rest of us, in the 7th grade, and interested in boys. She likes hanging around with girls in my grade so she can be a big shot and tell us all about how things are when you're in love.

I don't mind her so much, but Mary Anne doesn't approve of her and, of course, Caroline wasn't playing with us because she avoids Tessy, and I don't blame her for that. Anyway, Janice has a crush on Ronnie Carter, who lives on the other side of campus but who has been over here washing windows on the outside of our dorm for the past several days. Janice and Ronnie have been talking with her leaning out of a window next to whichever one he's been washing. She's gotten to do that because she's had a disease that I can't even pronounce, let alone spell. It makes her break out in red blotches on the trunk of her body, but not on her arms and legs. It's like measles, only she doesn't run a fever, she's just tired, and the doctor who comes here says that all she needs to do is take it easy for a couple of weeks and it will go away. So she gets to stay in her dorm room while the rest of us do our chores, and that includes Ronnie, who has been assigned to the windows.

So now they've got this big romance going and it's pretty interesting. Janice has been telling us everything they say to each other, and how she knows she likes him and how she knows he likes her. We don't get to be around the boys at all except during assemblies and on Sunday during church, and then they sit on the entire opposite side of the auditorium from us. Some of the older girls pass notes and the juniors and seniors have socials, but in our grades, there's not much contact and we're all curious. That includes me, I admit it.

Writing this all down has made me feel a little better, and I can tell that it's also taken me a while to get to my point. That must be a good thing because I was feeling awful when I started. But right now I feel like I can make it through all of this unless something outside kills me. Maybe if I grow up to be a writer, I'll be able to say what's really happened and what I really feel, and that'll make things better. I already know that writing makes dead people come alive again, so a writer is never alone. That's something to think about for the future.

Anyway, Janice was talking and the rest of us were listening, and Mr. Hodges appeared at the door of the school building. That's a long way away from where we were playing, but I clearly saw him look at me, jerk his head and disappear. I knew what that meant, so I said, "I promised to write my aunt and I better get to it."

The first thing I did was go to my dorm room and get my letter to be mailed to Aunt Rosa. Mr. Hodges mails them for me and I know he does it because Aunt Rosa writes back about things I've said. But, of course, he reads them first to make sure I haven't said anything I shouldn't have.

In the school building, the halls were deserted, and they're sort of creepy like that. I walked to the director's office quickly and opened the door from the hall, knowing it wasn't locked. I locked it behind me because Mr. Hodges always wants that. I try to do what I'm supposed to do and get it over with fast.

Mr. Hodges was sitting in his chair all twitchy looking when I closed the door to his private office. He said, "Lock it."

I said, "I did," and was sure he was nervous because of that remark. He had to have seen me turn the key.

Then he said, "Come here. I want to do it sitting down."

My mouth was dry, of course, but I said, "Okay. Here's my letter," and put it on his desk.

Well, usually I can just go off in my mind, and not remember anything between the time he opens his pants and when I use the towel. But this time, he already had his pants open and down and his snake was standing up. He said, "Lick it first."

I must have just stood still because the next thing he said was, "Do it," and he picked up a letter from Aunt Rosa and waved it.

So, I put my tongue on it. But it tasted salty and not very good. I took my tongue off and backed away.

Mr. Hodges got a mean look on his face. He picked up Aunt Rosa's letter to me again and he tore it in two and held up one piece in each hand. He said, "Karen, do you want to be able to read this letter?"

I nodded. So, I started again. But it tasted too salty and I gagged. He let me stop until I got my throat under control and then he said, "Never mind, just suck it," sort of through his teeth.

So, I closed my eyes and did. But when he was about to get it over with, he grabbed my hair and pushed my head down and moved real fast, himself. That's when I felt my tooth tear away. I couldn't yell because my mouth was full and I couldn't get my head up. Then he started moving a lot. All his sticky stuff came out in my mouth and he moved some more, but his snake got smaller and I got to take my mouth off of it and I swallowed. That's when I knew I was in big trouble. The tooth went down my throat, too.

I started crying. Mr. Hodges opened his drawer and handed me one of the towels he keeps in there. He said, "Karen, that wasn't so bad. Don't act like it was."

I wiped my face and my tongue and tried to stop sobbing with a couple of gulps.

He stood up and wiped his snake with another towel. While he was pulling up his pants and tucking everything in, he said, "You've really done me a service today and I won't forget it. Sometimes living with a grown woman can be too much for a man." Then he picked up the two pieces of Aunt Rosa's letter to me and said, "Here, I'm sorry I had to tear it. Don't make me do that again."

I took them. Then he picked up my letter to Aunt Rosa, read it fast and licked the envelope himself. Then he said, "I don't guess you have a comb on you?"

I shook my head.

He opened a couple of his drawers and then looked in his jacket pocket. He found one in there and sat back down. He said, "Stand still, you hair is messed up." He combed my hair squinting at my head like he was threading a needle. Then he took me by the arms and looked at me real hard. He said, "You look upset. Maybe you better sit down here until you look more pulled together."

I said, "I swallowed my tooth," and held the towel out to show him where there was blood.

He said, "How did you do that?"

"It was loose," I told him.

He shook his head. "Well, it'll come out the other end." Then he reached in his pocket and pulled out a quarter. He said, "Pretend like I'm the tooth fairy."

I didn't want that quarter. But I took it because I try not to cross Mr. Hodges in any way. I said, "I'm going back to the dorm. The other girls are out playing."

He said, "Okay. But try not to run into anybody."

I said, "Thanks for my letter." Then I left.

I didn't run into anybody. On the weekends some girls leave here for a few hours or even two days. They're visiting with people, so there are always fewer of us here on the weekends than at any other time. Also, the teachers are gone. The only adults around all the time are the seminary students who live with the boys and keep them away from our side of campus and Mr. and Mrs. Thurman. He's the building superintendent and she's the head cook. Other adults come and go and the monitors take extra duties, but the place isn't really busy and is lonelier than during the week.

I brushed my teeth and took a shower, which we are allowed to do any time we get dirty on the weekends. Then, I brushed my teeth again with my regular toothbrush, not the one I keep especially for when I've been with Mr. Hodges. I examined my mouth in a mirror. There's a hole on the left upper side where the tooth came out. I can feel a little ridge of a new tooth in there with my tongue. I'm doing that now again as I write this. It's hard not to.

But my real problem is that I'm not sure that tooth is really going to come out the other end, or if it does that I'll see it and will be able to stop worrying. What if it tears a hole in my stomach? Or gets stuck somewhere in my intestines? Or causes my appendix to burst? There are a lot of things that tooth could do to worry about. And that quarter doesn't make up for that worry. Anyway, I flushed the quarter down the commode.

39

I haven't felt any shame over what Mr. Hodges did to my tooth. I've just felt relief. It came out this morning. I'm not going to give the details, but it did, and I saw it and that's that. It happened before church, so even though I didn't get much sleep last night, I wasn't just miserable and I listened to the sermon.

On Sundays, Mr. Hodges doesn't preach, because, as I've said, he's not a real preacher, he just thinks he's one. We have visiting preachers, ones that I think are out of work. Nobody's ever said that directly, but when Mr. Hodges introduces them he usually says something like, "Rev. Buchanan was pastor at the White Castle Church in Jefferson County for twelve years," and usually there are complete strangers sitting on the front row. Sometimes they are the same people week after week. Then they disappear and new people come. But all the preachers seem to preach directly to the front row. I think they're trying out for jobs, like high school kids try out for teams.

The one this morning talked on suffering little children coming to Jesus, and, for once, I thought the sermon was right on the mark.

There are a lot of suffering children here. I'm not going to Jesus, but some girls, like Mary Anne, say they get comfort in him. I think she gets more torment than anything else, but she thinks Jesus is comforting, and what's comforting is different for different people. Two weeks ago, Aunt Rosa sent me a picture of Lauren Bacall. She often sends me movie stars' pictures, and I just tuck them away because we don't get to see movies except educational ones. But I put Lauren Bacall's picture under my mattress. She looks like Bella, and I get comfort from that.

The next time I went to see Mary Jayne after the one when she'd asked about Bella and me being in the bathroom, Rev. Cunningham went, too. That was the first time ever he'd done that, and I was surprised. Mrs. Cunningham drove us and he sat in the front seat and gave her directions, things like "Stop," "Watch out for that curb," and "Don't get close to that car." I could tell he made her nervous, and they both acted like they were hearing fingernails on a blackboard. About half the distance there, I just closed my eyes and went off somewhere else in my head. I don't remember where that was, but I do remember that when the car stopped in front of Mary Jayne's office somebody said something to me. And I answered by saying, "Uncle Mark came this week and you didn't tell me."

Both of the Cunninghams stopped like they were frozen. Rev. Cunningham had his hat in his left hand and he just held it in mid-air. Mrs. Cunningham had been putting the keys in her purse. I heard them drop, but she just looked at her husband, his hat, his arm, and the side of his face. It seemed like they stayed that way forever. Then they both turned around in the seat to face me, and Rev. Cunningham said, "Who told you that?"

I said, "No one."

He looked at Mrs. Cunningham and she looked at him and shook her head real hard. He looked back at me and said, "Don't lie to me."

Well, I could see the anger come up in his face from his neck, and I wanted to avoid getting slapped again. So I grabbed the door handle and said, "It was just a guess." I got out and I was all the way in front of the receptionist's desk talking to her before they came in the door.

When Mary Jayne came out to get me, Rev. Cunningham said he wanted to speak to her, and he went inside her office instead of me. He stayed in there almost a half hour. Mrs. Cunningham stayed outside with me, and she acted like that was what we always did and like there was nothing unusual about it. I didn't find that part surprising. That's what the Cunninghams did all the time, pretended whatever was going on was really something else or not happening at all.

Finally, Rev. Cunningham came out the door and Mary Jayne was with him. She looked at her watch and said, "Kit, we have a few minutes." I got up and went in.

She asked the usual stuff about how I'd been doing just to get the conversation going. Then she wanted to know how my sleeping was. I told her it was better because I didn't want to waste any more time. I said, "What did he want?"

She knew exactly what I was talking about, and I think to this day that Mary Jayne is an honest person although she can duck a question. She said, "I guess you're aware that your aunt and uncle want you to live with them?"

I said, "Aunt Rosa writes me about that all the time."

"Well, your uncle was over here on Wednesday visiting your father. He stopped by the office and we chatted. It was the first time we had talked. He seems like a nice man. So I called Mrs. Cunningham and told her he had come by. I was trying to get a feel for what they know about how you feel about your aunt and uncle. I should have asked you first, but I was really trying to get a little background to have a conversation with you. We haven't talked about your aunt and uncle. And I didn't expect to see Rev. Cunningham today, so there you have it." She held her palms out.

I said, "You still haven't said why Rev. Cunningham came."

Mary Jayne hesitated and she doodled on a piece of paper to keep her hand from shaking, I think. Finally, she said, "Kit, everybody is trying to figure out the best thing to do with you. Or what's best for you, is what I'm trying to say. Some people think maybe it would be best for you to live with your mother's family. But more people think maybe it would be better for you to go to a special school a couple of hours away. It's called Ashley Lordard. Rev. Cunningham just wanted to give me his opinion on that."

I had a good idea of what his opinion was. I said, "What does Daddy think?"

"I think he wants you to go with your mother's family, but he doesn't really get a say."

"He's my father!" I said in a louder than normal voice.

"Well, that's true. But his parental rights have been voided. What that means is that what he wants doesn't really count. I'm sorry. I should have told you that earlier, but it never came up." Her hand was really shaking then and she put her pen down.

I stood up and said, "So who owns me?"

Mary Jayne looked pitiful. She said, "Kit, nobody owns anybody. But sometimes when children's parents have been killed or can't take care of them for one reason or another, they become wards of the state. That's what you are right now."

I said, "I have a family."

Mary Jayne touched me for the first time ever and I let her do it, I guess, because I was so shocked I couldn't move. She put a hand on each of my arms. "I know you do. And your uncle seems nice. But people from the state have been visiting with them and with your whole family, and they've been trying to decide what to do."

I said, "Aunt Rosa hasn't said anything about that to me."

Mary Jayne let go of my arms and sat back in her chair. She said, "I imagine she doesn't want to get your hopes up. And sometimes this is a difficult thing for a family to go through. It's like being put under a microscope. You know what a microscope is, don't you?"

I nodded. "It's something that's used to look at germs. My family isn't germs."

Mary Jayne blushed and shook her head. She said, "No, of course they aren't. I shouldn't have put it that way. I'm sorry."

Our time was up right then, but I wasn't, for once, ready to go. Mary Jayne and I had a little tug-of-war about me having to leave and her having to talk to somebody else. But she won, and I left without any more information than what I've written down here.

I didn't speak to either of the Cunninghams on the way home. I just looked out the window and watched the rain. When we got to the house, Rev. Cunningham, who said he was driving because of the weather, let us out in the pull-up place in the driveway and then he drove off.

I didn't feel like saying a word to Mrs. Cunningham. It was clear to me that she was afraid of her husband and that it wouldn't do me much good to ask her for information. Also, I didn't know if I could talk to her without yelling, and children can't do that to adults, although adults do it to children all the time. But I also didn't want to miss any chance that I might have to get even the tiniest piece of information. So, I went in my room for a while and sat with the frontiersman. When I got calmed down enough, I went to the kitchen where Mrs. Cunningham was cooking dinner.

I said, "What's Ashley Lordard?"

She was at the counter and I don't think she had heard me come to the door. She jumped a little, and she turned around with flour on her hands. She said, "Sit down, Karen. Give me a minute."

I did as she told me because it seemed like a good idea. I was real upset and jittery and sitting would calm my nerves.

After she got the biscuits cut out, she washed her hands and sat down, too. I could tell she was trying to be nice, and to tell you the truth, she was a nice person, just married to a hateful man, which was, I know, a problem for her. She said, "Ashley Lordard is a boarding school run by a group of our churches to give a home to children who have lost their own families. It's run by a very nice man who is a friend of Rev. Cunningham's. And there are all sorts of children there. It's a place to live and a school all rolled up in one."

I should have asked her more questions because you get more information out of people that way than you do by telling them things. But I had had a hard day and I wasn't really in the mood to be patient. I said, "I'm not an orphan. I have a family."

She said, "I know you do. But Rev. Cunningham has talked to your grandfather. He thinks you should go to Ashley Lordard. He doesn't think your grandmother is up to looking after a child, and I understand you've never even met them."

I said, "I know my grandparents. You're lying."

Mrs. Cunningham's chin pulled in and I could tell I'd said the wrong thing. She frowned and wiped her hands in her apron. She said, "Don't talk like that or you'll have to go to your room."

I said, "Yes, ma'am. I'm sorry."

"That's better," she said. "I'm talking about your grandparents in Georgia. I understand you've never met them."

I said, "Why don't you talk to my real grandparents?"

Mrs. Cunningham's lips got as thin as a wire. She didn't say anything for a long time, although I could tell she was both wanting to and not wanting to. She finally said, "Karen, we all want you to be raised right. In a good Christian home with good values. You've had a hard start. It's essential that you get straightened out."

I didn't know what "essential" meant. But I understood the rest of it.

40

I wrote Aunt Rosa that weekend. It took me most of Saturday to get the letter to say exactly what I wanted, but I was pleased with it when I was through. I told her in BIG CAPITAL LETTERS that I needed for them to come get me. I didn't think anybody was going to let me see Daddy and there wasn't any reason to wait around hoping somebody would. I also told her that if she and Uncle Mark would come get me, I'd be good and go to school and help with the chores and they'd never be sorry. I'd grow up without causing them any trouble at all. I wanted to sound like an attractive child, not a whiny one, but I also wanted them to come very soon. That was hard to get across sounding exactly right, but when I was through with the last copy, I thought it was pretty good. I could tell writing was coming easier to me.

My main worry was getting the letter mailed without Rev. Cunningham knowing about it. Mrs. Cunningham had given me some stamps, and I had mailed a couple of letters right out in the mailbox like everybody else. But that was before I knew what Rev. Cunningham was up to, and sometimes he came home for lunch before the mail ran, and he checked the mailbox when he did. If he saw a thick letter to Aunt Rosa he might put it in his pocket. I know that sounds like I didn't trust him and that's exactly what I mean for it to sound like. On Friday night, he had asked me three times how I knew that Uncle Mark had been to visit Mary Jayne. I told him the same answer every time, the same one I told him in the car, but I could tell he didn't believe me and that made me think he'd be watching me even closer than usual.

I decided the best thing to do was to take the letter to church and give it to Uncle Russ. I was glad when Sunday came and I put the letter in a little pocketbook that some church people had dropped off with some clothes my size. I acted like I was proud of that pocketbook, but the real truth is that I don't like carrying one. However, you can't carry a flour sack to church. Even I realize that.

I sat in my empty space and Aunt Jean came in with the choir. She smiled and waved her finger and I waved an entire hand. Then I sat back and listened to the singing, thinking about how I never in my life thought I'd be glad to see Aunt Jean. When the preaching began it interrupted my thoughts, and I turned them to the sermon. Not to the words, which as far as I could tell didn't make any sense, but to how they were delivered. Rev. Cunningham liked to talk real loud and then repeat himself real soft. When he was real loud he sounded like he was making an announcement, but his soft voice was more like he was trying to convince people he had secret information that he was letting them in on. I couldn't see him from where I was sitting, but I knew exactly what his face looked like. When he talked in that voice he got a smile that said, I'm wise and you're stupid. That's what he tried to make his face look like on the outside, but if you watched him real close, his smile really said, Do what I say or I'll make you sorry. He didn't smile that smile just to me, he also smiled it to Mrs. Cunningham, and I bet to this day that she saw through it, too.

When the services were over, Aunt Jean filed out with the choir, and I could hear the people in the church leaving. Just for a second, I got sort of a panicked feeling that Uncle Russ wouldn't come see me. But that didn't last. I heard boots and knew they belonged to him.

He had seen Daddy again. He said that Daddy said not to worry about him, just to do what everybody told me to do and everything would turn out all right. Uncle Russ said that in sort of a mumble and I could tell he didn't believe it, but had promised he'd say it. So I said, "Does that mean I can live with my aunt and uncle?"

Uncle Russ was hunkered down on his boots and he looked at the wall of the church that had a drape on it. He said, "Kit, they're trying to get a fix on that."

I said, "I know." Then I reached into my pocketbook and got out my letter. I said, "That mean old preacher wants me to go to an orphanage. But my aunt and uncle want me. I need to get this letter to them."

Uncle Russ turned red. He was ruddy colored to begin with, but I could tell he was even redder. He said, "You probably shouldn't call the preacher names." But he took the letter.

I said, "I don't know how old he is, but he's mean for sure."

Uncle Russ looked at me directly. "Why do you say that?"

"He slapped me."

Uncle Russ pulled his chin in and his eyes squinted. He said, "Are you kidding, Kit?'

I shook my head.

"Why?"

I knew better than to say for no reason. But I couldn't hardly say it was because he could see into my heart and realized I was glad Mrs. Burnett was dead. So I said, "I don't know. He didn't give a reason."

Uncle Russ bit his lip. Then he said, "Now, Kit, accusing Rev. Cunningham of slapping you is a serious thing to say. And it's just a little bit hard to believe."

I said, "It's true. I wouldn't make it up. I want to go live with my aunt and uncle."

Uncle Russ stood up. He said, "Have you told anybody else this?"

I said, "I didn't think anybody would believe me."

Uncle Russ looked at me long and hard and then he hugged me. He promised to mail my letter.

Rev. Cunningham didn't come home from the church with Mrs. Cunningham and me that Sunday. We were dropped at the house by a man and a lady. But we had a roast that was pretty good eating, and we got to listen to the radio in peace. Mrs. Cunningham wasn't bad to be around. She had two grown daughters who were living off somewhere else, so she had raised children. When I think back on her now I wish I had made more of an effort to get to know her. I've gotten to where I can spot loneliness way off on the horizon, and she was just as lonely as anybody I've ever met. I bet she's still lonely today, and still without any hope of deliverance. She can't divorce like Bella did because she's married to a preacher. There's just no climbing out of that kind of hole.

Monday afternoon when I went back to see Mary Jayne, she surprised me by telling me she had talked to Daddy. It was the first time she had ever seen him in person and she said they had a long conversation. I couldn't imagine Daddy having a long conversation with anybody, but I didn't say that, I just asked her about what.

Mary Jayne said Daddy didn't want me to live with his parents and he was glad that wasn't a possibility. He wanted me to live with Aunt Rosa and Uncle Mark. He told Mary Jayne that Mama's family was made up of good people. She asked me to tell her about them.

I told her every detail I could remember, both from my own knowledge and from Aunt Rosa's letters. In the letters, Granddaddy's health was a big topic. He didn't like to go to the doctor and Aunt Rosa or Aunt Lou had to take him when he went. But he was a World War I veteran and could go to the VA and see the doctors there. Aunt Rosa was real proud that he was allowed to go to the VA and thought it was good medicine. She also thought that he was healthier than he had been in a long time and said that he had stopped drinking everything except beer. But I didn't tell Mary Jayne about the beer. I just said that he liked lemonade.

I told Mary Jayne about Grandma, too. She was feeling real good, and her chickens were laying lots of eggs, and her cow was giving enough milk to feed the calf and have some left over for cooking. The garden was producing enough vegetables to feed the entire family and the cantaloupes were coming on. I wanted Mary Jayne to get the hint that if I went to live with my family I'd have plenty to eat.

I spent a lot of time telling her about Aunt Rosa and Uncle Mark saving up for their television, which they were doing at that time. Aunt Rosa had a lot of programs she was planning on watching on a regular basis and they were not programs about Indians, they were programs about white people. I also told Mary Jayne about the new curtains Aunt Rosa had cut out and made. I had never seen them, but I told her that they were sheers, and I think she knew what sheers were. I was pretty sure that sheer curtains are something that normal people have in their houses, or want to have in their houses. I wanted Mary Jayne to know that my aunt and uncle were as regular as totally white people.

I also told her that Aunt Lou was pregnant, which was the really big news and I should have said it first. But the idea of another child in the family wasn't something I liked to think a lot about. I didn't tell Mary Jayne that. I just told her that the baby was due in the winter and Aunt Lou was sewing up a storm and so were Aunt Rosa and Grandma. I also didn't tell her too much about Uncle Dennis except that he was a mechanic and could fix anything with his hands.

The last thing before I left, I told Mary Jayne I'd bring her some of Aunt Rosa's letters and she could read for herself what a good family I have.

41

Besides talking about the misuse of the English language, Miss Reynolds's favorite topic is not blurting out in class. She mentions it every time anybody besides her blurts out. When she blurts out, she's just giving directions. I'm reminding myself of this because what I really want to do is blurt out what happened after I told Mary Jayne about my family. But in this case, I know Miss Reynolds is right. I need to be calm and take my time and write everything down just like it happened.

Which was that Miss Davis came the next morning. She stayed for two and a half hours each time she visited and about half of that time we spent on arithmetic, some on spelling and some on geography and history. We spent almost no time on reading, my favorite subject. While she was checking my spelling, Rev. Cunningham, who was lazy and never went to work very early, came into the dining room and said he was taking Mrs. Cunningham to get her driver's license. A few minutes after that, they left and Miss Davis started talking about the Constitution.

The Constitution is pretty boring, and I had already studied the founding fathers once before and had figured out that the entire country was stolen. So I hadn't remembered much of what I read about the Constitution, and Miss Davis was going over all of it again. I was trying to listen, but I was having a hard time until she got to the part about the three parts of the government: the executive branch, the legislative branch, and the judicial branch. Then, I realized the Constitution really did apply to me. I asked her about the court system.

Miss Davis said there are federal courts and state courts and they are different systems. She said that federal courts settle all the big questions, like Brown vs. the Board of Education. I knew what that was and that it was important. I read the paper every day at the Cunninghams' and had heard Rev. Cunningham tell a man on the phone to quit worrying about it, it would never take hold. But I wasn't interested in the usual big questions. I was interested in Daddy's trial, which was the big question to me. So I asked Miss Davis which court system his trial was going to be in.

Her eyes got big and round and she said, "Well, Kit, tell me a little bit about your father's trial and maybe I can answer you better."

I wasn't taken in by that for a minute. I knew I was being kept away from everybody except just a few people, and I had a theory that it was probably because there was a lot of gossip going around and they didn't want me to hear it. I also felt that even Aunt Jean (who I had decided was a decent person) was curious about what was going on with me. And I imagined that Miss Davis wasn't any different from everybody else. So I said, "I don't know much about it except that it's happening real soon."

Miss Davis closed the history book and put both her hands on top of it. She said, "Are you going to testify?"

I said, "What about?"

"To get your father off for killing that Bella woman," was her reply.

Well, I was shocked. I hadn't even thought about testifying in court. Nobody in the world had said anything about me testifying and I didn't know anything about how to do it. The whole idea, plus hearing Bella's name said out loud, must have just sent me off somewhere in my head. The next thing I knew Miss Davis was shaking my arm real hard. I realized what she was doing and that she expected me to say something. I said, "Daddy shouldn't have killed her."

Miss Davis let go of my arm then. And she said, "So she didn't do anything to you?"

I said, "You didn't even know her. Killing is wrong." But then I realized that if I said any more it would get Daddy in more trouble, so I stopped there and didn't say anything else.

Miss Davis said, "If she did terrible things to you, Kit, you need to tell people."

I just froze. And I stayed that way. I think she tried to shake my arm again, but I wasn't coming back even if she shook my brains out.

The next thing I remember was sitting in my room with the frontiersman. We just looked at each other and we weren't really in the room, we were in the forest looking for Indians to take us in. The frontiersman isn't the kind of frontiersman who shoots Indians or anybody else. He is the kind who wants to marry an Indian woman and settle down and have little brown children that he plays with all the time. And he also wants to fish and play with bears and foxes and eat berries and wild onions and other things in the forest. He and I talked about that a lot.

I was still shocked over what Miss Davis said and I didn't pay much attention to Rev. or Mrs. Cunningham that day or the next. Miss Francis still came on Wednesday mornings, and I checked out some books, but I don't remember what they were. However, on Thursday after Miss Davis left, Mrs. Cunningham said she needed to go to the grocery before lunch and was going to drive the car to get there. Rev. Cunningham was working on his sermon and she asked me to go with her. The thought crossed my mind that riding with Mrs. Cunningham might be dangerous, but I didn't really care. At that point, dying didn't seem like such a bad idea. I didn't want to testify. I still didn't know what to say.

We did go to the grocery together and didn't get killed and we bought food that we generally didn't get to have, potato chips and some Coca Colas. Mrs. Cunningham didn't say so directly, but I knew I wasn't supposed to say anything about them and I thought we'd probably eat and drink them together sometime when Rev. Cunningham wasn't around. I enjoyed the store, and it sort of got me to feeling like there was a little hope in life again.

My mind had been off so much that I was behind in my homework. So after we came home from the store and ate lunch, I did a bunch of arithmetic problems. Then I read some. I didn't think anything else about the trip to the store until after supper when I decided I'd use the old cigar box I kept my school supplies in to take Aunt Rosa's letters to Mary Jayne's office. When I opened the drawer I kept the letters in, I was thinking up a lie about the cigar box in case anybody asked me what was in it. And at first, I thought I had just opened the wrong drawer. I opened another one. Then, I stopped thinking about the cigar box and panicked.

I looked everywhere, even in places I knew I had never put the letters and in places I knew they couldn't be. I got to breathing hard and panting. I had seen Randy do that on hot days when he had run too hard, and he had always stopped and hung his head down and held his tongue out of the side of his mouth. So, that's what I did. It took my mind off my letters and I thought about Randy and becoming him and then I realized for the first time I hadn't even thought about what happened to him and who was keeping him. That thought scared me even more because it made me wonder what else I hadn't remembered to think about. I started panting again and had to start all over in calming myself down. But I did it. I remembered then that my letters had definitely been in the drawer on Wednesday night.

It was about my bedtime when I went to the living room. Rev. and Mrs. Cunningham were sitting in chairs across from each other reading. I said, "My letters from Aunt Rosa are missing," and I looked at Rev. Cunningham when I said it. I saw the smile flicker in his eyes.

Mrs. Cunningham said something, I don't remember what, but I could tell she was confused. She said a couple of other things, but my attention was on the preacher. He finally said something. It was, "What letters?"

I said, "The ones in my dresser drawer," and I stared at him real hard.

He acted flustered. He said, "Why, Karen, I hope you aren't accusing us of taking anything from your room."

I said, "They're not there."

He said, "Well, I don't know anything about them. I didn't even know you had any letters." Then he went back to his reading.

Mrs. Cunningham got up. She said, "Let me help you look for them." And she passed me and went into my room. I went in after her and closed the door behind me.

She said, "I'm going to go through your drawers. Maybe you've just mislaid them." I just watched her. Mrs. Cunningham was trying to be helpful and also, I know, trying to decide what to do. She was so used to pretending that it was hard for her to do anything besides that, but deep down she knew there was a snake in the house. I think a lot of times when there's a snake in the house, at first people don't want to believe it and hope it's just a rope or a stick. But, eventually, if there's one inside, you have to deal with it.

And that's what Mrs. Cunningham did. After she went through every drawer and the closet and looked under the bed, she walked right past me without saying a word, and went to the living room and said something to Rev. Cunningham in a low voice. After that, she went outside and got in the car. A minute or so later, he went outside and got in the car, too. When the car backed out of the garage, she was driving.

But when it came back, he was driving. Sometimes the snake wins.

42

The next morning when I went to the kitchen nobody was around. Usually, Mrs. Cunningham was fixing breakfast and Rev. Cunningham was in there reading the paper. But the only sign of life that morning was the smell of coffee. I got a bowl from the dish rack and used a stool to get some cereal. The paper from the day before was on the table. President Eisenhower was under the headline, standing up in a car, smiling and waving, but he looked tired to me. I had read that paper before, but I read it again from the front page to the comics and noticed that the crossword puzzle hadn't been done. Nothing else happened except that I finished my breakfast. I washed my bowl and went to my room.

Of course, I had been listening while I was eating and reading. The Cunninghams were in the front bedroom. I could hear just a little movement and talking, but not enough to make out what was being said. So my mind had moved from them to my own problems. I had been pretty upset and had had a hard time sleeping, and in the dresser mirror my face didn't look much better than President Eisenhower's. But I gathered my hair into a ponytail and slipped on a dress and went to the bathroom. It was between my bedroom and the Cunninghams', and I was hoping while I was in there I could pick up some clues about what was going on. I dumped the toothbrushes out of their glass and stepped in the bathtub and put the glass against my ear and the wall. That worked for Nancy Drew, but it didn't for me. I couldn't even remember which end of the glass was supposed to go against my ear and which went against the wall. And it didn't seem to make any difference.

About 9:30, I began to get even more worried. My appointment with Mary Jayne was at 10:30 and I really needed to see her. But the house stayed quiet and I didn't know what to do. I had never knocked on the Cunninghams' bedroom door or even been in their room. My mind started whirling around in a circle and I couldn't think straight. I was in my room in my chair, and while I was still in that state, their door finally opened and I could tell by the footsteps that old preacher had come out.

The phone was in the hallway between my room and theirs and my door was wide open. So I heard him call Dr. Fletcher's office. He didn't talk to the doctor directly, but he left a message that Mrs. Cunningham was sick and he wanted to know if Dr. Fletcher could come out to the house. Then he made another call. It was to Mary Jayne's office. He said that I couldn't make my appointment that morning. Then he put the phone down and didn't even look in my room. He went back to their bedroom and closed the door. After a while, he came out again, went out the back door, and left in the car.

Mary Jayne had given me her telephone number on my first visit, and it hadn't been stolen. I crept out into the hallway and pulled the phone into my room. It had just barely enough cord that I could close the door. I asked the receptionist lady if I could talk to Mary Jayne and she said she was with a client. Aunt Rosa and Aunt Lou had brought me a Mickey Mouse watch on one of their visits. I looked at it. In 15 minutes she was supposed to be with me. I told the receptionist lady that I was Kit Crockett and would call Mary Jayne back in 20 minutes, and told her not to let her call me.

To tell you the truth, the receptionist acted like I called every day and when I got off the phone I felt calmer than I had in some time. I got my writing pad and pencil and sat in my chair and made a list of the points I wanted to make to Mary Jayne. The list read: 1. Rev. Cunningham stole my letters. 2. Rev. Cunningham slapped me. 3. I hate to tell you but Rev. Cunningham doesn't like you. 4. I want out of here. It's like being in prison.

When I got Mary Jayne on the phone, I told her all of that with my hand cupped over my mouth and the receiver. She didn't say much at first. Then she said, "Kit, I'm going to try to help you. I don't know if I'll be successful, but I'll try. You hold on to that."

I said, "I will."

Mrs. Cunningham didn't come out of her bedroom for lunch, so I made myself a peanut butter and jelly sandwich and did arithmetic problems. Miss Davis came at 2:00. We always did my lessons at the dining room table, and when we sat down she looked around and into the kitchen. I knew she was looking for Mrs. Cunningham, but I didn't want to say she was sick. I had gotten afraid people were thinking I could read minds. But while she was going over my papers, Miss Davis asked, "The Cunninghams haven't left you alone, have they?"

I said, "He's gone off somewhere. But Mrs. Cunningham is here. She's lying down."

That seemed okay with her, and we got right down to work on math and spelling and didn't let up until 4:30. But twice while we were working, I heard Mrs. Cunningham come out of the bedroom. I think she went to the bathroom.

Right when Miss Davis was going out the front door, Dr. Fletcher and Rev. Cunningham pulled up in separate cars. I hadn't seen Dr. Fletcher since my first day at the Cunninghams', and after he spoke to Miss Davis I held the door open for him. When he got inside, he put his hand on my shoulder and asked me how I was doing. Having him there was an instant relief to me, but right then Rev. Cunningham came through the door. So I said, "I think my stomach hurts."

Dr. Fletcher said, "I'll talk to you after I see Mrs. Cunningham." Then he followed Rev. Cunningham into the front bedroom. I went out on the front porch and sat in the swing.

They were in there a long time. The sun was starting to set before I heard Dr. Fletcher ask Rev. Cunningham where I went off to. They were in the living room by then, but I didn't hear his reply. When Dr. Fletcher came out on the porch, Rev. Cunningham stopped at the door and looked at me.

Dr. Fletcher said, "Albert, I'll call you in the morning." And then he didn't say anything else. Rev. Cunningham and I both knew he was telling him to go away. He smiled that fake smile and shut the door.

As soon as Dr. Fletcher sat down, I told him about my letters and about Rev. Cunningham slapping me. He said those were serious something (he used a word I didn't know), but I got the sense of what he was saying. I said, "I know."

Then he said, "Why do you think he would do those two things? What would be his reasons?"

Those were hard questions. I didn't know the complete answers. I said, "He doesn't want me to live with my family."

Dr. Fletcher looked puzzled. He said, "Tell me more about that."

"That's why he stole my letters. I was going to show them to Mary Jayne to prove my family are regular people and love me. But he stole them so I couldn't do that, and then he pretended like he didn't even know I had any letters."

"Well, Kit, maybe he didn't know you had letters," was what he replied. "A lot of grown-ups don't pay much attention to what children are doing, and Rev. Cunningham is a busy man."

That showed me right there that he didn't know Rev. Cunningham very well. I had never seen the preacher do anything at all except read and write and talk like he knew everything. He didn't actually work. I said, "He knew I had them. It wasn't any secret."

"Well, how would he know you were planning to do something with them?" is what he asked next. And to tell the truth, it stumped me. He couldn't have known unless Mary Jayne told him or unless he was like me and sometimes knew things there wasn't a logical way to know. I didn't think either of those possibilities had really happened, and I didn't know what to say, so I changed the subject. I said, "Mrs. Cunningham knew I had letters. And she looked for them and then they went off in the car last night."

"They went off in the car?"

"Yes. Last night after she looked for my letters and didn't find them."

Dr. Fletcher got real still after I said that. He just looked off into the front yard where the shadows were getting long, and I let him do that without adding anything more. Finally, he said, "What about the slapping? Was that on the face or the bottom?"

I said, "My face."

Dr. Fletcher put his hand to his brow and sort of pinched his forehead. He said, "Kit, why would he do that?"

I said, "I don't know for sure. He was talking about going to the river to wash away my sins and about Daddy not having any moral authority and Mrs. Burnett getting killed. It was all mixed up together."

I wanted to keep Dr. Fletcher on the subject of Rev. Cunningham, but the next thing he said was, "Kit, do you know why your father killed Mrs. Burnett?"

I was sort of shocked that he said that. But I shouldn't have been. Uncle Russ had wanted to know the same thing, so it was a normal curiosity. I said, "It hasn't been proven that he killed her."

"Well, he's confessed to it," was what Dr. Fletcher said next.

That was news to me. And I had to think about it. It took me a while to talk again, but when I did, I said, "If he said he did it, why doesn't somebody ask him why?"

Dr. Fletcher sighed. "People have. And he won't say."

I just stared out into the shade of the trees. I don't know where my mind went off to, but the next thing I heard was Dr. Fletcher saying, "Jack says that he killed your friend because she was doing things to you that adults shouldn't do to children. And that Mrs. Burnett saw her doing that when you were in the bathroom with her." He didn't say that as a question. It was more matter of fact.

I said, "Mrs. Burnett was a snoop."

Dr. Fletcher got stern like a teacher then. He said, "Well, that may be. But it's much more serious for an adult to do unnatural acts with a child than it is to snoop around somebody's house."

I wanted to tell Dr. Fletcher that Bella was just trying to get me cleaned up in the bathroom. But I didn't know if I could say Bella's name without crying, or even at all. And while I was feeling around inside myself to see if I could do it, I realized if I said that, it would make Daddy look like he had killed Bella for no reason. But if I didn't say that, then Dr. Fletcher and everybody else would keep on thinking that Bella was a terrible lady rather than somebody who loved me and didn't mind showing it. Right then I realized that I was like an animal trapped in a corner.

43

After Dr. Fletcher left, I went to my room. I stayed there until Rev. Cunningham left in the car, then I went to the kitchen and made a peanut butter and jelly sandwich and I took it and a glass of milk back to my room. Having two peanut butter sandwiches in one day was fine with me, and by the time Rev. Cunningham came back I was in bed with the door closed, pretending I was asleep. But I was really worrying about how I could say anything at all that wouldn't hurt Daddy or Bella, one or the other.

The next morning I woke up hearing humming. It was female humming, and I decided even with my head still on the pillow there was a colored woman in the house and that she was Rev. Cunningham's solution to Mrs. Cunningham being sick. That wasn't surprising, because it's what most people would've done. Help was common in town and even in the country and the fact that Mama didn't have any was sometimes mentioned by the women who brought us their cooking. They said things like, "Peggy, maybe if you had some help, it'd be easier on you." They weren't talking about helping out themselves, or even Mama's family helping, they were talking about colored help. "Help" only meant colored, it didn't mean anybody else.

When I went into the kitchen, the help turned around and looked me over. She had big whites to her eyes and her skin was a different shade of brown than Grandma's, or mine, or the rest of my family's. Other than that she ran to the skinny side, not real skinny, just not fat. She said, "What do you want for breakfast?"

I said, "I can make my own," and took a skillet out of the drying rack.

She said, "I'll make it for you, baby."

I couldn't remember anybody calling me "baby" in a long time, and it took me by surprise. But then I remembered that's how colored people talk, and I said, "I don't mind. What's your name?"

She said, "Cararethea."

I said, "Mine's Kit. What kind of name is Cararethea?"

"My mama done give it to me. Named after two of my aunties. Auntie Carrie and Auntie Theodosia." She went back to washing the dishes.

I got bacon and eggs out of the refrigerator and checked the oven to be sure biscuits were warming in there. I said, "Do they call her Theodosia?"

"Naw. We call her Auntie Theo. It's easier."

Cararethea was wearing yellow rubber gloves. And she had on a white blouse with ruffles on the sleeves, and a dark skirt. Her shoes were broken down, but that was the only way you could tell she was poor. She carried herself straight and her head was level. I decided right there, standing at her back while I was cooking, that she was a good addition to the house. I said, "How's Mrs. Cunningham?"

"Doctor ain't been 'round yet. We'll have to see."

"Have you been in to see her?" My bacon was crinkling and I turned it.

"I cleaned her up first thing this morning. She's limp."

I found that surprising. In my imagination, Mrs. Cunningham had been sleeping, but not limp. I said, "How come?"

"The Reverend says it's most likely her heart." Cararethea pulled the plug on the drain and the sink made a sucking noise.

"I thought she just had a cold or something," was what I said then.

"Nope. Pale as a ghost." She picked up a drying towel.

I started to say, "You're just not used to how pale white people can get," but then I realized Cararethea had probably taken care of sick white people before. Colored women have to work. So I said, "Maybe she's just off her feed." Cararethea made a humming noise that I took for a no, and I got my bacon out of the skillet and cracked my eggs open.

While I ate breakfast, Cararethea took to dusting and I read the paper from the day before. I was through with the funnies and trying to find five blackbirds hidden in a drawing when I heard a car crunch the gravel outside and a door slam. Rev. Cunningham was in the bedroom with Mrs. Cunningham and could see who drove up. He let Dr. Fletcher in the front door before he even knocked.

I didn't have anything particular to do, so I got a book and went out to the front porch. I was reading my fourth or fifth Hardy Boys. I don't remember exactly which, but I was pretty deep into it when a white van with writing on the side pulled into the drive. I realized it was an ambulance because one came for Mama a couple of times. I stood up. I don't know why. It seemed like the right thing to do. Two men got out.

Dr. Fletcher met them at the door and told them, "She's in the front bedroom." Then he said to me, "Kit, if you stay where you are, you can see Mrs. Cunningham before she goes to the hospital."

I said, "Yes, sir," and sat back down and waited. In a few minutes, Dr. Fletcher came back to the door and held it open. One of the ambulance men came out holding one end of a stretcher, and they both stopped when they cleared the door. I hadn't seen Mrs. Cunningham since the night I discovered my letters were stolen, and to tell the truth, she looked just as pale as Cararethea had said. She put her hand out and I took it. I said, "Thanks for helping me." Right at that moment, Rev. Cunningham came to the door. Mrs. Cunningham squeezed my hand and the ambulance men carried her off the porch.

Since I'd told him I knew about my letters, I hadn't really been directly eye to eye with Rev. Cunningham except for a second when Dr. Fletcher was there. But we looked at each other then. I could tell even with the screen between us and with a fake smile on his face that he was mad. I didn't know at the time if Cararethea was going to be spending the nights, so I got frightened right then about being left alone in the house with him and him being so mad at me. I would have to leave, even if I had to strike out across the fields alone. I would go past the pecan trees and find a place to hide. I would take the frontiersman with me.

I was plotting my escape when Rev. Cunningham came out of the house with Dr. Fletcher. He didn't look at me. Dr. Fletcher did look, and he gave my arm a squeeze and said, "Mind Cararethea."

They both got in their cars and drove off, and I began to relax. It sounded like Cararethea would be around. I went in the house, where she was taking the sheets off of the Cunninghams' bed, and I asked her, "Are you going to be taking care of me?"

She said, "We'll see."

I said, "I'm not much trouble," because I wanted her to stay. Then I helped her put new sheets on the bed just to show her that and also to try to get to know her. You want all the allies you can get. It doesn't matter if they're a different race. My family had taught me that.

I was thankful for every minute Rev. Cunningham was out of the house. But I didn't know when he would be coming back, so after we changed the sheets, I sat down at the dining room table where all of my school work was still laid out, and I wrote a letter to Aunt Rosa. I told her the developments and that I was afraid to stay in the house with Rev. Cunningham alone. They needed to come get me.

Later that afternoon, I started to get to know Cararethea better.

She had a husband and two little boys and could read and write, and she liked to listen to the radio. She found a station that was broadcasting all the way from Chicago, and that night we listened until way past my bedtime and she told me about all the singers and sang along with them. I had never been around anybody musical before. It was fun.

44

Cararethea slept on the couch, and the next morning when I got up Rev. Cunningham still hadn't come home. It was Sunday, and I needed to go to church to see Uncle Russ and Aunt Jean and give them my letter to mail. But Cararethea and I didn't have a car, and even if her husband, Herb, came to get us we'd have to go to the colored church because Cararethea said she wouldn't let me out at the white church. She didn't say directly she was afraid of Rev. Cunningham, she just rolled her eyes, shook her head, and said, "Rev. Cunningham don't wanta see the likes of you prissin' up the aisle while he's concentratin' on his preachin'."

I said, "I don't priss."

She looked me over. Then she said, "No, I don't guess you do. I'll get us some preachin' on the radio."

I said, "That's not the idea."

Cararethea's brow knotted. She said, "Well, what is the idea?"

"I've got people I've got to talk to at church."

"Don't we all," she said.

I could tell that coloreds could be just as difficult as Indians and white people in their own way and decided that people with more than one race mixed up in them were probably the easiest to get along with. That made me think of Bella all of a sudden, and I stopped worrying about not going to church for a minute and looked at Cararethea to compare them. They were about the same age and height and maybe the same weight, but where Bella was curvy, Cararethea had angles. And there was a different feel about the two of them. Bella was full of mystery; it just oozed out of her, like a perfume. Cararethea, who I didn't know nearly as well, seemed more everyday. I could imagine her with her two little boys in her own house without any trouble or real information. But Bella, I couldn't imagine her any place other than the cabin, even in New Orleans, and I couldn't, or won't, see her anywhere after that. She just lived at the cabin. And I decided right then and there that I would never go past that cabin again, no matter what, because I want Bella there, and since she's not I won't be able to bear it.

When Cararethea got a colored preacher on the radio, he made me stop thinking about Bella. I was glad in a way, but also was glad to have had just a few minutes of thinking about her, because I hadn't thought about much her in a long time. The colored preacher was more lively than Rev. Cunningham, but he used that same yell at you and then get quiet kind of voice. But his words rolled and drew pictures in the air. He preached about a river carrying people away, and I felt myself caught up in the flood.

Rev. Cunningham came back in the late afternoon, but only to get new clothes. He gave his dirty laundry to Cararethea and she gave him a list of groceries to pack in. He told her that Mrs. Cunningham was resting peacefully and that the doctors expected a full recovery, but he didn't say exactly what happened to her and I didn't ask him. I didn't even directly see him. I just listened to them talking through my open door.

Monday morning while I was still eating breakfast, Mary Jayne called. I was really glad to talk to her and I told her we'd need to have our visit on the telephone because I didn't have any way to get to her office. She told me not to worry, she was coming to see me. That made my heart jump with some hope. And it made me feel like Mary Jayne was really on my side and would help me escape. Maybe even that afternoon. I decided a bath was in order.

So later, I was clean and dressed up in clothes that were my own but that I hadn't had on in a while, and I had my letter for Mary Jayne to mail to Aunt Rosa telling her what was going on, just in case she wouldn't take me away right then. I also had decided not to pack, because that could bring on bad luck. I really didn't know what Mary Jayne had in mind, just what my hopes were.

So I had done everything I needed to do and was sitting in the front swing when a blue car pulled in the driveway and stopped. A man was driving it, but Mary Jayne got out of the passenger's side and waved real big. I hadn't expected to see a man with Mary Jayne, and he wasn't anybody I had ever seen before, but he walked right up to me with a big smile and held out his hand for a shake. He said, "I'm David Wayne Bumpus, your daddy's lawyer."

I said, "Please to meet you, Mr. Bumpus," just like I shook hands all the time.

The three of us settled on the porch, Mr. Bumpus in a chair and Mary Jayne and me in the swing. Cararethea brought us a pitcher of tea and set it and a tray of glasses on a table between Mr. Bumpus's chair and an empty one.

Mary Jayne led off the conversation by saying, "Kit, your daddy's trial starts this week, and Mr. Bumpus needs to ask you some questions, because children can't testify in court. You need to tell him the absolute truth. He wants to help your father as much as he can, but the truth is always better than a lie, particularly in court. Do you understand?"

I nodded. I felt like all of a sudden a burden had been lifted off my shoulders. Finally, somebody had a rule about children that benefited me.

Mr. Bumpus talked next. He said, "Now, Kit, I want to ask you first about Mrs. Burnett. Can you tell me anything about her?"

I told him the same thing I had said before, that she was mean and that she killed the guineas and that she was always stealing around on her neighbors' property, but that she didn't want anybody on hers. Mr. Bumpus listened to what I said and took notes on a pad he had pulled out of a briefcase. Then he said, "Do you know why your daddy killed her?"

I shook my head, but I said, "Because she was mean, I reckon."

He winced. Then he pushed his glasses up against his face better. "Did you tell your father Mrs. Burnett was mean to you?"

I tried to think back and remember if I had said anything at all to Daddy about Mrs. Burnett, but I couldn't think of anything in particular. I said, "Maybe if you told me about when he killed her, it would help me remember something."

Mr. Bumpus and Mary Jayne looked at each other for a long time. Then Mary Jayne said, "Kit, your father says Mrs. Burnett came to y'all's house on that Sunday morning on her way home from church. She told him that she had seen you and your friend in the bathroom and that you didn't have on any clothes. She said the woman was doing things to you she shouldn't have been doing. Then, evidently, he and Mrs. Burnett went together to your friend's house and there was an argument. We're not sure who said what. But your father shot your friend during that argument, and then he shot Mrs. Burnett."

I couldn't hardly bear to think about Daddy and Bella arguing, so I didn't dwell on that. I went straight in my mind to him shooting Mrs. Burnett. I said, "She probably said something to make him mad."

Mr. Bumpus said, "Well, that's a reasonable assumption."

I wasn't quite sure what that meant, but I said, "She didn't like me. Maybe she said something about me."

Mary Jayne and Mr. Bumpus looked at each other and smiled like that was important information. "Do you know what that could have been?" Mary Jayne asked.

"I don't know. She didn't like me visiting Bella, and she told me one day to go home."

"Did you go?" Mr. Bumpus said.

"No. Bella told her she invited me and I stayed."

Mr. Bumpus bit the end of his pen. Then he said, "Kit, do you think Mrs. Burnett thought you liked Bella too much and maybe, I don't know how to put this, maybe she thought you enjoyed Bella and maybe she said that to your daddy? Do you know what I mean?"

I said, "I did enjoy Bella."

They looked at each other again, but that time they frowned.

45

Another friend of Mr. Hodges, a Rev. something or another, was the preacher today. He told a story about an old man who held a little bird in his hands behind his back and asked a young man to guess if the bird was dead or alive. The young man said, "It's in your hands," and that preacher smiled just like Rev. Cunningham used to and repeated that line two or three times. I took a fast dislike to him, but the story is the most interesting one I've heard in a while. I know just how that bird felt cooped up inside those sweaty hands. The old man was hiding what he was doing, playing games with everybody, and all the time he was willing to close a fist on that bird and snuff his life out for no reason except, and this is important, to look wise and in control. That's exactly what Rev. Cunningham is like. And that's the reason that I didn't get to live with my family. I understand that now. And I will set down here how I got the information that's the way it would turn out even though I didn't understand it at first.

On the Wednesday morning after I talked to Mary Jayne and Mr. Bumpus, I was in my room deciding which new book from Miss Francis I was going to start when I heard a car pull into the drive. Cararethea must have been cleaning the living room and seen it come in. She called, "Kit, baby, come here," even before I heard a door slam.

I put my books down, went into the living room, and found her at the front door. She said, "Lookee. You know them folks?"

I looked out the window. Uncle Mark was stretching and Aunt Rosa and Aunt Lou were getting out the back doors. I yelled and busted out of the screen.

There was a lot of confusion after that, everybody hugging and talking over each other. But when we got into the house, we settled at the dining room table and Cararethea brought us some sweet tea.

They had come for the trial and had a plan and needed my help. They wanted to keep me with them so we could be together and people could see us as a family. Uncle Mark thought that might help them get custody of me and get Daddy a fairer shake from the jury. He said, "Kit, the way I figure it is this: Jack's going to have to spend some time in jail. There's no getting around that. But they won't give him a long time for killing that woman from New Orleans. His real problem is Irene Burnett." I nodded because I knew that to be true, or at least that nobody really cared about what happened to Bella. "Bumpus says he thinks he did pretty well selecting the jury. Only one Bible-thumper in the group, which is a miracle in itself. About half of any case is who's on the jury. So if they can get a look at you, they might just remember that Jack was a father protecting his daughter and think things just got a little out of hand."

I knew from Frank Still's trial that the law wasn't cut and dried, more just whose opinion won out, so what Uncle Mark said made sense to me. I said, "I bet Mrs. Burnett drove him to it."

They all three leaned in, and Aunt Rosa, who was sitting next to me, put her hand on my shoulder. She said, "What makes you say that?"

"She would tell you what to do and then call you names."

"Did she call you any names?" Aunt Lou said.

"No. But she called my friend Jezebel."

Aunt Lou looked to Uncle Mark and he leaned back in his chair and frowned. Aunt Rosa squeezed my shoulder and said, "Let's don't tell them that. That could make Mrs. Burnett look good."

I still didn't know much about Jezebel, and I didn't know what that meant. But talking about Bella hurt. I didn't mind dropping the subject. I said, "Will I get to see Daddy in court?"

Uncle Mark said, "We don't know yet. We're not sure they'll let you in. They've sort of got you in jail, too."

I said to Aunt Rosa, "Did you get my letter yesterday?"

She said, "No, honey, when did you mail it?"

"I gave it to Mary Jayne on Monday."

"Well, if she didn't mail it until the afternoon, it'll probably come today."

I said, "Then you don't know that Rev. Cunningham stole my letters."

They all leaned in again and their eyes got big. Aunt Lou said, "That rat," and Uncle Mark said, "Tell us about that." I told them the whole story and about the slapping, too.

Even before I was completely through, Uncle Mark was up pacing the floor and rubbing the back of his neck with his hand. And Aunt Lou and Aunt Rosa threw questions at me, including about who all I'd told. They chewed on the whole thing for several minutes, and said things to each other that I didn't entirely understand. But the drift of their conversation was that we'd have trouble getting anybody to believe all that. I knew Uncle Russ had had the same trouble, but I was fed up with adults who wanted to believe in lies. I finally said, "Why wouldn't people believe it? It's true."

They all looked back and forth then. I thought for a minute nobody was going to answer me. But finally Aunt Lou said, "A lot of people want to believe in preachers, Kit. So it's easier for them to get away with stealing and lying than it is for most folks." She arched an eyebrow and tilted her head.

Uncle Mark said, "I sort of wish you hadn't told anybody but us."

I was startled by that remark, and hurt some, too. I said, "Don't you believe me?"

He sat back down. "Kit. I do. I believe you for sure. But it just makes things harder."

I had no idea what he was saying, and it must have shown on my face.

He said, "Rev. Cunningham's not going to want that out in the community. Don't tell anybody else. It'll make him an even worse enemy. He'll have to protect his reputation. We may need to pretend it didn't happen."

That made the hurt even deeper. And it made me mad, too. I said, "I thought you loved me." I sounded whiny even to myself.

Uncle Mark turned red in the face and put his elbows on the table and his hands on his forehead where he was losing his hair. Aunt Rosa said, "Honey, we do," and Aunt Lou said, "Kit, you're too young to understand that people pretend things that aren't true all the time."

I did understand that. I knew Rev. and Mrs. Cunningham pretended all the time. But I didn't think any of us should pretend things to protect that mean old man. I said, "Why should Uncle Mark pretend." It was more of a statement than a question.

Aunt Lou shook her head. "I think I've just confused things. Somebody else try."

Aunt Rosa said to Aunt Lou, "I'll tell her what Mama would say." Then she said to me, "Kit, do you remember learning in school that America was an empty land waiting to be discovered by civilized people? And that the country is built on freedom and justice and liberty for all?"

I nodded.

"What do you think that means for Indians?"

That was an easy question. I replied, "I think that's a lie for Indians."

"That's what we're trying to say. It's a lie that everybody pretends is true. Even we pretend sometimes, because to do anything else is too dangerous. And that's what we need to do about the stolen letters and the lying and the slapping. Telling the truth about those things will get you in trouble. We can just hope he doesn't know you've already told it. He'll be fit to be tied."

I let that sink in. But I felt again like an animal trapped in a corner. If I told the truth about almost anything it would make everything worse for me or for Daddy or for Bella, who was dead to everybody else but was alive in my heart. I got real quiet and still. The adults got up and moved around.

I think my mind went off. I don't remember exactly what happened next. But some time later Cararethea came into the room and said to Uncle Mark, "He told me to call the church if you folks showed up."

Uncle Mark said, "Did you?"

Cararethea shook her head. Then she said, "Sometimes he comes home for lunch, from what I understand." She sort of tilted her head and the whites of her eyes got big.

Uncle Mark said, "Got it," to Cararethea, and to my aunts, "We need to get outta here."

They promised to come back in the evening, and Uncle Mark said they would see Mary Jayne and try to talk to some people down at the courthouse and get a motel room. They were also going to try to see Daddy. Uncle Mark slipped some dollar bills under the sugar bowl on the dining room table and they all sort of rushed out the door.

When the car was out of sight, Cararethea picked the bills up and slipped them inside her brassiere. It was the first thing I had seen her do that reminded me of Bella, and I smiled. Cararethea said, "Lord, child, you're growing up too fast."

I hadn't understood everything that had gone on and I wasn't sure if that was a compliment or not. But I understood about the money and whose side Cararethea was on. And that afternoon I had some hope that everything could turn out all right.

46

They came back to the house and got me for supper. Rev. Cunningham still wasn't home, but I think they would've come even if he had been. We're not cowards, we just get the lay of the land. And by then they had been in town. They'd talked to people. And everybody knew they were around.

We went to a place I had never eaten at before called Jasper's. It was right across from the courthouse, and we took a table with a window that overlooked the sidewalk. I sat next to Aunt Lou, who was big in the stomach with that baby. I had ignored the baby in the morning, but there was no way not to notice it at supper. I had never said anything about a woman having a baby before and couldn't remember anybody else doing that either, except when Aunt Rosa wrote me the news and then later when she wrote that Aunt Lou had been sick in the mornings. I knew those two things had something to do with each other. So after we ordered, I said, "Is the baby still making you sick?"

Aunt Lou smiled and said, "Not anymore. Do you want to try to feel it move?"

I didn't really. I didn't want anything to do with the baby. But I
didn't want anybody to know that. While I was sort of frozen about
what to do next, Aunt Lou took my hand and placed it on her stomach.
The baby kicked or something. It was a feeling like a toad cupped in
your hands. I smiled, and I thought to myself right at that minute, now
I'm pretending like everybody else. But that didn't seem that bad. I
was glad to be able to do it because that baby was a bother to me, no
doubt about that, but to everybody else it seemed like a good thing. I
thought I could get used to it if I could just get away and live with my
family. I'd only feel bad about it if it got to be with my grandparents
and aunts and uncles and I didn't.

They had seen Daddy, Mary Jayne, Mr. Bumpus, and the judge, all
four. And I could tell they were trying to make the best of what they'd
been told. But I wasn't going to get to see Daddy and I wasn't going to
get to sit in the court. I was going to get to be with them, and sit outside the court. They were going to take turns sitting inside and out, so
one of them would be with me all the time. That seemed important to
them and I was all for it, but I wasn't afraid to be alone in town. I knew
people, and alone in town isn't nearly as bad as alone in the house with
somebody who steals from you and could hit you at any minute.

While they were telling all of that, Mr. Simmons, the newspaper
reporter man, walked in. Uncle Mark jumped up, shook his hand, and
introduced him to my aunts, although he'd already met Aunt Rosa.
Then Mr. Simmons sat down at the end of the table facing the window. A waitress came right over and handed him a menu. We were
through eating, but Aunt Rosa said he should eat whatever he wanted
and Uncle Mark said to put the food on his tab. Mr. Simmons ordered
collard greens and beans and corn pudding, and said his gall bladder
was acting up on him. After that, they settled into the kind of talking
adults do when they're showing each other they're on the same side
and want to be friends.

But when the cigarettes came out, Mr. Simmons said to me directly, "I bet you've been missing your dad."

Everybody at the table got quiet and it seemed like the whole restaurant did, too. I said, "Pretty much. Have you seen him?"

He nodded. "He said to tell you that you're a fighter."

That wasn't at all what I had imagined Daddy would say if he had one thing to say to me. I said, "He did?"

Mr. Simmons nodded. Then he said, "I understand you were fishing when it all happened."

I nodded.

He took a long drag off his cigarette and looked up at the ceiling. He said, "Now, I'm trying to recollect, does that bayou back up on Mrs. Burnett's land?" Then he looked over at me again.

I wasn't fooled, but I didn't mind, either. He had convinced me that he was on Daddy's side while he was trying to convince my aunts. I said, "The bayou's on an easement."

Mr. Simmons smiled. "An easement? You don't say. Where'd you learn about easements?"

I had to think back. I couldn't really remember where I first heard about easements. Then I recalled Uncle Joe telling Mama that the government was going to take part of his land for the river easement. They had talked about that a lot. It had made them both mad. I said, "I always knew about them."

Mr. Simmons seemed pleased and drew on his cigarette again. Then he said, "Can you remember anything about Mrs. Burnett that would help your father?"

I said what I always said. "She was mean."

Mr. Simmons said, "Well, to tell you the truth, Kit, some people might agree with you about that. And I want to help Jack if I can."

I must have sighed real deep. I know I felt tired all of a sudden. And it must have shown because Aunt Lou put her arm around me and pulled me up closer to her stomach and that baby. I said, "I'd make something up if I knew what to make."

Mr. Simmons said, "And believe me, I'd put it in the paper if it would help. The only living war hero in this town is sitting in jail for killing somebody after we all praised him for doing that again and again. It doesn't sit well, not just with me, but with a lot of folks around here."

I hadn't thought about the war part. I didn't even know much about it. And the only thing I knew about Daddy being a hero was that Uncle Mark had once called him that. It'd never really occurred to me that Daddy had killed people before Bella and Mrs. Burnett. I found that sort of shocking. I went off somewhere in my head. The next thing I remember I was standing on the front porch with Cararethea waving good night to my family. But after they drove away and we went inside the door it came up in my mind that if Daddy had learned to kill people in the war, it might be hard for him to stop shooting once he got started, particularly if the people were mean.

47

My family picked me up again the next morning. And we went to Jasper's again. When we came in, people were drinking coffee, eating breakfast, and reading the paper. There were three men at the table we had taken the night before, and they all got up at the same time and introduced themselves to my aunts and uncle and said howdy to me. One of them was Mr. Elliot, the feed store owner. They gave us their chairs and the waitress came over, cleared all their plates, and wiped the table. There was a lot of moving around, but by the time everybody settled down and the new plates arrived, I realized we were the center of attention.

We ate with a lot of introducing and talking, and people giving their opinions and wishing us luck. It seemed to me that the entire town was on Daddy's side and I began to feel that it didn't matter who he had shot, he would get off because everybody liked him. I didn't think that was a far-fetched idea, because Frank Still got off after killing Uncle Joe.

At a few minutes to nine, Uncle Mark and Aunt Lou left to go across the street to the courthouse and the men in the restaurant left at the same time. They also went across the street and into the courthouse. That left Aunt Rosa, me, and the waitress there, and the waitress was busy clearing off tables.

Aunt Rosa said, "I believe being pregnant has made your Aunt Lou more outgoing. Usually, it works the other way."

I had no idea what she was talking about. I said, "Yeah, I know."

We sat there for a while with Aunt Rosa drinking coffee and reading the paper and me doing math problems. Miss Davis was due because the deal Uncle Mark made with the judge was for me to continue my lessons throughout the trial. She came about 9:30. But to tell the truth, except for checking my problems, she didn't do anything but drink coffee and talk to Aunt Rosa. I began to see that Aunt Rosa could make anybody like her just by being nice to them and making them feel special. I watched her do that with Miss Davis and it kept me entertained. Adults can be interesting when they forget a child is around.

At noon everybody came out of the courthouse and into Jasper's and Miss Davis stayed to hear the news because she was like everybody else. People were interested in the trial, and Jasper's was as busy as a hive of bees. The morning had been spent with Daddy's lawyer and the district attorney standing before the judge and jury and explaining how they agreed that killing Bella was justifiable homicide but disagreed about the killing of Mrs. Burnett. The district attorney said it was murder in the second degree and Mr. Bumpus said it was voluntary manslaughter. They also said how they would present evidence in Bella's death.

I don't mean to sound here like I'm educated in being a lawyer and I may be misusing the English language. But, really, I've heard a lot of legal words again and again, and when people get in a pickle, they talk about the same things over and over, trying to get a different angle on them. So although nobody explained the difference to me, I figured out that justifiable homicide was better for Daddy than voluntary manslaughter and that voluntary manslaughter was better for him than murder. But I never got the part about the second degree.

48

Last night, several of us played jacks. This was after supper and homework, but before bedtime. We were playing for money, which is the way we usually play, because almost nobody has enough to buy batteries off the battery queens unless we win it from somebody else. I'm pretty good at jacks, quick with my hands, and Caroline's good, too. She and I and a girl named Donna were the only three left. The pot was about 52 cents, and with 50 cents somebody will sell you two batteries, so it was real jacks, not just fooling around.

We were playing a game where you had to throw the ball, hit the floor with the palm of your hand, say "bang" at the same time, and then pick up your jacks. We call that fancy bang, and Donna went first and completed her turn without making a mistake. Caroline went next. She was on threesies on the way back down when she missed a jack and only grabbed two. Donna squealed. She has a high voice that goes, I think, with being real skinny. But I grinned myself because Caroline rarely makes a mistake at jacks, especially on an easy move.

But when Caroline handed me some jacks and the ball, I noticed something unusual. Her hand was shaking. I looked at her face. It was as calm and smiling as always. But I knew I wasn't mistaken about the hand, and when I started my round, I got only to foursies going up before I missed, too. Donna won the entire pot, and we broke up to go to our closets.

Caroline's bed and closet are the farthest from the door in our room, and mine are the fourth from the door, so we have four beds and closets between us. All those girls were already in their closets or in the bathroom, and Donna had gone to her room across the hall. I pulled my top off over my head because I like to be ready for bed before I get in my closet. Caroline did the same thing with hers, and when she did I noticed bruises on the pale underside of her left arm.

I put on my pajamas. But instead of going to my closet, I rearranged things on my bedside table until Caroline went to hers. I waited until she had been in there for a few minutes, then I gave her door my special knock, three quick taps and then two more. We all have our own taps, and if the person whose door you tap on taps the same thing back, you can go in. I don't know how that system got started. It was here before I came.

Anyway, Caroline tapped my tap back and I went in and sat down on the floor with her. It was dark in there, but not smelly, because Caroline's clean and smells like an Indian. I said, "I'm sorry you lost."

She said, "Thanks," but she didn't say anything else, like "I'm sorry you lost, too." And that wasn't like her. I waited a little longer. Then I said, "I know what he's doing to you."

I heard her take a deep breath. But she said, "I don't know what you're talking about."

I said, "I'm talking about Mr. Hodges. I know what he's doing to you."

She didn't say anything for the longest time. Then she said, "I still don't know what you're talking about."

The thing about talking in the dark is that it's easier to tell if somebody's lying than it is when you're talking in the light. I don't know why that is, but it has something to do with their voice. Also, I knew Caroline was lying anyway, just by what she said. I said, "I'm talking about the marks on your arm," because I didn't want to say the other stuff.

Caroline said, "Oh, he was just trying to get me to class."

I said, "I know. He tries to get me to class, too. I've had the same marks. They're from his fingers grabbing real hard and pulling."

She knew exactly what I was saying because that's how he does if you don't get enough of his snake in your mouth. But she didn't say anything and we just sat there in silence in the dark for a long time. Finally, I said, "I wonder how many of us he's trying to get to class," because that's the best way to ask Caroline a question.

She was so quiet for such a long time that I began to think she wasn't going to answer. I waited, because that's what you do. I'm used to it. It's being polite.

Finally, she said, "I think it's just the Indians."

Well, I bet if the light had been on, my eyes would have shown the whites like Cararethea's used to. That was a shocking statement. And I didn't move while I tried to think out what it meant. I couldn't come up with anything that wasn't just terrible, so I blurted out, "Why?"

And Caroline didn't wait. She said, "I don't know. I may be wrong. That's just what I think."

Right then, we heard the monitor announce 10 minutes to lights out. I decided not to try to talk to Caroline anymore, and just went to bed and laid there awake until the 11:00 monitor came by. She was 10 minutes late, but after she finally came, I got in my own closet and tried to sleep. But all inside, I was like birds flying up from the field. I've been like that ever since. I can't think it out and I can't settle down and I'm hardly getting any sleep. I couldn't even write that night. I'm some better now, except for my stomach, and I think it might settle if I take my mind off of things here and put more down about what happened in the trial.

49

On the afternoon of the first day, Mr. Graham, the district attorney, laid out the case against Daddy for killing Bella. He said it was justifiable homicide, and the state wasn't going to ask for punishment. All of that sounded both good and bad when Uncle Mark and Aunt Rosa came back over from the courthouse and told Aunt Lou and me about it. It sounded good because I didn't want Daddy in jail. But it sounded bad because I couldn't stand to think about Bella being dead, and talking about her being killed was the same thing as talking about her being dead. I just went off in my head and didn't even think to ask questions.

There was a lot of commotion in Jasper's. I could feel that even with my mind someplace else. Everybody around me was talking, and the restaurant was pretty full. Somebody brought me a coloring book and crayons and I began coloring a picture of some bears in the woods that was mostly green and gold and, of course, brown for the bears and the tree trunks. I stayed inside the lines, except for on one foot of a mama bear, and I was almost through with the picture when things got noisier. I looked up and my mind shifted back to inside the room.

Rev. Cunningham was standing in the middle of it, about ten feet away. He was the center of attention, and people were shaking his hand and he was saying things like, "Thank you, thank you." Mr. Bumpus, Daddy's lawyer, was standing right by his side. That looked suspicious to me. I didn't know why anybody on our side would have anything to do with that old rat.

Aunt Lou was sitting across from me eating a sandwich and watching everybody. I said, "That's the preacher."

Aunt Lou kept chewing because her mouth was full, but she nodded.

I said, "What's he doing here?"

She washed her food down with some tea and said, "He testified for your daddy."

I said, "What does he know about anything?"

Aunt Lou picked up her sandwich again. She said, "He knows what Mrs. Burnett told Jack that led up to the killings."

I said, "How could he know that?"

"She told him, too. They'd been talking about your friend for a while. Rev. Cunningham told Mrs. Burnett to tell Jack everything that she'd told him."

That's where I made my mistake, some say. But I didn't think about it. It was just a natural reaction, and to tell you the truth if I had it to do over again, I'd do the same thing. There's just so much a person can stand. And you know it down deep inside your body before you even know it in your head. I've thought about it a lot since, and wondered, if I'd kept my temper would it have made any difference? But I found out pretty quickly afterwards that Uncle Russ and Mary Jayne had already told that old preacher what I had said about his slapping and letter stealing and lying, and he had denied all three. So, if Uncle Mark was right, and I think he was, then I would have been sent to Ashley Lordard anyway, and not just because of what was said about my family, and not because of what I did, but because that old preacher was going to have to save his reputation, and the best way to do that was to lock me away here with his friend. I may be fooling myself about that, and it may really be my own fault like some people have said. But I will write down right here what I did, and anyone who reads this can decide for themselves.

As soon as Aunt Lou told me that Rev. Cunningham had put Mrs. Burnett up to telling Daddy whatever it was that made him so mad that he killed Bella and her both, I got up from the table. I weaved through people and tables until I got a good angle and a clear path. Then I put my head down. I ran straight at that evil old man like a charging bull and I butted him smack below his belt. He screamed bloody murder. Then he fell over backwards flat on the floor. He curled up in a ball, moaning and groaning, beet red in the face.

After that, all hell broke loose, as they say. People scrambled this way and that, and somebody grabbed me from behind, and yelled, "Don't kick him, Kit." I think that was Mr. Bumpus, but it could have been somebody else. But the important thing is that nobody brought out any knives. So I got carried away, but not cut up. I fared better than Uncle Joe. And I've lived to fight another day.

50

That stopped the trial. Judge Prescott was presiding over both Daddy's situation and mine. And somebody, him I guess, decided they'd better give me some attention before things got out of hand completely. So, I didn't have to go back to the Cunninghams'. I spent the night with my family at the Starlite. They got an extra room, and Aunt Lou moved over to sleep with me, and it was in that room that we gathered. Uncle Mark had bought us a whole chocolate meringue pie at the restaurant and had talked the waitress out of some little plates and four forks. We had to use his pocket knife, but Aunt Rosa said, "You make do with what you have," and washed it before and after she cut the pieces.

We talked a little about what I should say to the judge if he decided to talk to me. But there were differences of opinion about that, and they couldn't agree. Finally, Aunt Rosa said, "It just depends on what he asks. But tell the truth, Kit. That's usually the best solution."

Aunt Lou said, "Except when it's not."

They all laughed. And I did, too. I might be a child, but I know the truth of that.

The next morning we all got up, dressed, and returned the plates and forks when we ate breakfast. Then we went over to the courthouse. I had never been inside it before, and it was dark for a building. The wood was brownish-red and the floors were green. There were big lights that looked like white balls and were hung from the ceiling by chains. People were sitting on benches along the walls on the first floor and other people were going in and out of doors. When I walked by, everybody stopped what they were doing and looked at me.

The judge's chambers were at the top of a long flight of stairs that turned a corner halfway up. When we got to the second floor, we went in a door with the judge's name written on it. Mary Jayne, Mr. Bumpus, Dr. Fletcher, Uncle Russ, and Aunt Jean were in there waiting in chairs in front of a secretary. While we were talking to them, Rev. Cunningham and some other people came in. He spoke or nodded to everybody else, but he didn't look at me, and nobody said anything except for hellos. Rev. Cunningham told the secretary that they'd wait in the chairs in the hall. I didn't know any of the people with him, but Uncle Russ told Uncle Mark that, except for one, they were members of his church. He didn't know who the stranger was, and neither did anybody else at the time. That man turned out to be Mr. Hodges.

People took turns going in to talk to the judge. Dr. Fletcher went in first, but after him I can't remember the order. However, everybody, including all those people with Rev. Cunningham and my aunts and Uncle Mark, went in. Even Miss Davis showed up before noon. After they'd all had their say, later in the afternoon after we'd eaten sandwiches brought over from Jasper's, the judge called me in.

His office was light compared to the rest of the building. The windows were open and the walls were painted white. When the secretary opened the door for me, the judge stood up. He didn't look like what I'd expected to see. For one thing, he was tall. For another, he was young. He didn't even look as old as Daddy, and I had been imagining an old man with white hair. But Judge Prescott's hair was dark brown, and while Daddy's hair and the hair of most of the men in the town was either crew cut or a burr, Judge Prescott's hair was full and longer. He had a lot of it for a man. I liked him.

He said, "So, you are Kit Crockett!" like he was meeting somebody special.

I said, "Yes, your honor," because everybody had told me to say "your honor" when I talked to him.

He said, "Have a seat in this chair," and he pointed to one right beside his desk and sat back down in his.

I sat down and looked around. He had papers framed on the wall and pictures of himself shaking hands with different people. I inspected everything, then I looked at him. He said, "I've heard a lot about you."

That seemed about right. He had been talking to people all morning, and I knew it was about me. I didn't know what to say, so I didn't say anything.

He said, "Can you tell me why on earth you head-butted Rev. Cunningham?"

I said, "He's caused me a lot of trouble."

The judge nodded. Then he said, "But he testified for your father."

I said, "Did he testify why Daddy killed Mrs. Burnett?"

The judge's glasses were on his desk, and he reached over and moved them. Then he said, "Well, no he didn't."

"Then no matter what Rev. Cunningham said, Daddy's going to jail. He wasn't that big of a help."

The judge nodded. He said, "The jury and I will decide if your father goes to jail, but I take your point." Then he picked up his glasses and tapped them on his desk. He said, "I hear you want to live with your family."

I looked at him straight in the eye. "Yes, your honor, I do."

"It would help, Kit, if you could show a little remorse."

I said, "What's that?"

"Well, it's like feeling sorry for your bad deeds."

I said, "I do feel sorry for my bad deeds."

"I'm talking about head-butting the preacher in the groin," is what he said then.

I looked out the window. There was a big maple tree out there and its leaves were starting to turn. I thought: How hard can it be to say that I'm sorry for knocking the preacher down? I could turn over a new leaf. I looked at the tree while I thought about that. But I couldn't get any words to come to my lips that sounded like anything but a lie. And I knew you couldn't lie to a judge, or you had to go to jail yourself. Finally, I said, "I owed him one. He slapped me."

The judge took a sigh so deep that I could see his body move out of the sides of my eyes. Then he said, "So I've heard."

I looked straight at him then. I said, "And he stole my letters and lied about it."

The judge picked his glasses up again and he tapped the palm of his hand with them. He said, "Apparently, he did."

I was surprised. I said, "You believe me."

He said, "I do."

"Then can I live with my aunt and uncle?"

"Well, I'm not going to send you back to live with the preacher, that's for sure. But Mrs. Cunningham has had a heart attack, so that wouldn't be a good option anyway. But I've got a problem, Kit."

"What is it?"

"Well, Rev. Cunningham denies he's done any of what you've accused him of. And he's a respected man in this town. Most people won't believe he's done anything but been a Good Samaritan to you. And he's come up with a place for you to live at his church's expense. It's a place where you can get a lot of special attention and maybe get straightened out."

I didn't know what a Good Samaritan was, but I've found out since, and it's not a good description of Rev. Cunningham. I said, "My family can straighten me out. I'm not that crooked."

The judge smiled. Then he said, "Well, maybe not. But you've been through some rough things, and when that happens to a child, it's the court's responsibility to try to make that up to you."

I wasn't sure what he meant, but it didn't make me feel too good. I said, "My family can do that."

The judge sighed again. He said, "Do you know who King Solomon was?"

I shook my head.

He said, "That, Kit, is part of the problem. King Solomon was a very famous king in the Bible. All children need to know who he is. And there's a famous story told about him that's much like the situation we're in here." He put his glasses on then. "Two women came to the king. Each one claimed to be the mother of the same baby, and each claimed that the other woman was lying about the baby being her child. Solomon didn't have any way to know which one was the real mother. So he asked one of his guards for a sword and he held it over the baby. He said that since he didn't know who to believe, he'd just cut the baby in two and give half to each woman."

I found that idea truly alarming. I said, "I don't want to be cut in two."

The judge smiled again. He said, "I'm sure you don't. And I didn't mean to threaten that. But the fact is that judges often have to split the difference and try to please both parties."

"I thought judges were supposed to do what's right?"

Judge Prescott blushed a little then. He said, "Right is hard to determine sometimes. Rev. Cunningham believes that you getting a good Christian upbringing is the right thing to do. And to tell you the truth, about ninety percent of the people in this town believe that, too. I'm not entirely sure they're right. But I don't know that they're wrong, either. And you do need to fit in better. I don't think it can hurt you to go over to the place Rev. Cunningham is suggesting. You could get some education and some good moral values, and then you could go live with your family."

I said, "My family has good moral values."

Judge Prescott took a deep breath and blew out so that you could see his lips flutter. He started to say something but stopped himself. I wondered what it was he thought he shouldn't say. But you can't ask people that. It's not polite, and they lie, anyway.

But I could see things weren't going my way. So I said, "If I said I was sorry about the head-butting, would it make any difference?"

I guess one of Judge Prescott's hips was tired. He shifted in his seat. Then he said, "Well, I wouldn't believe you, so probably not."

I wouldn't have believed it, myself. So he was at least being honest. I said, "How long would I have to stay?"

"Technically, in this state you'd only have to stay until you're sixteen. You're nine now, I believe. That's seven years."

"My family could forget about me in seven years."

The judge wasn't quick to answer. But he finally said, "Not if they love you as much as they say. They'll wait for you, Kit."

He seemed sorry for what he was doing to me. And I was really, really sorry, myself. I felt the tears come up in my eyes and throat and there wasn't anything I could do to stop them. But I can cry without making any sound, and that's what I did. I just sat there and cried until my chest got in sort of a heaving motion and a tear dropped down onto my skirt. Judge Prescott put his hand on my shoulder then, and he said, "I'll tell you what. I'll review your case every year. And if you behave and if things cool down here, I'll let you go live with your family."

I folded over and put my face in my hands and cried and cried. I made a noise, but I didn't care. And I couldn't have stopped myself, anyway.

51

It's been four days since Caroline and I talked about Mr. Hodges getting us both to class. We've hardly spoken to each other. She's just acted like nothing ever happened and I've been trying to get those birds in my stomach to settle down and to think up a plan. Most of the details are worked out, but I need to get some equipment together and to convince Caroline it's the right thing to do. That'll take a day or two, so I'll write down here the rest of the story about how I came to Ashley Lordard.

Uncle Mark and Aunt Rosa went and got all my stuff from the preacher's, including the most important thing I own, the frontiersman. We stayed in the Starlite over the weekend. Grandma, Granddaddy, and Uncle Dennis came over and joined us. I slept in the bed with Grandma and Granddaddy slept in the other bed, and it was the most comforting sleep I'd had in a long while. Grandma smelled like Mama, and she slept with her arm over me. She also braided my hair, because my aunts wouldn't do that before and she said it didn't matter now.

During the days, she told me a lot of things I've found useful ever since. It was like she was trying to tell me everything she knew about who I am and about how to survive in case she didn't get another chance. I knew what she was doing and it made me real sad. She could see that, but she went on, and she told me more than once, "We're not broken people, Kit. We're people who plot and wait. Then, when the time is right, we take our shots." That was good to know. It has kept me going forward more than once. It has also kept me out of trouble, because I can keep my mouth shut while I bide my time and know it's for a reason. The things Grandma told me are things they don't teach you in school, and I'll use some of them on the way out of here.

Uncle Dennis had to go to work on Monday morning, and Grandma and Granddaddy aren't the kind of people who will sit in a room packed with whites, especially after what happened to Uncle Joe. So Uncle Dennis drove them back home Sunday night, and on Monday morning the trial started again. I stayed over at our table by the window at Jasper's, and my aunts switched off sitting with me just like before. People came through the door, straight over to us, and reported what was going on. Mr. Bumpus put Daddy on the witness stand on Monday afternoon and asked him to describe that Sunday morning when the killings took place.

He told the jury about Uncle Russ coming over with his mower to get fixed and about how we all talked about the fish. He said that Uncle Russ went home after I went fishing because he needed a part for the mower and thought that he had one there. It was while Uncle Russ was gone that Mrs. Burnett came through on her way back from church. I think what she said to Daddy was said in court, but nobody said it to me. They all just said that Mrs. Burnett told Daddy what had been going on at the cabin.

I didn't ask about that then and I haven't asked about it since, but I did ask what Daddy said about why he killed Mrs. Burnett. Mr. Simmons, the newspaper man, read it from his notes. He said, "Mr. Crockett said that he had just shot Bella Bowing and that Irene Burnett was laughing like a crow. He had the deer rifle in his hands and he guessed he just pulled the trigger again."

When Mr. Simmons first read that, the only thing I could think about was that Bella's last name was Bowing. I had never heard it before, and it was news to me. I said it over and over in my head to see how it sounded, if it seemed natural in my ears or like it didn't fit. I decided it did fit, that there was a flow to it. And Bowing sounded sort of Indian. More than Granddaddy's last name, which is Glory, and Uncle Dennis's last name, which is Smith.

By the time I got that worked out, Mr. Simmons was talking to somebody else, but he was still standing next to me, and I tugged at his sleeve. He said, "Yes, Kit?" and looked down over the tops of his glasses.

I said, "Would you read that again?"

He did. Then he said, "Does that make any sense to you?"

I said, "I told you she was mean. She got him to kill somebody for her and then laughed about it."

Everybody around quieted down. Then Mr. Simmons said, "Say that again."

I did. And all the grown-ups looked at each other. Nobody said anything for the longest time. Then Aunt Lou said, "You have a way of putting it that makes it real clear." And Mr. Simmons took his pencil from behind his ear, and he wrote down what I said. I know that was what he wrote because it was in the paper the next day.

The next morning, the jury started talking to each other. (Right now, I can't remember the special name for that.) They talked through most of the day. People came and went from the courthouse to Jasper's, back and forth, and they all got wet and had to shake off because it rained all that day. Everybody in the restaurant was grumpy and moody and drinking too much coffee and smoking too many cigarettes. The place got to smelling so bad that a couple of times I went outside and stood in the doorway. That's where I was when Aunt Jean came out the front door of the courthouse and waved her arm high in the air. I waved back and turned and pushed in the door. I yelled, "The jury's coming in."

We all got to go. Even me. The courtroom was as dark as the rest of the building, and it, too, had benches in it like it was a church. But in front of the benches were tables and there were two rows of chairs behind a rail on the left and a great big cabinet in the front of the room and a door. We were just getting settled in our seats when Sheriff Hawkins came through that door, and Daddy was right behind him. He had on handcuffs. I don't know if it was seeing them or seeing him that made me do it, but I started crying. Aunt Rosa's arm was around my shoulders and she pulled me to her and whispered, "We're going to be brave for your father." I took a deep breath then. And Daddy looked at me. He smiled and waved his fingers mostly because his hands were locked together.

After Daddy came in, other men came in, too, and they all sat down at the tables in the front of the room. One of them was Mr. Bumpus and another was Mr. Graham, the district attorney. But except for them and Sheriff Hawkins, the rest were strangers. After they came in, another man opened the same door again, and a line of men came in and took the chairs at the side of the room. Right behind them, the judge walked in, and the man holding the door said, "All rise." Some of the people hadn't sat down yet, but everybody who had got up. When the judge sat down at that cabinet, everybody else sat, too.

There was some talking at the front of the room between the judge and some of the other people. Then the judge said, "In the case of the state versus Jack Crockett," and some more words I didn't understand until he said, "Bella Bowing." Then the man who had held the door went over to one of the men at the side of the room and got a little piece of paper from him. He took that little piece of paper to the judge. The judge read it. After that he called out names. Every name he called out, one of the men at the side of the room stood up and said, "Guilty, justifiable homicide."

When the last man said that, there was a little grunting and nod-ding in the audience. Aunt Rosa squeezed me and said, "That's good." Then the judge said, "So be it," and hit his desk with a hammer.

The next thing he did was the same thing he did before, only this time it was about Mrs. Burnett, and when the first man stood up, he said "Guilty, voluntary manslaughter," and a man in the au-dience said, "This is a crime." The judge stopped everything then and you could tell he was mad. He said, "There'll be order in this court, or I'll fill the cells." Things got graveyard quiet real quick, and nobody hardly breathed. Finally, the judge said, "Proceed." The rest of the men stood up, and each one said, "Guilty, voluntary manslaughter." After the last man was through, the judge hit his desk again. Then everybody started talking, and the adults around me started shaking hands and patting each other on the back. Aunt Rosa squeezed me real hard, and when I got loose from her I made a beeline for Daddy. He had his back toward me, but Sheriff Hawkins saw me coming and said, "Jack, here's your daughter." I slipped under the railing and grabbed Daddy's waist.

I held on for dear life. But Daddy said, "Kit, here, let me see your face." And he squatted down and put the circle of his arms over my head. He said, "Squat, Kit. I'm gonna lose my balance."

So I squatted, too. And we must have looked like puppies play-ing with each other because we were hugging, but we were off-balance and squirming because Daddy couldn't hug in the usual way with his hands cuffed and we kept wanting to look at each other's faces as well as hug.

I don't remember what we said, but I do remember the hugging well and Daddy's face. I remember them every night when I go to sleep in my bed or my closet, and I remember them every morning when I wake up.

The judge didn't sentence Daddy until after I came over here to Ashley Lordard. But the evening when that verdict came in, a lot of people, including Mr. Bumpus and Mr. Graham, ate with us at

Jasper's. Even though Daddy was guilty, he wasn't guilty of murder, and everybody, including Mr. Graham, thought the judge would give him a light sentence. They all were happy about that. But except for Aunt Jean and Uncle Russ, no church people were there. And in the middle of the dinner, Aunt Jean said, "Russ and I are gonna try out the Methodists."

52

Today is Sunday, so we had church. The sermon was given by another friend of Mr. Hodges, a short man with red hair, who seemed nervous to me. He talked about honoring your father and mother. I honor mine. But I've got a lot of other things on my mind, so I didn't think much about that except to wonder why anybody would pick that topic when a lot of kids here probably don't have fathers and mothers and others have parents who are mean to them and some, I know for a fact, have perfectly fine parents that just happen to be Indians.

We have more free time on Sunday than on any other day, so today I finally talked to Caroline. I waited until after dinner, but I ate a lot because I'm trying to fatten up. I also stole some crackers. Most of the girls here steal crackers all the time and take them to our dorm rooms. They don't consider that real stealing because the crackers are for us. But we get talks about not taking food to our rooms because so many girls hoard it that some closets and drawers smell all the time. Also the mice problem is bad, particularly in the fall and winter. I don't know why I'm writing about this tonight, except food is on my mind, and I'm worried about going hungry. But my point is really about stealing. I'm normally real cautious against it because so much has been stolen from me.

This writing is getting a little choppy and if Miss Reynolds were grading it, she'd mark "ORGANIZATION" in red all over the pages. But I can't help it. I'm nervous. And I want to get everything written down before I go. Also, sometimes I read back over what I've written the night before, write it again better, and flush the first writing down the commode. I can't do that with this last piece, so it will just be as it comes out, and I'm nervous, as I said before.

Caroline has a secret place that she goes to outside. She's not the only one. I do, too. I'm not going to say where mine is, but hers is in tall grasses down in one of the little low spots that's never been cultivated. I didn't want to sneak up on Caroline, so when I got to within hearing distance I started singing "The Yellow Rose of Texas." I picked it because it's been all over the radio for some time and I know all the words. I can't sing very well, but that has its advantages because my voice doesn't sound like anybody else's. And Caroline, instead of laying low like I figured she would, popped up and said, "Kit, are you drunk?"

I stopped singing and walked into the grasses. What I found in there was interesting, but nobody's business but Caroline's, so I won't put it in here. I will say that we sat down in a spot that wasn't wet, even though it was low, and that had been built up in a strange way that could be Comanche. When we got settled, and after Caroline saw I wasn't drunk, I started telling her my plan.

Caroline isn't a person who finds fault or asks many questions. In fact, it's hard to tell what she's thinking. But the first thing she said was, "And you're doing this now," which is her way of asking me why.

I told her that I'm fed up. He won't stop unless somebody stops him. And Linda and Susan will be next.

She said, "What makes you think that?"

That was a direct question. Coming from Caroline it sort of threw me. And I didn't want to say because I'm not sure I'm right. It will probably take me my whole life to figure it out for sure. But it seems to me that unless something big happens to change them, most people act the same way again and again. Uncle Joe liked liquor, and kept drinking it. Daddy kept carving frontiersmen, even when he had plenty. Rev. Cunningham was always pretending one thing and really doing another. And Bella had liked Priscilla, that girl in New Orleans. I hate to think about that, but it's true. I said, "Even if I'm wrong, two of us are too many."

Caroline said, "Kit, you're going to get us killed."

I already know three killed people and I don't want to know any more. But instead of getting off the path thinking about that, I said, "Not if you help me."

She said, "No, really. Listen to me. You know how girls come and go around here."

"Sure," I said. "That's normal."

"It may be for some. But I can show you two graves."

"Where?"

"Over the ridge. There's a thicket. In there."

"How do you know they're girls?"

"I don't. They could be boys. But they're there. One, I think, is pretty old. There's grass over it. But you can still tell the earth has been moved around. The other one, you can still see shovel marks where they tried to pat the ground down. And that grass isn't like any of the other grass."

That knocked me completely back. I felt my heart pounding. And I must have lost the color in my face or something, because Caroline reached out and put her hand on my arm.

I don't know how long we sat there. Comanches can sit still as long as Cherokees can. And although I went off in my head, it wasn't to the graves. I was trying to get away from them. I don't like graves in general, but those in particular I couldn't bear to think about. I was afraid they would steal my courage. I still am. But I finally felt my breathing get regular. And felt, too, that Caroline was breathing the same as me. We were going in and out together.

When I could speak again, I handed her a little slip of paper with Uncle Mark's telephone number on it. I told her, "I'm going to try it anyway. I need for you to call my family. I'm going to leave my frontiersman and my letters from Aunt Rosa in my closet hidey hole. It's in the floor under the tackle box my grandma gave me for Christmas. When they get here, show them where they are so they can take them. I don't want them left behind. Particularly, my frontiersman. I've got to keep him."

"I don't see how that will help," she said.

I said she would have to trust me. If I told her any more it would be dangerous for her.

She said, "You can burn a Comanche at the stake and she won't say a word."

I figured that was true. I also think that Comanches know something about burning people at stakes, but I didn't say that. I said, "That's why I'm trusting you."

I'm going to end this part here. The next part I'll write and take with me. In fact, I'll take this part, too. If they find out Caroline knows about the graves, she'll be next. Caroline, thank you. We're true friends. And if we don't get killed, we'll be friends forever. Or we'll be friends forever even if we do get killed.

53

The hardest part of this is leaving the frontiersman behind. He doesn't have a gun or any protection. But I think he'll be in less danger here than he will be with me. And if I'm successful, I'll see him again.

I've gathered these things together: my flashlight, extra batteries I've bought or won (not stolen), matches, fishing line, hooks and weights from my tackle box, crackers, my knife, my picture of Lauren Bacall, a few things like soap and toothpaste from my bathroom kit, and $1.32, which is all of my money.

One of the things Grandma taught me that weekend at the Starlite was, if you're ever lost, or if people drive you from your home on a Trail of Tears, pay attention to the earth and the growth of the trees. Flat land shows you're in a river bottom. Straight thin tree lines grow around turned land, but bunches of trees grow around water. That made sense to me because that's how the land and trees are around the bayou and the river. But I didn't know until Grandma told me that's true other places, too. She also told me always get to the water. You have to have water to keep going, and you can catch fish there and shoot or trap animals that come to drink. She also said to go downstream, not up. Downstream always leads you to people.

But my plan is not to get to people too soon. When Caroline calls my family, they'll come to the school. And they'll start looking for me. But I want other people to be looking for me, too. White people particularly, because everyone pays attention to what white people say. Once they form a posse, or whatever they call it when they're looking for kids, and after they look for a while, when they find me or when I find them, there'll be a lot of law enforcement officers around and probably at least one social worker.

Everybody will ask me a lot of questions. I'll be glad to answer them this time. And I'll have something to show them as evidence. Not the frontiersman. Because he's a decoy. He's not in my real hidey hole. All the other pages I've written are. So, if you're reading them, you know that Mr. Hodges didn't realize I have another hidey hole. He didn't find those pages and destroy them. Also, Caroline didn't get murdered. And I didn't die. I located a river and followed it downstream. I fished and ate crackers. I didn't starve or drown. I took the people who found me to my real hidey hole, which is in a piece of furniture in an old shed. They got my papers out of there and they read all about what's been going on here at Ashley Lordard.

After that, with any luck at all, they'll give me to my family. Daddy will get out of prison. And Mr. Hodges will get in.

ACKNOWLEDGMENTS

I wrote the bulk of this book in 2006 and 2007. I had a successful international career as a consultant then, and I had decided a few years before that, as busy as I was, I could either make time for writing or for talking about writing, but I couldn't make time for both without giving up my career. That work is important to me, and I like to think it's helpful to others, so I kept on with it and spent my "free" time in my basement writing alone, with very little input, except for a few friends who read drafts for me. This book was written so long ago that I can't remember exactly who that was, but I believe it might have been Gretchen Brown, Lana Dearinger, Laura Derr, Rona Roberts, Martha Helen Smith, Sue Weant, Judy Worth, and Julie Young. If I have left somebody out, I apologize. I've changed computers and email servers over the years, and can't locate that record anywhere except in my head. If I've thanked you and you didn't read this manuscript for me, I'm sure you've helped me in some other way.

Because I'd made the choice to write instead of talk about writing, the first actual professional writer to ever see this manuscript (or any other fiction of mine) was Roxana Robinson, my instructor at the first writing workshop I ever attended, the 2007 Wesleyan Writers'

Conference. I was nervous, of course. Didn't have any idea what an actual well-known, high-caliber, up-east author would say about what I'd been up to in my basement in Kentucky. What Roxana said was, "Already a good writer," when she inscribed her book, *Sweetwater*, for me. So I'd like to thank Roxana in particular. Not only were those encouraging words, they were the very first ones I'd ever heard from a professional author of stature. They kept me going for a long, long time before I actually got published.

I'd also like to thank my editor, Nicole Angeloro, for her helpful, light touch, and for her banter, which I always enjoy and which makes our exchanges, trade-offs, and compromises fairly friction-free. And, of course, I want to thank my agent extraordinaire, Lynn Nesbit. I didn't show Lynn this manuscript until the First Nations boarding school scandal broke in Canada, because I'd realized years earlier that the few people I'd submitted it to didn't really know what I was writing about. But, in 2021, Lynn did. And she loved Kit like I do and was anxious to get her into print.

ABOUT THE AUTHOR

Margaret Verble is a citizen of the Cherokee Nation. Although she was raised in Nashville, Tennessee, most of her family is in Oklahoma, and some still own and farm the land on which her first two novels are set. Her first novel, *Maud's Line*, was a finalist for the Pulitzer Prize for fiction in 2016. Her second, *Cherokee America*, was listed by the *New York Times* as one of the 100 Notable Books of 2019 and won the Spur Award for best traditional Western. Her third novel, *When Two Feathers Fell from the Sky*, is set in Nashville, and was selected by *Booklist* as one of the 10 Best Adult Novels of 2021.